LOVE YOU FROM A-Z

LINDA CORBETT

One More Chapter
a division of HarperCollins*Publishers* Ltd
1 London Bridge Street
London SE1 9GF
www.harpercollins.co.uk
HarperCollins*Publishers*
1st Floor, Watermarque Building, Ringsend Road
Dublin 4, Ireland

This paperback edition 2022
1
First published in Great Britain in ebook format
by HarperCollins*Publishers* 2022

A catalogue record of this book is available from the British Library

ISBN: 978-0-00-855456-9

Printed and bound in the UK using 100% Renewable Electricity
by CPI Group (UK) Ltd

For Andrew, my hero

Chapter One

As a child, Jenna Oakhurst had believed in Happy Ever After. It was what happened in all the best stories, where everything worked out perfectly in the end. Later on, having observed her own parents' marriage and after experiencing a bit of the world for herself, she decided that Happy For Now was probably the best one ought to expect. Later still, after dating Mr Conceited, Mr Unreliable, and one excruciating evening with Mr I-like-dating-women-with-big-boobs, her romantic expectations were further downgraded to Happy For Now With Compromises. Which probably explained why she ended up cancelling her hair appointment in order to spend Saturday afternoon helping Matt empty a storage unit somewhere on the outskirts of Swindon after he had blown a large part of his redundancy payment on a new money-making scheme.

'So how on earth are you going to shift this lot?' asked

Jenna as they examined the proceeds of Matt's latest purchase.

'Most of it will sell on eBay,' replied Matt confidently. 'Parry's been doing it for the last couple of years.'

Jenna's eyebrows raised slightly. 'And this is the same Parry who transferred his pension savings into an investment scam?'

'That was an accident.'

Jenna resisted the urge to respond. In her opinion, Parry's tips should be severely restricted to include only those with no serious financial consequences, like best buys in toilet roll, but she knew better than to criticise Parry. Her boyfriend's best mate was blessed with a winning smile, but would make Del Boy look like a cautious investor.

'I still can't see how buying abandoned storage units makes much money though. You could still do this'—she swallowed the word hobby—'as well as a part-time job, couldn't you?'

Matt lifted a couple of heavy-looking boxes onto the platform trolley. 'I know you're worried and you don't like taking risks, but I'm not your dad; the money side of things will be fine, honestly.'

Matt's job as a kitchen-fitter might not have earned as much as a senior accounts clerk, but at least it had been a regular wage over the last eighteen months. Jenna reminded herself that it was *his* money he was wasting; as long as he could still pay his share into the joint bills account, it wasn't up to her what he did with his money, although she doubted he would have bought the units at all had Parry not highly recommended the idea in the first place.

Two weeks ago, Matt had bought a unit full of building materials and plumbing gear, and this week's purchase was hardly more exciting. In fact, the contents of storage unit seventy-four was a right old mix of stuff; it was as though someone had scooped up half the contents of their home and just dumped it in an untidy pile. The biggest item by far was an old-fashioned mahogany display case with glass panels in the front and cupboard storage underneath, which was wedged at the back behind lots of boxes. It reminded Jenna of the furniture in Great-Aunt Mary's house.

There were also a couple of bar stools with pale green seat cushions and two tired-looking dining room chairs. Stacked around them were a number of utilitarian cardboard boxes, many of which had seen better days and looked as though they had been packed in a hurry. What appeared to be picture frames poked out the top of one box, and another seemed to be full of kitchen stuff. Presumably, one of the boxes contained the cameras that Matt had been enthusing about yesterday and which he was convinced were the star items of this purchase. Jenna was highly sceptical that anyone would abandon valuables in a storage unit but was happy to be proved wrong.

Unable to help with the heavy lifting, Jenna sorted out the boxes and put any loose items into the spare black bags she had brought along with her, while Matt took charge of the platform trolley.

Over the next hour, with rest breaks, they steadily emptied the storage unit, and Matt made a number of trips back and forth to the van. Both the van and trolley had been loaned by Parry, although the latter looked suspiciously like the ones they used at the garden centre on the Haxford Road. At least they were more useful than some of Parry's dubious financial tips.

The teak display unit was the last item to be taken out, but luckily it separated into two parts and – with Jenna holding the trolley steady – Matt managed to lift off the glass panelled top.

'I'll take this bit first,' he said, laying the unit down carefully. 'The base will have to be a separate trip. Do you want to check it's not full of heavy stuff?'

Jenna checked in the cupboard compartment underneath and saw only one box. It was A3-size in a colourful dotty design, about fifteen centimetres deep, and with a magnetic flip-over lid. It was the sort that you would buy to put a nice gift in, or store something special. She lifted it out, surprised at how light it was.

'Matt, look at this, isn't it pretty?'

'It's a box.'

Jenna gently tipped it and heard a sliding sound. 'Ladies and gentlemen!' she announced in her best impression of a seaside entertainer. 'Do you want to guess what's inside? Or do you want me to … open the box?'

'We're not contestants on a game show. You can inspect it later; just stick it on the trolley.'

Jenna grinned and pulled a face. 'Spoilsport.' She had already decided she was going to keep this box as recompense for giving up her afternoon.

'Right, I'll be back for that last bit and then I reckon we're done here.'

While Jenna waited for Matt to return, her thoughts trailed back to the display case that had reminded her so much of the one that had stood proudly in Great-Aunt Mary's front room. Mary didn't believe in entertaining children by sticking them in front of the television so had steered Jenna and her sister towards more imaginative games instead. Jenna often wondered in later years whether that had, in part, been intended as a distraction from the problems at home.

The best game was when Mary carefully lifted out a selection of her china figurines and animal ornaments, and then encouraged Jenna and her sister to come up with a story using these items. Jenna's were always tales of heroic deeds, daring escapes or romantic proposals. Of overseas travel to far-flung lands, or saving the planet in true superhero style. Disability was never an impediment in that imaginary world – a world now confined to the pages of an old exercise book and hidden away somewhere with all her other treasures.

The unloading of Matt's treasure went a bit quicker as they could park directly outside their garage, where Matt planned to store everything. They didn't use the garage as

Jenna's car normally sat on the road, and Matt had sold his as he'd been using one of the company's vans most of the time.

The block of garages sat in a squat concrete row behind the flats as though the architect had wisely decided to hide them from view, and Matt had fitted a good quality padlock to theirs so it could be used for his trade tools. And now for his new auction purchases.

'Well, that's the lot,' said Matt as he stretched his arms up above his head. 'I don't know about you, but I've done enough furniture-shifting for one day.' He patted the garage door, which reverberated unnecessarily loudly. 'Good haul. I'll drop the van over at Parry's and then tomorrow we can start sorting through everything.'

Jenna watched him drive off. It annoyed her that she'd been roped into this venture; this was *his* grand plan, he could sort things out by himself. She combed her hair back with her fingers as she briefly thought about her cancelled appointment. She had already made enough of a sacrifice.

It was as she made herself a late lunchtime snack that she remembered about the decorative box, and she headed down to the garage with the spare key. Ten minutes later, she was back inside with the mystery box, which she placed on the small wooden coffee table in the lounge. She touched it reverently. Despite her curiosity, she felt reticent about rummaging inside. This was the sort of box you bought to put special things in, not just everyday knick-knacks, and what if it contained certificates? Or valuable items?

Matt would argue that that was why he bought these lots, in the hope of making money. Although you were honour bound to return any personal documentation, it was that promise of treasure buried in amongst all the tat that encouraged people to flock to these auctions in the first place. Jenna couldn't see the attraction of storing anything personal or valuable anywhere other than in your own home, but conceded that others might have reasons for needing temporary accommodation for their possessions.

She tentatively opened the box. On top lay a piece of white, folded needlework material. As she picked it up, Jenna realised it was a part-finished cross-stitch project. She carefully opened the material to see what the picture was.

In the middle, there were numbers from one to ten and underneath, a partly completed alphabet in the style of a traditional sampler. Around the outside the sampler was divided into rectangular shapes. Around a third had a pattern or design inside, and the remainder were empty. There were some half-finished flowers as well, but without a photo of the finished design, it was impossible to work out what it was going to look like. She'd never felt inclined to anything crafty, but Evie loved that sort of thing. Maybe she'd call her sister after she'd finished exploring the rest of the contents.

Underneath the material, she found a variety of postcards from around the British Isles and further afield. There was one of colourful Dutch bulb fields, and another from Iceland, depicting what looked like a giant blue iceberg. There was also an assortment of objects that looked remarkably ordinary: a packet of serviettes, a blank picture frame, a soft toy in the shape of a puffin, a small model church, an empty tin of Scottish shortbread, and a number of fridge magnets, which were mainly of specific buildings. Why keep all this stuff in storage instead of at the bottom of a drawer? The box seemed too big for such a small collection of things. There were no threads for the sewing either.

At the bottom of the box was a sheet of white, stiff paper – lining paper of some sort – but it didn't sit quite flat. Jenna lifted it out and underneath was a cream-coloured envelope addressed to a Miss Isla Price. A quick examination showed that it was still sealed, and immediately a dozen questions spun around inside her head. Why didn't Isla open this letter? Was it bad news? Was it connected to the other objects? And more importantly, why was it hidden right at the bottom?

Jenna grabbed her phone and took a few pictures before calling her sister. As it was the middle of the afternoon, Evie was probably cleaning hutches or attending to one of her many rescue guinea pigs. Sometimes she couldn't just drop everything when the phone rang, but today Jenna caught her sister at a good moment.

'So what do you think?' she asked, after giving Evie a rundown of the contents. 'It's rather random, isn't it?'

'And it was all in a box in this storage locker?'

'Yes. Matt's marvellous investment. That sounds like the title of a Roald Dahl book, doesn't it?'

'So what was in the letter?'

'It's sealed. You can't just go round opening other people's private correspondence.'

'You can when you've paid for it,' argued Evie.

Jenna was unconvinced and after promising to keep her updated, she went in search of the contact details for StoreSafe. It was a Saturday afternoon, so she was surprised to get through to a person rather than an answerphone, but it sped things up. The rather bored-sounding person on the other end of the line informed her that the unit had been auctioned off because the person who had rented it had defaulted on payments, and had not responded to any email or written communications. It was therefore safe to assume that any old address found on an old envelope in an old box was no longer relevant or useful, so no, they didn't need her to send anything back to them.

Now what? While she decided what to do, she made some space at the bottom of her wardrobe for the box. It was late afternoon by the time Matt reappeared, carrying one of the more ordinary-looking boxes from the garage.

'I'm going to start with this lot,' he announced, dumping the box down on the kitchen worktop. 'This looks like a decent camera – some of them sell on eBay for over £160. There's also accessories and all sorts in this box so I'm going to do some proper research before I flog it all.'

'But what about the personal items? There's a box of postcards and knick knacks I was looking through earlier.'

'Nah, there's no value in that rubbish. We'll sort out what can be sold, and put the rest into boxes for the charity shop and the dump. You can choose which pile to put it in.'

'Doesn't it feel a bit weird though, selling off someone else's stuff?'

'But it's not someone else's now, is it, it's mine. And I'm perfectly entitled to sell off my own gear if I want to.'

Jenna couldn't dispute the legality of the argument. Or the business transaction. Presumably Isla Price had understood the terms and conditions when she originally rented the storage space. But she remembered how, as a child, she had bought a book from a jumble sale, and it had obviously been a Christmas present for someone as written inside the flyleaf it said: *Happy Christmas John, with love from Nan and Grandad.* Even at the time she felt as though the book wasn't truly hers and that she ought to return it, despite not having any means to do so.

Her thoughts stubbornly remained on the box with the sealed letter for the rest of the afternoon. Basically, if Isla wasn't at that address any longer, the only way to contact her would be through whoever had written that letter.

She waited until Matt was busy on the computer later that evening before fishing out the letter that she had carefully replaced at the bottom of the box. If she opened it, she would have to own up to being nosey, but if she didn't open it, she'd never find out how to contact Isla, and her treasures would end up at the charity shop. Or worse, in the bin.

With Evie's words ringing in her ears, she carefully slid her finger under the seal of the envelope and pulled out a folded piece of A5 lined paper that looked like it had been torn from a notebook.

24 Harcourt Drive
Kings Hampton

Dear Isla,
I know we haven't spoken in some time, and I'm sorry I didn't live up to your expectations.
Can you please return the things of mine that are left at the flat? I'll come and collect if it's too much hassle for you.
We had some great times though, didn't we?
Best wishes,
Henry

Jenna's imagination fizzed into overdrive. This was obviously a relationship of some sort, or even a marriage gone wrong. It sounded as though Isla had finished it, but why didn't Henry live up to her expectations? Did he love her too much? Or not enough? What things had he left behind? And were they the objects that were now sitting in their garage?

A feeling of guilt slowly seeped into her consciousness. Even though the relationship was over, this Henry was still thinking about the good times they'd had together. He sounded like a nice person actually. Thoughtful. She allowed her imagination to scamper around a bit more as she wondered what he looked like; was he the sort of dark-haired, gorgeous hunk who worked out every morning in the gym and spent his earnings on designer clothes? Or was he a fair-haired geek who did clever things on computers and in his spare time crowd-funded holidays for hard-up families? Being her own imaginary jilted lover, she was very sure that he was not the sort of guy who'd ask his girlfriend to accompany him to Swindon to shift boxes instead of having a relaxing afternoon at the hairdresser's. She had only made the appointment in the first place because of that bonus.

Use it to treat yourself, her boss Adam had said. *This fella of yours doesn't appreciate how lucky he is.* Jenna smiled. Adam regularly grumbled that his own partner seemed to think the word 'budget' meant minimum spending requirement. Being awarded March's employee of the month meant far more to her than the two-hundred-pound bonus though. That wasn't a salary payment for doing a job, it was something far more personal and precious: Achievement. Recognition. Respect. You couldn't buy those things.

She hadn't told Matt about the bonus, but why should she? Did he tell her what he spent his money on when he sold his car? Her thoughts returned to Henry. Was he careful with money or did he flash it around like James

Bond at a casino? Cherry-picking the best bits of both scenarios, she pictured a handsome, dark-haired man in a tailored suit who was wealthy but not spendthrift. The good thing about imaginary heroes was that they could be perfect like the ones in her childhood stories. Real-life ones were a different matter.

There was no date on the letter, so she picked up the envelope and squinted at the postmark to see if the date was decipherable, but it was heavily inked, and very smudged.

Even after Jenna had returned the letter to the box, the words stubbornly stayed in her head.

Can you please return the things of mine that are left at the flat?

Isla had never even opened this letter so she wouldn't know that Henry needed them back.

As Jenna cleared up later that evening, she wondered again about what things he was referring to. She told herself he was just referring to a few mugs and a change of clothes, or maybe a shelf of toiletries. After all, he was a bloke – the ones she knew didn't collect boxes of knick knacks and cuddly toys. But what if he was referring to something else? She tried to tell herself his request might not have anything whatsoever to do with the items in storage that Matt had assured her were bought legitimately. So why did she feel guilty by association, and why did she feel the irrational urge to contact Henry to find out whether he ever got his possessions back?

Chapter Two

Going in to work on Monday mornings often felt like a bit of an anti-climax after a busy weekend, but Jenna didn't expect to be greeted with a groan of despair.

'Oh no! I was sure I was right.'

Jenna stopped midway through removing her jacket and looked at her two colleagues who were studying her intently. 'About what? Have I missed something?'

'You *are* the something,' replied Alisha with a cheeky grin. 'We had a bet on Friday afternoon about what you'd spend your bonus on. I was sure it would be either a hair appointment or manicure; you sneaked out to make a phone call so it had to be something personal.'

Jenna extended her arm and splayed her fingers. 'As you can see, sadly no manicure, although that would be a lovely treat.'

'Definitely,' agreed Alisha. 'I think we need a

lunchtime nail bar. There must be room somewhere in this building.'

'Excellent idea. I'll let you suggest that one to Adam,' laughed Jenna.

'So come on, what's the plan for the bonus?' asked Denise. 'There's a chunky KitKat resting on this so we need to have an answer. And don't tell me you spent it on Matt, otherwise you will have Auntie Denise to answer to.'

Denise was the longest serving member of the Accounts team at Confederated Financial Solutions and had been married and divorced twice, had brought up three children and was famed for her compassion and common sense. Everyone regarded her as a cross between a surrogate mother and agony aunt.

Jenna forced her mouth to curl up into a smile. 'It's a work in progress.'

Her answer was met with a collective groan, but she refused to be drawn into further speculation. In order to change the subject, and as she waited for her computer to wake up, she regaled her colleagues with Saturday's van adventure and her subsequent discovery. As the rest of the team trickled in, there were several pauses and reca-pitulations and, as expected, given the choice of processing last week's company expense claims or discussing Jenna's mystery letter, there was little competition.

'So you don't know anything about this Henry?' asked Denise. 'Was there a photo?'

'No, nothing like that.' She was secretly glad about

that as she'd already grown rather attached to her dark-haired, suit-wearing hero.

'So you don't know how old he is either?'

Jenna frowned. That was something she hadn't considered. She had automatically assumed Henry was in his early thirties like she was, but there was nothing to indicate that. And she had no idea how old the letter was, so Henry might have moved on and be married with kids by now. For some reason she didn't like that idea.

'So do you know which items he wants back?' asked Alisha.

'Nope.'

'But don't you want to find out?'

'She doesn't need to return anything,' piped up Jamie, the junior administrator whom Jenna was currently in charge of training up. 'They've paid for everything.'

'But this poor guy doesn't even know the stuff is in storage, never mind sold to someone else,' argued Denise.

'So what exactly was in this storage unit?' asked someone from a neighbouring team whose chair was now swivelled round to better participate in the conversation.

Jenna felt like a contestant on *The Generation Game* memorising items on the conveyor belt as she tried to recall the items Matt had stacked on the trolley.

'But there are lots of things in the boxes that haven't been sorted yet,' she added.

What she didn't mention was that watching Matt open up all the boxes like an overexcited kid on Christmas morning felt somewhat distasteful.

'So are you going to contact this man?' asked Denise.

'Of course she isn't, haven't you seen those creepy stalker films?' Jamie replied vehemently. 'The woman agrees to meet him in a windswept, isolated wasteland and then aaaargh'—he put his hands round his own throat, grimacing theatrically—'nobody ever finds out what happened to her,' he finished in a raspy voice.

'You must watch some horrible films; it's a miracle you can sleep at night,' Denise said, reminding Jenna of Great-Aunt Mary. 'Ignore pip-squeak in the corner, I think it sounds like something straight from the pages of a romantic novel.'

'So what will you say if he asks you where his things are?' asked Denise's neighbour Paveen, joining in the discussion.

'I honestly don't know,' said Jenna. 'But if there are things that are maybe sentimental to him that Matt doesn't already have his eBay eye on, I think he has a right to have them back.'

'The trouble is, Jenna doesn't even know what things he's asking about,' explained Denise. 'It's all a bit light on facts.'

'A bit like this expense claim from our esteemed Sales Account Manager,' said Jenna, tapping at her computer screen with the end of her biro. She tutted loudly. He had submitted a claim for airport expenses without supplying further details, plus a flight to Edinburgh when he could have taken a cheaper train (with the added bonus that he would not then have had to waste money at the airport while waiting around for his flight). And he'd booked first class! Under normal circumstances, the company would only reimburse the cost of a standard fare. Some people clearly thought they were above the rules and could do what they liked without bothering to check what company practice actually was. Apart from being plain old wrong, it showed a total lack of respect.

As she drove home later that day, her thoughts returned to the letter. She had two choices really; either ignore it and put the whole box in the charity shop pile, or … or what? Contact this mystery man and say, hey, you don't know me but my boyfriend has just bought all your ex-girl-friend's abandoned property, some of which may or may not belong to you. Just the thought of that made her feel more than a little queasy, and this letter would have to be worded very carefully, and would need plenty of fore-thought.

She continued to think about it most of the way home, and all through dinner, until Matt asked for the second time whether her hip was playing up again, as she seemed very uninterested in the fact that he'd already sold the boxes of Italian tiles and got a reasonable bid for some of the other plumbing items. Apparently, Parry had recommended adding in an option to make an offer on some of the items, as it sped up proceedings. Cash in hand, according to Parry – who was fast becoming

Haxford's modern-day Nostradamus as far as Matt was concerned – was worth far more than stock piled up in the garage.

After they had eaten, Matt headed back to his computer to carry out more research, and Jenna wondered whether this was what she had to look forward to from now on. She was as much an advocate of hard work as the next person, but she believed in earning money the honest way, not off the back of someone else's misery.

She also preferred emailing to writing. It was more immediate and one could be slightly less personal than you would otherwise have to be if one was writing a letter, which felt not only old-fashioned but slow. However, this time there was no alternative.

Her letter was both brief and vague. She explained that an acquaintance of hers had come across a box of personal items that belonged to Miss Isla Price, which had been in storage, so would he please email her if he had a contact address for Isla? She included her email details as well as her postal address, but omitted any reference to the letter addressed to Isla, thereby side-stepping the need to address the question of returning his belongings. The thought of explaining how she'd come across his address was already causing anxiety. She'd deal with that one when he replied. If he replied.

It was three days later that the message popped into her inbox. She'd been checking her personal emails at lunchtime when her eye was drawn immediately to the name HenSom in her inbox. It took her a few seconds to work out that this was probably Henry. Instantly, she experienced a small rush of adrenaline as she stared at the name. What was she afraid of? She told herself it was purely a business transaction; she had some personal items to return to Isla, that's all. It was not linked to any items Henry wanted returning, and nothing whatsoever to do with the fact that she was hugely curious about her dark-haired, handsome, hard-done-by hero.

She stabbed the screen and quickly scanned the email before shoving her phone back in her bag. Five seconds later, she retrieved it and sent her sister a quick text.

Got a bit of a problem. Can I come over and see you after work?

Jenna was on edge for the remainder of the day. She was quiet with her colleagues, and when Sales Account Manager, Ian Ransome, emailed demanding to know why he was only getting seventy per cent of his costs reimbursed, she replied attaching a copy of the company's expense policy with a suggestion that he read that first before making any further claims. He may have the title of Sales Account Manager but he didn't actually manage anyone and in any case, the company afforded all the sales team that title – presumably because 'Sales Person' didn't sound important enough. Jenna wasn't scared of his bluster; not for nothing was he nicknamed Mr Rant by the team, and as she herself had said on many previous occasions, she was more than happy to go toe-to-toe with that man – provided she used her good foot, obviously.

It was a relief to just get away from the office and as she made her way back to her car, she felt some of the tension leave her body.

The office of Confederated Financial Solutions was situated south of the river on a modern industrial estate. It was a four-storey building, its outward-facing structure mainly steel and glass, with a roof terrace largely used by the maintenance team as an overflow storage area, and the local pigeon population as a toilet.

Jenna had joined the company as an office junior after leaving school, progressed to accounts clerk and then worked her way up to her current position. She had seen many corporate changes over the years, but she rarely felt the urge to seek new employment, even when she didn't always agree with the changes.

She supposed that having a childhood marred by endless house moves and often being uprooted from school just as she had started to make friends had left her with a deep-seated need for continuity. It helped her to feel she belonged somewhere, unlike Evie who had seemed to just drift from job to job after leaving school, until two years ago when she gave up on work altogether to set up a guinea pig rescue with her best friend and partner, Kaitlyn, known to most people as Kat. Jenna had to concede that while her baby sister had a somewhat chaotic lifestyle and she didn't have two pennies to rub together most of the time, at least she was now happy and content.

Evie and Kat lived in a converted farm building a few miles east of Haxford's town centre, and away from the bustling commercial area, the touristy Old Town and suburban New Town area. Technically the postal address was still Haxford, although Jenna sometimes thought of it as the end of the world. As she drove towards her sister's home, she gazed at the flat, open countryside, with low hedgerows, wide expanses of ploughed fields and grazing land. Even though it wasn't yet the end of March, she could see signs of spring everywhere.

A few houses nestled in amongst the green landscape, which were useful journey markers and in the early days, helped Jenna to work out when to slow down and flick on her indicators. It was even easier to find now that there was a large sign erected in one of the fields opposite the turning, which advertised a national chain of house builders with the words *Coming soon – 200 new homes* in a large, bold font. On the other side of the road was a more modest handmade sign.

SAVE OUR GREEN BELT
protect our countryside
no more cars or pollution!

Jenna turned into the tree-lined gravel track that led up to a single-storey stone farmhouse. She parked at the front and looked around for her sister.

The house had originally been part of a series of farm buildings but had suffered fire damage during the 1990s recession. The farmer had used the insurance money to turn the main building into a residential property but having budgeted for his refurbishment rather frugally, he then found difficulty in selling it as a luxury renovation, and opted instead for renting it out. Much of the adjacent land was still used by the farmer for grazing, and concerns had been raised in the past over developers trying to build houses in Nethercott Lane as the likely dust, noise and fumes could disturb his cows.

According to Kat, sometime in the past this had been designated a protected area, but based on the new sign she saw on the way in, Jenna assumed the developers had managed to find a loophole.

In addition to the main house, there were two smaller buildings off to one side. One looked like it had started out life as a potting shed before being converted by Evie and Kat into a storage area. The other was a large, barn-type structure that, if one was being polite, could be described as rustic, and which had had long since weathered to a dull grey-brown colour. It was here that their large family of rescue guinea pigs lived. A few years ago, Evie and Kat had added on an equally rustic homemade covered area so that they could do outdoor jobs without having to worry about the weather. Attached to the wall was a painted board that said: *Welcome to Little Paws Guinea Pig Rescue.*

The farmhouse had retained one area of grassland, which had probably been intended as a lawn when the building was first renovated. Since Evie and Kat had no use for anything ornamental, it now had a secure perimeter fence so it could serve as an outdoor run for the guinea pigs.

Jenna headed in the direction of the barn. She was wearing office shoes rather than something sturdier, and she walked carefully across the uneven gravelled area. Even before she reached the door to the barn, she could hear the endearing wheeking of all the guinea pigs. She poked her head round the open door and her nostrils detected the familiar, sweet smell of fresh hay.

The barn, or 'Piggingham Palace' as Evie jokingly called it, was a multi-purpose structure about twenty-five feet in length. On one side there were any number of sturdy plastic crates piled up amongst odd bits of furniture like a badly organised junk shop, alongside which sat numerous wrapped hay bales like a wall of environmentally friendly insulation. There was also a battered looking fridge, which they had acquired second-hand, and which was used to store fruit and vegetables for the guinea pigs.

On the other side there were two tiers of wooden hutches, where the male residents lived as well as those females who – for reasons of age or infirmity – needed their own space or required medical care. It resembled a sort of guinea pig Alcatraz but with five-star facilities and friendly wardens, and the furry occupants peered out squeakily in the hope that the unexpected visitor might be bringing veggie treats. At the far end of the barn was a large L-shaped pen where Evie and Kat kept the majority of their healthy female guinea pigs, including a few permanent residents. Nearby was a scuffed wooden table, which served as workspace for both paperwork and guinea pig inspections, and a large butler's sink.

Jenna spotted her sister at the sink, bent over a yellow plastic bowl. She was wearing jeans with holes in – holes made by a guinea pig rather than a fashion designer – and a navy blue hoodie that was covered in animal fur. Her blonde hair was scooped messily into a ponytail. As children, people had often commented on how unalike they were, as though it was some sort of mystery that they looked so different, rather than just the randomness of genetic inheritance. While her sister had a delicateness about her features that masked her physical strength, Jenna's alert expression often gave the appearance of seriousness to those who had never seen her mischievous grin. The one feature they had in common was their grey eyes, apparently inherited from their father. He had left home so many years ago now that Jenna could barely remember what he looked like, never mind what colour his eyes were.

As she approached, Jenna noticed a small squirming guinea pig in the bowl. 'I'm not even going to ask whether that piggy is enjoying itself!'

'Hi, sis. This poor little thing arrived in a batch from a

charity rescue with several big bald patches, so Ginger Nut here is having an anti-fungal shampoo.' Evie talked as she worked the lather into the animal's fur. 'Honestly, some people really have no idea how to look after an animal – look at the state of her.'

Evie carefully held up the ginger and white piggy so that it was facing her. 'Don't you worry, you're soon going to be a gorgeous cuddly piggy again.' She added some air kisses for good measure, and nodded in Jenna's direction. 'Pass me that towel over there so I can wrap her up while the medication works.'

After carefully placing the piggy in a high sided plastic crate, Evie turned to her sister. 'Now we can talk for ten minutes.' She rinsed her hands, then pulled over a wooden chair, which complemented the junk shop ambience, and brushed off some loose strands of hay. 'Is that clean enough for your posh office clothes?'

Jenna carefully perched on the chair while Evie plonked herself down on a partially opened plastic-wrapped bale of hay. 'So I'm guessing this is about that box of stuff you found?'

Jenna nodded. 'And you know that letter I mentioned? Well, I opened it.' She paused.

'And what?'

'Well, it's a bit awkward you see, because he was asking Isla for his things back, and I don't know whether they were included in the storage lock up.'

'Who's "he"?'

'Oh, sorry, this bloke called Henry. I think him and

26

Isla were together at some point. Anyway, he sounds quite reasonable, he just wanted some items returned.'

'Which Matt has bought, so you now own,' Evie argued. 'Well Matt does really, but you know what I mean.'

'Ye-es, but it feels a bit wrong, doesn't it, when you know it could be someone else's stuff. Anyway,' Jenna continued before her sister had time to answer, 'I couldn't get any details from the storage company – they said she'd moved away – so I wrote to this guy Henry instead.'

Evie's eyes widened as she stared at her sister. 'You're mad!'

'And today he replied.' Jenna fished her phone out of bag and located the email. 'He says thanks for getting in touch – that's nice, isn't it? – and could I check to see if we have any of his things, which he helpfully listed for me.'

'So that spotty box belongs to him, does it?'

'No, he didn't mention that at all. But he says there are a couple of books he left behind, plus some random stuff, and a'—Jenna checked the email again— 'a Nikon D3200 DSLR camera and tripod.'

'Oh shit.'

Jenna tucked the phone back in her bag. 'Now you see the problem. He's asked if we could meet up as I'm not that far away.'

'How does he know where you live? You didn't put it in the letter, did you? Jenna, he could be god knows what sort of person! And you tell me I'm the one who's away with the fairies!'

'You sound like Jamie,' Jenna laughed. 'The thing is, Matt has already started to list things on eBay. And what do I say? Excuse me, can I keep that expensive-looking camera?'

'What's this about an expensive-looking camera?' asked Kat, striding into the barn. Matt had once commented (in private) that Kat looked like the sort of person elderly people crossed the street to avoid. Rather unfairly, in Jenna's opinion, as she knew Kat to be a very kind-hearted person who was fiercely loyal to all her causes, but she had to admit that her pale face, thickly arched eyebrows and short-cropped dark hair could be described as somewhat striking. Possibly stretching to star-tling. People occasionally tried to take advantage of Evie, but no one messed with Kat.

Unlike Jenna's light-coloured work shoes, Kat was wearing sturdy, black ankle boots and dark coloured throw-it-all-in-the-wash clothes. She would lay odds that neither of them owned anything that said *dry clean only* on the label.

Evie quickly brought Kat up to speed with the details as she rinsed the medicated shampoo from Ginger Nut, expertly dried her off sopping wet fur with kitchen paper and then wrapped her in a clean towel and handed her to Kat.

'So do you want to meet him?' asked Kat as she continued towel-drying the guinea pig. 'It isn't as if you have any obligation to return anything. It sounds like he split up with this woman and left his stuff behind. More fool him. Maybe the poor woman was desperate to get away.'

'It'll just be for five minutes. Aren't you even the least bit curious to know what happened?'

'No!' chorused Evie and Kat.

The guinea pig let out a loud squeak of protest and burrowed deeper into the towel.

'See, even Ginger Nut thinks it's a bad idea,' said Kat, offering the piggy a piece of cucumber in recompense. 'Look, if you're really set on doing this, pick somewhere like a tea shop with a busy afternoon trade. Keep your phone charged and switched on, and wear shoes you can run in.'

'She can't run in any shoes,' replied Evie, stating the obvious.

'Fine. Something she can slip off and bash him over the head with then.'

Chapter Three

J enna opted not to tell Matt why she was suddenly filled with the urge to go shopping the following Saturday, but he didn't object. On the contrary, he seemed delighted and assured her that he'd have plenty to do on his stock assessment.

Following her chat with Evie, she'd sent a quick email arranging to meet Henry at two o'clock in The Cup and Saucer tea shop in Kings Hampton. It seemed safer than meeting in Haxford town centre where she could inadvertently bump into a friend or work colleague, and then have to explain what she was doing. She wasn't even sure she could explain it to herself yet, but it pained her to think of throwing out someone's personal items without at least notifying them. She would return the items, and then Isla could do with them as she pleased.

The whole question of Henry's items, including the

thorny problem of an expensive camera, were as yet far from resolved. And as for this afternoon's rendezvous, it was hopefully only going to take fifteen minutes. A cup of tea and a slice of cake, obtain address for Isla, ignore difficult questions about missing items, job done.

With Kat's advice still ringing in her ears, she made sure she was wearing a comfortable pair of trainers although she was sure that she wouldn't need to remove them at any point. In fact, as she pointed the car towards Kings Hampton, it was beginning to feel more of an adventure and less like a foolhardy operation. This time last week she and Matt had returned from Swindon with a van load of boxes of someone else's belongings. Now with any luck she might be able to stop feeling guilty about it, even though it was neither her responsibility nor her fault.

Kings Hampton lay a few miles to the north-east of Haxford but following the post-war housing expansion, the two areas had almost grown together. However where Haxford had developed a commercial base, Kings Hampton still retained its residential appeal with an exclusive price tag to match. If Henry lived in Kings Hampton he was probably seriously well off anyway, so why was he bothered about a camera?

Jenna found The Cup and Saucer without too much trouble and made a pretence at studying the notice in the window while she dithered for a few seconds outside. *Pretend this is a business meeting*, she decided. That felt much safer. She knocked up a quick agenda in her head:

1. Meet and greet
2. Ask how he knew Isla
3. Ask whether he has any contact with her

Out of habit, she almost added *Any Other Business*, but unlike the monthly department meetings she attended, which frequently felt like they went on longer than the Jurassic period, there would be no AOB on this occasion.

She pushed open the door and stepped inside. The smell of freshly ground coffee and warm pastries filled the air and despite having had lunch, Jenna felt peckish again. The walls were painted in a duck-egg blue colour and filled with framed pictures of what looked like pre-war Haxford, which she pretended to study while looking around. She suddenly realised that she had no idea how to identify Henry. And as Denise had pointed out, it could easily be an older person's name; there were several older couples already seated at smart looking limed oak tables. There was also a group of mums with young children, but no solitary males. Maybe he came with someone? Was her James Bond-esque imaginary male already here or not?

'Can I help you?' asked a polite voice.

Jenna turned to see a woman wearing a pale blue apron.

'I was looking for someone,' she admitted sheepishly.

The waitress pointed towards the back of the shop past the counter. 'There's more seating back there. I'll be over in a jiff to take your order. Mind how you go.'

Jenna refrained from pointing out she always minded where she went, and headed in the direction of the pointing finger as it seemed less conspicuous than hovering around. The back of the shop was painted in the same colour but in place of the framed prints, there were large murals of ornamental vines covering the walls, which made it feel like one was in the middle of a French orangery. Large picture windows on the back wall provided natural light.

Jenna sat down at a table that enabled her to look through to the front of the shop. She was a few minutes early so from here she would get a good view of anyone arriving. To give herself something to do, she picked up her phone and pretended to flick through her emails, while surreptitiously looking around. Thankfully many of the tables were taken already and there was plenty of background chat, so she felt less self-conscious as she waited.

There were at least two family groups, and in the corner there was a large table of women talking animatedly over each other. By the window, a young woman sat with headphones on typing intently onto a laptop. On a neighbouring table was a man, in his thirties she guessed, with what Evie called pop star hair: short at the sides and longer on top swept back from his face. He glanced up for a second and smiled at her.

Jenna immediately stared down at her phone lying on the fake limed oak table as a warm rush of heat flooded her cheeks. He would probably think she was staring. She hated it when people did that to her. Could that be Henry? Should she go and ask? She'd feel silly if it wasn't. She halted mid-fluster as a new email pinged onto the screen. It was from Henry. Probably cancelling, she thought with some relief. He's realised this is a daft idea. Now she had an exit strategy with a clear conscience.

Hello there! Is that you?

Jenna turned her head the smallest amount so that the man with pop star hair was just about in her eye line.

He grinned and gave her a small wave. 'Hello,' he mouthed and pointed at the seat opposite with a wide-eyed questioning look.

Jenna slowly pushed her chair back and got to her feet as the waitress bustled over. 'Have you changed your mind, love?' she enquired politely.

'Just moving seats,' mumbled Jenna and scurried over to the vacant chair.

'It's okay,' said Henry to the waitress in a reassuring voice. 'Can we have a minute?'

For reasons unknown, Jenna's insides churned round faster than the cotton spin speed on her washing machine. 'Um, sorry … yes … hello, I'm—'

'Jenna would be my best guess,' replied Henry with a grin. 'You've obviously worked out who I am.'

Well, that was agenda item one totally messed up. Why was it that discussing expense claims with company directors was no problem, but saying hello to a complete stranger in a tea shop was suddenly complicated? *It's a business meeting*, she reminded herself.

Jenna straightened her shoulders and made proper eye contact with her new acquaintance. He actually had a very attractive face and what her mum used to call smiling eyes. His swept back blonde hair emphasised a high forehead that gave him a youthful professor sort of appearance. Certainly nothing like the James Bond hero she had created in her own head. Her mum always used to say she had too much imagination. He didn't dress like her imaginary hero either who wore smart, tailored suits. This Henry was dressed in faded jeans and a navy-and-white-striped rugby shirt with a crumpled collar.

'It's good of you to meet me,' Henry said, breaking the silence. 'I guess you must have loads of other things to do.'

'As you do too, no doubt,' replied Jenna, wondering why she found it so difficult to make natural conversation.

Henry smiled. 'Sadly I don't, so this counts as excitement in my diary these days.' He paused as if he was studying her. 'So, shall we order first?'

Henry ordered afternoon tea complete with clotted cream scone, and Jenna chose a toasted teacake. As if by common consent, they talked about general non-contentious matters for a few minutes, remarking on the recent showery weather (typical British default conversation, thought Jenna wryly), whether they had lived long in the area, and how Haxford Old Town got too busy in the summer once the tourist season was underway. The waitress returned with their order and Jenna took a bite of her cinnamon spiced teacake.

'So then,' Henry said as the waitress bustled away, 'I'm totally intrigued as to how you found my address – are you a friend of Isla's?'

The teacake turned to sawdust in her mouth; Jenna coughed a crumb from her windpipe and took a sip of her tea. 'No, I'm not.' She frowned. 'Oh crap, how can I explain this?'

Whichever angle she came at it, it still sounded callous and money-grubbing to her ears, but Jenna explained with a few hesitations and stumbles how Matt had bought a storage unit at auction that had belonged to Isla, and (without mentioning the box or its contents) that she came across his letter. She felt her face flush as she admitted how she'd opened it in an attempt to trace Isla, but he didn't seem angry. If anything, he looked quite pleased.

'I had wondered,' he said, when her explanation trailed to a halt. 'It's my parents' place, you see, so it's rare that anything arrives there addressed to me. I'm glad you decided to write though.'

Before he could ask anything else, Jenna quickly posed a question of her own, to which she suspected she already knew the answer. 'So how do you know Isla?'

Henry gave her a brief, sad smile. 'Ex-girlfriend. We'd been together for a couple of years. We had a shared love of travel, but...' He looked down for a moment and scooped up a stray splodge of jam with his forefinger. 'Well, let's just say I wasn't what she wanted.'

His mouth turned down in a rather dejected manner, and Jenna felt rather sorry for him. She couldn't imagine living with someone who didn't share her outlook on life. Matt might be less romantic than other men, but he was at least practical (most of the time) and until his recent financial venture, hadn't done anything to give her cause for concern.

Having confirmed the relationship between Isla and Henry, Jenna decided to steer the conversation towards agenda item number three.

'So… I presume you don't have any contact with Isla?'

Henry picked up his teacup and took a sip before replying. 'Short answer: no. I suspect she's moved away based on what you've told me about the unclaimed storage lock-up. I realised I'd left some bits over at her flat but by then she'd stopped replying to messages or picking up phone calls, so I ended up writing to her, but I heard nothing back. I heard through a friend of a friend that she'd met someone who works as a guide for an adventure tours company, but I've no idea how long that's been going on.' He pinched his lips for a second. 'I expect they're trekking in Nepal or some other remote part of the planet.'

For a brief moment, a wistful expression crossed his face, and Jenna wondered whether it pained him to think of Isla on the other side of the world. 'Isla originally talked about a temporary split – that was February before last – but with hindsight I wonder now whether she hadn't already met someone else as I never saw her again. There was this Australian backpacker we met in Iceland…' He shrugged. 'Anyway, that's all in the past, but I think I mentioned in my email there's a camera and other bits, which I left at her flat; most of it I can live without, to be honest, but the camera has sentimental value – it was a present from my parents.'

Henry busied himself pushing the crumbs round on the plate as a silence fell over the conversation. He didn't ask the most obvious question, which was: was it in the storage unit? Closely followed by the equally problematic: can I have it back? Perhaps he sensed that this was a difficult issue for both of them, given that her boyfriend now legally owned his property.

What should she say? Play dumb when she knew this was a precious family gift? She hadn't received anything from her father for her thirtieth birthday last year – not that she expected to as she hadn't seen him for years – and her mother hadn't been able to afford to give her lavish presents, nor would Jenna have wanted her to. But what if she had? And how would Jenna then feel if she had split up with Matt and he hadn't returned them? Evie had given her a pendant in the shape of half a silver heart with the words *big sis* on it, saying that she would always wear the matching one saying *little sis*. It was of little monetary value on the antique jewellery market but the thought of it being sold or given away to someone else made her cringe.

'I haven't seen a camera yet, but Matt hasn't finished going through all the items. I promise I'll look for you.'

She was rewarded by a smile of immense gratitude, which made her insides tingle. 'Thank you. I know we only met forty minutes ago, but this means a lot.' Henry hesitated for a few seconds. 'Would it be presumptuous of me to ask if we can meet up again?'

Before Jenna could reply, Henry rushed on. 'Not because I want to pester you or anything but I have zero social life at the moment so it's just in case you want to feel sorry for me.' He grinned. 'And of course I'd be fascinated to know what you find in all the boxes.'

———————

So would I, thought Jenna ruefully as she drove home a short while later. Henry had seemed really nice though. Very easy to talk to. Not a serial killer, thank you, Jamie. Just normal. Quite a bit faster on his feet than she was, as she found out when she followed him out to the car, but he quickly adjusted to match her pace, and didn't do that surreptitious staring thing that people often did.

She arrived home to find Matt sitting on the sofa, his iPad in hand and the sports channel blaring out in the background.

Jenna pointed at the television. 'Are you actually watching that?'

'Yeah. And checking bids at the same time.'

'And how's it going?'

'Not bad. Several people are watching the household items, and I've already got a few bids on the gatefold table and the display cabinet. But look at this!' He jabbed the screen. 'That camera already has four bids and it's got another week until it ends. I told you that would be valuable.'

Jenna moved closer so that she could look at the screen over his shoulder. Was that camera Henry's? Or just another one of Isla's unwanted items?

She thought about her bonus and made a quick decision. 'Matt, would you mind if I bought one of your cameras?'

Matt's shoulders stiffened. 'Buy it? Why?'

Jenna affected a nonchalant shrug. 'I just thought it would be nice to own one, that's all.'

'There are dozens to choose from online.'

'I know, but you have some here.'

'They're all listed now. And don't think I can't see what you're trying to do.'

Jenna grabbed the arm of the sofa to steady herself. 'I don't know what you mean,' she said in a shaky voice.

'You think I'm not capable of making money out of these auctions.'

'No, that's not—'

'Look, it's great that you're interested but I want to do this by myself. I don't need my girlfriend buying things to help out. Just because you work in finance doesn't mean I don't know how to run a business. I promise I know what I'm doing, okay?'

Jenna had made a promise too and she intended to keep it. Matt was just being pig-headed, and she resolved to do some research of her own. But what she would do if she actually found Henry's camera was another matter entirely, and not one for which she currently had an answer.

Chapter Four

Henry's email arrived within a few hours of their meeting. It was brief and to the point, thanking her for coming over to meet him and for agreeing to look for his camera. It seemed ironic that a complete stranger who had been seriously inconvenienced by Matt's activities was thanking her for donating an hour of her time, while Matt was happy to commandeer almost an entire day of hers to empty a storage locker, with absolutely no thought to any plans that she might have had.

Matt had already announced he was spending the evening putting up more items for auction. According to the gospel of St Parry, items finishing on a Sunday evening stood a better chance of attracting higher bids, so Jenna had left him doing his research. She had some of her own to do and having already clocked his eBay seller name, she disappeared into the bedroom with her laptop.

She felt ridiculously guilty just nosing through Matt's

eBay shop even though he ought to be pleased that she was showing an interest in his fledgling business. With Henry's email from the other day open on her phone, it didn't take long to locate the Nikon camera. A quick check online suggested new it would cost over £400. Good condition second-hand ones could reach over £200 and bids currently stood at £165.

The tripod that Henry had listed only had one bid of £50, but there was a just over a week until both auctions ended. There were other items on Henry's email but after a thorough search, Jenna could only find one match against Matt's eBay sales, and that was a coffee table book entitled *Landscapes of Britain*. It was entirely possible that some of the items on Henry's list had already been chucked in the charity shop box. Alternatively, they could be in the queue waiting to be added to Matt's eBay shop, which would mean they were still languishing in one of the boxes in the garage. After she closed everything down, Jenna lay back on the bed and wondered why she was even getting involved.

If it hadn't been for her curiosity, that box of knick knacks would have ended up at the charity shop by now, or the dump. She would never have even seen that letter, never mind read it. By contacting Henry, she had unwittingly involved herself, but now the problem was what to do, if anything. Legally, the position was unequivocal: the articles belonged to Matt and if the past had taught her anything, it was that legality always won out over sentiment. But from a moral standpoint it wasn't so clear cut.

Matt had bought Isla's unwanted goods, but the issue here was that not all of them were Isla's. So why did it bother her so much? After all, this was Matt's business venture, and Henry and Isla split up fourteen months ago, so she could just reply to Henry and tell him it was too late and everything was sold, or as good as.

The trouble was, she didn't want to. Her thoughts kept returning to earlier that afternoon and how Henry had been so thrilled by her promise of trying to help. She felt like she was doing something useful for someone. She wondered whether she could persuade Matt that he had a moral duty to return the camera. But then she would have to explain how she knew it wasn't Isla's in the first place, and that she had met up with a complete stranger for afternoon tea to discuss the matter behind Matt's back. Although it was all perfectly innocent, she didn't need to be any sort of soothsayer to see where that conversation would go. Matt always had been a bit testy about her having male friends.

She needed a Plan B. Some way to help Henry without inconveniencing Matt, while also satisfying her own conscience. Jenna prided herself on her decision-making abilities reinforced by a strong, ingrained sense of right and wrong, and in her mind there was really only one obvious answer.

Chapter Five

'You want to do what?!' Evie stared at her sister. 'You must be off your rocker – you can't drag me into this! Why can't you ask one of your friends? Or work colleagues?'

'Because they'd think I'm mad,' Jenna replied honestly. 'And I know what you're thinking,' she continued hastily, 'but I just feel this is the fairest thing to do. I can't explain, it just feels wrong when I know someone's belongings are sitting in our garage.' Jenna gestured helplessly.

'So you want me to use your money to bid on a camera that Matt bought as part of a job lot, so that you can give it back to its original owner. Which bit of that sounds like a sensible idea to you?' Evie opened up one of the hutches and gently scooped out a long-haired, toffee-coloured guinea pig which she passed to Jenna. 'Sit down and hold Snickers for a minute, would you, so I can clean his cage. The water bottle must have leaked overnight.'

Jenna carefully took the animal while Evie shovelled wet shavings and hay into a large plastic dustbin. 'Look, I know you don't think it's a great idea—'

Evie let out a bark of a laugh. 'That's the understatement of the century.'

'But will you do it? Please? I hear what you're saying, but this was a sentimental present from his family and he had no idea it was just left behind to be sold off with loads of other stuff.' Jenna skilfully turned the guinea pig round so that he was no longer chewing a hole in her jumper and gave him a gentle rub behind his ear. 'Do you remember that time we moved house and we were told we couldn't take all our toys and we had to choose what to take and what to leave behind? How grateful would you have felt if the person who moved in had decided to return them to us?'

'They were just things, Jenna.'

'But they were *my* things!' Jenna could still recall writing her name in the front of each of her books in case any got left behind.

'Anyway, I assume this Henry isn't a freckle-faced little eight-year-old boy, is he?' Evie asked as she scattered fresh bedding in the clean cage. 'He must realise this isn't your problem.'

'Of course he does. And he's probably closer to thirty-eight than eight. He's very nice-looking actually.' Jenna immediately felt her cheeks flush. Why did she just say that? She busied herself stroking the guinea pig who had quietly decided to make a start on chewing her other sleeve.

'Come on, Snickers, it's time to go home,' announced Jenna, avoiding eye contact with her sister as she waited for her face to return to a normal temperature. Jenna put the guinea pig back in the clean hutch and watched as he scuttled into his hidey hole, from where happy, squeaky sounds emanated.

'Someone's pleased with their fresh pile of hay,' said Jenna with an amused smile.

Evie fished a bit of chalk from the pocket of her jeans and scribbled the date on a small chalkboard attached to the door of the hutch.

'So what's that other date in red?' asked Jenna pointing at the board.

'He's going for the snip when he's old enough,' replied Evie. 'Then he can be re-homed with some nice girlies, can't you Snickers? We'll find you a lovely forever home.'

'Don't you feel a bit sorry for him though? He probably doesn't realise he's going to have bits of him removed.'

Evie rolled her eyes. 'If you saw some of the places we've rescued animals from, you wouldn't ask that. Honestly, some people buy these as pets for their kids without any idea about how much work is involved so they let them breed and before you know it, there are dozens of them, all stuffed into horrible, cramped conditions. The last rescue we did, there were dead baby pigs in the hay, it was appalling.'

Jenna had often wondered whether Evie was more attached to her animals than she was to many humans, but Evie certainly wasn't overly sentimental about them. She wasn't sentimental about objects either, something that was readily obvious from the state of the farmhouse, which, in its less tidy phases, bore marked similarities to the interior of the barn. Jenna wondered whether having moved from place to place so many times had desensitised Evie to the loss of her possessions; in Jenna's case, it had certainly had the opposite effect.

Evie carried a large, red, plastic trug over to a partially open bale and began filling it with lumps of the compressed hay. Jenna knew that Sunday was always a busy day at the rescue as it was when most visitors arrived. Although the individual cages were cleaned on Saturdays by a small army of volunteers, the pen that housed the majority of the female guinea pigs was always given a thorough clean first thing on Sunday morning in readiness for the arrival of visitors, which with any luck would lead to successful adoptions. Jenna pushed up her sleeves and helped fill a second trug with shavings as she regrouped her thoughts for another attempt at persuasion, this time with added leverage.

'So, Miss Tough Negotiator, if I throw in an offer of free labour, would that help sway the balance?'

Evie gave her a tight smile but there was a definite twinkle in her eye. 'It might. Make me an offer.'

'Next Sunday morning. Two hours.'

'Pass.'

'Three hours then.'

'Next.'

'You drive a hard bargain,' Jenna grumbled as she pushed the trug over to her sister.

'Never look a gift horse in the mouth,' replied Evie. 'Or in this case, that should be a gift guinea pig helper.' She grinned and Jenna couldn't help but join in.

'Okay, two Sundays of my choosing, two hours apiece.'

'That'll do nicely.' Evie picked up a short, concertinaed fence that was propped up against one of several storage cupboards. 'Give us a hand with this and then you can tell me again what I need to do.'

It was rare to visit her sister without being roped into something animal-related but at least Evie didn't treat her like she wasn't capable of doing anything. As a child, Jenna had sat on the sidelines during many children's parties where someone's parent had been worried about letting her join in the games in case she fell over and hurt herself. With hindsight, she could see it was probably well-intentioned but it took away her right to decide things for herself.

Evie carefully stepped over the edge of the large pen that stretched across the end of the barn and immediately triggered the impatient squeaking of around two dozen guinea pigs who rushed over expecting food. No matter how many times Evie maintained it was just cupboard love, it never failed to bring a huge grin to Jenna's face as she watched the spectacle of her sister being mobbed by the cutest little whiskery furries. With Jenna holding one side, Evie carefully unfolded the fence until they had almost partitioned the pen into two separate areas, then Evie shepherded all the guinea pigs into one half of the pen.

'Door's closed, little piggy-wiggies, until the chambermaid has finished cleaning.' Evie gestured to her sister. 'So come on then, what do I have to do? And it better not be complicated as you know I'm no good with computer things.'

As Evie cleaned the pen, Jenna outlined her plan.

'Honestly, it's totally idiot-proof. I'll send you a link to the item and confirm the amount to bid. It looks as though there are already a couple of people interested so if I can get you to put in your bid right at the end, there's less chance of being outbid. There's just one thing I haven't mentioned.'

'Which is?'

'I would need you to use Kat's eBay account.'

'Why? We live together, what difference does it make?'

'Because, little sis, Matt will recognise our usernames. Kat could update her postage address to her parents' one before you place the bid.'

'So now you're dragging Kat into this as well?'

'Please, Evie, just ask her if you can use her account.'

'It matters that much?'

'I know it sounds mad, but I've been turning this over

and over in my head and it just feels like this is the only way to satisfy everyone that won't cause an argument.'

Evie didn't reply immediately and Jenna knew that was her way of thinking about things. She watched as Evie finished spraying pet-friendly cage cleaner and wiped over all the sides and corners of the pen with kitchen paper. Several furry faces were watching her eagerly through the guinea pig version of the Berlin Wall and proffering the occasional squeak of protest.

'Okay,' she said finally. 'I'll speak to Kat; I'm sure she won't mind. But what about Matt?'

'He'll just be pleased that he's made another sale. He won't have to know it's me, and he'll actually make more money if we outbid anyone else. Henry will be pleased to get his camera back. You get to help out your extremely grateful sister, and I don't have to worry about this anymore. Everyone's happy, job done.'

'You make this sound very simple.'

'It is, little sis. Come here, I want to give you a big hug to say thank you.' Jenna leaned over the side of the pen and pulled Evie into her arms. 'You are the best sister in the whole world.' Jenna sniffed carefully at her shoulder. 'Even though your sweatshirt does smell more eau de guinea pig toilet than eau de toilette.'

'And so are you. Which is why I know I can be honest with you. I know what you're like when you've promised to do something, but you don't owe Henry anything.'

'I know, but—'

'I just don't want to see you get hurt, Jen, but it's your choice and your money.'

Jenna allowed Evie's words to reassure her as she drove home. It *was* her choice and moreover it was her money too. Her £200 bonus to be precise, which should have been spent eight days ago. Instead, her appointment got hijacked and she spent the morning pratting about with boxes. And it was Matt who had splashed his redundancy on what amounted to little more than a hobby, without even telling her.

No matter how many times she reminded herself that it was his money he had wasted, it still annoyed her, and even though he wasn't the most demonstrative person on the planet and got prickly when she offered to buy the camera, she did care about hurting his feelings. Nevertheless, if he could spend several hundred pounds without telling her, so could she.

Chapter Six

Having made her plans, Jenna waited until midweek before contacting Henry again. She dithered over what to write and whether to mention their meeting. If she wrote that she had enjoyed it, would he read too much into it? After all, he was just a friend, albeit a very new and rather good-looking one. In the end she opted to stick to facts.

> *Hi Henry,*
> *Just to let you know that I think the camera is here some-where but haven't seen it yet as there are boxes of stuff everywhere – my boyfriend has bought a shed load (literally) of items. It will take me a few days to sort out, but I'll get back to you asap.*
> *Jenna*

It niggled at her conscience a bit as she was convinced

the camera on eBay was his. However, she needed to buy herself some time and it was true that she hadn't actually *seen* it in the flat.

The reply popped up later that morning, although calling it a reply was doing it a disservice. Henry had emailed a photo of what looked like a Nordic woodland on a dark night. The black trees were silhouetted against a night sky that was lit up by huge swathes of green and blue, purple and pink, in a fantastic display of the aurora borealis. In the background the night stars dotted the sky like tiny flecks of white glitter. Underneath the photo were the words: *Thanks Jenna, really appreciate that. You are a star!*

Jenna smiled as she gazed at the amazing photo and wondered if it was one that he had taken. At least someone appreciated her, unlike Sales Account Manager Ian Ransome (alias Mr I Rant), who was doggedly pursuing the balance of his expense claim, which he maintained Jenna had rejected without due cause.

'You look happy,' observed Denise. 'Sex text from Matt, was it?'

'God no! He doesn't do things like that.' Jenna laughed as she tried to imagine Matt composing anything remotely resembling a sex text.

'Well, that idea obviously tickled your fancy!'

'Matt's not prone to spontaneous gestures, although he's very good at unblocking sinks, which is possibly more useful,' Jenna said with a grin.

'Did either of your husbands ever send you romantic messages?' Alisha asked Denise.

'Not messages as such, but husband number one did bring home flowers regularly. I thought it was desperately romantic until I found out that he nicked them from outside florists.'

For several seconds, no-one could speak for laughing.

'And don't go getting any ideas, Jamie Dalton, that is *not* how to impress a woman,' added Denise firmly.

'My boyfriend sent me a Valentine's card last year,' said Alisha. 'He wrote, "you sparkle in my life like the biggest diamond".'

'That's more like it,' said Denise. 'I hope he buys you an actual diamond next year. And maybe Matt will get one for Jenna too.'

Jenna laughed. 'A diamond? You must be joking! The closest I'll get to a diamond is on a pack of playing cards. He doesn't go for all that flowers, champagne and chocolates stuff, but on the plus side he's very practical around the house. And he doesn't nick things,' she added, which prompted another round of laughter. 'Anyway, romantic gestures and all that stuff, it's not real life, is it? That's what happens in books and films.'

'But there's more to romance than that,' Denise said carefully. 'Sometimes just talking, sharing experiences, helping each other – those things can be romantic too.'

The last thing Jenna and Matt had done together was the packing up and subsequent unloading of Isla Price's abandoned storage unit, and she wasn't convinced that was the sort of shared activity Denise was referring to.

And from her side at least, it was about as romantic as cleaning the bathroom.

Even their first meeting was more practical than romantic; they had both been guests at a friend's wedding reception, during which the fire alarm had gone off. With the lift out of order, Matt had helped her down the stairs and prevented the stampede of slightly drunk guests from accidentally knocking her over. Once outside they'd got chatting and discovered that they shared the same determination to get on in life, and had both had to deal with family troubles. It wasn't love at first sight – more of a joint agreement, she supposed – but it meant being able to leave home and, more importantly, be independent. Sure, there were compromises but ones that at the time she'd been willing to make.

Her thoughts meandered over to her afternoon tea with Henry. Despite mentally filing that under 'business meeting', she often found herself thinking about him in idle moments; she admired his happy-go-lucky demeanour, and that gorgeous smile, which made her go all tingly inside. He must have thought she was very serious, but he probably hadn't grown up like she did, and her past was not something she viewed with rose-tinted glasses.

She also found herself wondering about his relationship with Isla. They must both have had plenty of money to do all that travelling around, even if they had found work along the way. She had been lucky if there was enough money in her family for the occasional school trip. Her school had had a support fund, which was basically a charitable means of ensuring children whose parents couldn't afford things didn't miss out, and Jenna was aware that she and Evie had often been its beneficiaries. They were the free school meals kids. Money didn't buy you happiness, her mum used to say, but in Jenna's opinion it certainly went a long way to providing you with a better life.

Over the next couple of days, Jenna and Matt separately but regularly consulted eBay to see how bidding was going. Matt was delighted to have sold a further two items, although the palaver involved in packing the things up hardly seemed worth the effort, in Jenna's opinion. She kept that to herself, along with her covert checks on the camera. No further bids had been placed, much to Matt's chagrin, and Jenna emailed Evie on Saturday to let her know that she should place her bid later on Sunday afternoon and to watch out for texts.

Bids had not increased beyond the £165 she had observed earlier in the week but even so, by Sunday afternoon Jenna was becoming increasingly anxious. She was aware from Matt's regular breakfast monologues on eBay strategies that people often snuck in last minute bids in order to win the auction, but she couldn't ask Evie to do any of that down-to-the-last-second sniping stuff. The auction finished at 4.23 p.m. and she wanted to make sure Evie got the details in good time.

Hi little sis, just checking everything okay your end? Can you bid no more than £210 for the camera? Please put in bid any time between four and quarter past. Do you need me to send over the link again?

The reply came back ten minutes later.

Stop panicking! All good here. Snickers sends a squeaky hello to Auntie Jen xxx

How the hell could she be so calm? Jenna tried to find things to do to keep her mind occupied as she watched the minutes crawl past. Matt was thoroughly engrossed in watching his auctions, and gave Jenna a running commentary on how they were doing.

'That display cabinet's just sold,' he announced triumphantly, punching the air with his fist. 'That's another forty-nine quid to add to the total. Parry reckoned I'd only get around thirty.'

'Fancy that. How are you going to post it?'

'The buyer is collecting, obviously. And the DVD boxset of the *Hunger Games* has two bids. We'll need to start saving boxes to post all the smaller items. It's important to know which size parcel you are sending.'

Jenna tuned out of the impromptu and ungripping tutorial on what constituted a small or medium parcel size and played a few games on her phone instead. If she hadn't already made up her mind, this afternoon perfectly illustrated what would pass for home entertainment on Sunday afternoons if Matt continued with his new hobby. The only thing she could hope for was that the work involved in parcelling things up and taking them to a courier or parcel depot would soon cause the novelty to wear off.

Her phone was stubbornly silent, but she continued checking for messages on an increasingly regular basis. After what felt like three boring afternoons' worth of time had elapsed, two things happened simultaneously. Matt punched the air again and shouted 'Woo-hoo!' just as Evie's message pinged through.

All done. Won the auction. Just have to pay £180.

As Evie never had any spare savings – every penny went on guinea pig food or vet bills – Jenna had already electronically transferred two hundred and twenty pounds over to Evie's bank account. It allowed for Evie to do a last-minute increased bid. Jenna always believed in having a back-up plan.

Thanks sis, you've been brilliant. Keep the balance for Snickers' op.

'Guess what?' said Matt excitedly. 'The camera's just sold for a hundred and eighty pounds. I told you there was some decent stuff in those boxes. I'm going to see Parry later and update him on how it's all going. Do you want to come with us for a celebratory drink?'

'No thanks, I won't gatecrash your lads' night out.'

'But you won't be gatecrashing; when you're with us, you're one of the lads, aren't you?'

Jenna wasn't sure whether she was supposed to be flattered by that comment. 'I've got things I need to do.'

'No problem. You can always change your mind later on.'

Matt fetched a beer from the fridge. 'At this rate, every Sunday will be a celebration.'

'Well, until you've sold everything,' said Jenna. 'Then you'll be back to fitting kitchens. Or if you're bored of that, scouring the job ads,' she added.

Matt took a swig of his beer. 'Don't be so sure about that. Parry and I reckon there's ways of making this more profitable. Not that it isn't already,' he added quickly, 'but I know you worry about money—'

'Only because we have to pay the rent every month—'

'So I've been keeping a spreadsheet of the profit from each sale. I'll show you later and then you'll be impressed for a change.'

'I was impressed with your job,' said Jenna, feeling stung by his comments.

It was okay for Matt. He grew up in a working-class household like she had, but his parents had saved for things they wanted, not bought them on credit that they couldn't afford to pay back. Nor did he have to hide his treasured possessions because sometimes strangers walked into your house without any warning and took things away while your parents stood by and did nothing.

'Have you never wanted to just chuck it all in and do something different? Take a few risks?'

Jenna shook her head. 'Not with my job, no thank you.'

'Sometimes you have to spend to accumulate. And I have now accumulated a hundred and eighty smackers, as the buyer has just paid.' Matt rubbed his hands together. 'I like it when people pay promptly. Let's see where this is being posted to.'

Matt tapped at the iPad. What should have been a few seconds of reading extended into several. And then several more.

'I don't understand this,' said Matt, finally breaking the silence. 'You'll never guess where the camera is being posted to.'

'Erm, Taunton,' suggested Jenna with a flutter of nerves in the pit of her stomach. 'Cumbria. Hartlepool. Brighton. How the heck should I know?'

'The address is Farm Cottage, Nethercott Lane, Haxford. Does that sound at all familiar?'

The flutter turned into a sharp stab of anxiety, which pulsed through Jenna's body. Evie had promised to change the posting address; she had double checked that fact only two days ago.

'So why would your sister or her gothy friend be buying an expensive camera when they're continually sponging off you? They don't go on holidays so what do they want a camera for?'

'Does it matter now they've paid for it?'

For a brief second, Jenna hoped the topic might be closed.

'Yes, it does. And when I deliver it in person – because I'm not spending several quid posting this when they're only the other side of Haxford – I'm going to damn well find out what's going on. I bet they've got more money than we thought. When I lose my job and try to do something that actually makes us money, you get all disapproving—'

'I only suggested you keep some sort of reserve—'

'But that pair only have to spin you a sob story about some poor, ill-treated guinea pig and you fall for it every time and keep bailing them out.'

'They don't spin me a sob story – where's that come from? And why wouldn't I want to help my sister?'

'I'm just saying there's more to it, that's all. And I intend to find out what that pair are up to.'

'They're not up to anything,' retorted Jenna angrily.

It was one thing asking Evie to bid on something, but she couldn't let her sister take the flak for this. This had clearly not gone according to plan and if Matt stormed up there doing a bull in a china shop impression, he'd upset Evie for no purpose. He ought to hear the truth from her.

'Matt, this is nothing to do with Evie. I asked her to do the bidding.'

Matt leapt to his feet. 'You? Is this the same camera you wanted to buy off me?'

Jenna nodded and took some deep breaths to reduce what was fast turning into a flood of anxiety. Matt could be reasonable. Provided she could explain this properly he would understand. 'Yes, and now you've got more money than if I'd bought it in the first place.'

'You bought the bloody camera?' repeated Matt, glaring at her.

'Just let me explain; the thing is, that camera belonged to someone else and—'

'Yes, the person who owned the storage locker. Which is now me.'

'No. It belongs to Henry.'

'Who the hell is Henry?'

'Do you remember that spotty box I found? Well, there was a letter at the bottom of it, asking for some things to be returned. I just felt it was the right thing to do. I didn't want to spoil your business venture so I used my own money – my bonus actually – to buy it back. That way everyone's happy.'

'Happy?' Matt gestured wildly with his arms. 'Are you deluded or something? Of course I'm not happy! You've gone behind my back, made me feel stupid. How do I know you haven't been seeing this Henry behind my back too?'

'I met him once, that's all.'

'Great. So what does that mean?'

'It doesn't mean anything. Call it a business meeting if

it makes you feel any better.'

'But it wasn't, was it?'

Jenna sighed. 'Matt, you probably went into a hundred different kitchens doing your job; did I ever accuse you of eyeing up some bored housewife who wore sexy underwear in order to liven up your day job? No, because that's just plain stupid. So why don't I deserve the same consideration?'

Matt picked up his wallet, shoved it into his pocket and grabbed his jacket.

'So that's your answer, is it? You're just going to stomp off?'

'I'm meeting Parry like I told you earlier. The camera's in the box over there.' He pointed to the corner of the room. 'You can sort out the delivery yourself.'

The door banged shut after him.

Jenna grabbed the nearest sofa cushion and chucked it at the door. 'Bugger off then, you stupid, pig-headed man!' How dare he talk about her sister like that? Accuse her of playing the sympathy card while squirreling away sums of money. It was utterly ridiculous.

'Good riddance!' she shouted at the door. 'I used my own bonus to pay for that camera and this is your fault because I didn't get to spend it on myself!'

Jenna rubbed angrily at a stray tear. She had done the right thing. Even though her plan had backfired somehow, she clung on to the unassailable facts: Matt had made his sale, Henry had his camera back (or as good as) and Evie had a bit of spare cash for her troubles. The thought of

Evie made her reach for her phone. She needed to speak to her in case Matt decided to get in first.

'Evie, it's me – Jenna. Thanks for bidding on the camera. You haven't heard from Matt, have you?'

'No, why?'

'He … well, he's found out. The delivery address wasn't Kat's parents' place, it said Farm Cottage. I'm not blaming you, I just wanted to let you know in case he asks any questions.'

'But he's okay about it, is he?'

Jenna pinched her lips for a second.

'Jen?'

'I'm fine. Don't worry about me. I just wanted to let you know.'

With Matt safely out of the house, Jenna removed the camera and while she was at it, she took her time and examined the contents of the other indoor boxes to see if she could identify more of Henry's belongings. Maybe tomorrow she would check the boxes in the garage as well, but it would be as well to let the dust settle first. She found the book *Landscapes of Britain* and was tempted to just take it. After all, she had earned Matt an extra fifteen pounds on that camera by increasing the bidding. However, after checking the inside to make sure there was no inscription or dedication, she took a quick photo of it and put it back in the box.

She sat back down on the sofa and put her feet up; her leg ached after crawling round on the floor. The inactivity gave her an excuse to mentally replay the argument.

Aside from the unjust accusations about Evie, Matt had got right out of his tree when she mentioned Henry. So it was okay for him to go meeting other people and buying expensive items without telling her, but she was not allowed to meet up with a person for the purposes of righting a wrong. She never gambled, but if she had, she'd have bet a sizeable sum of money that if Henry had been a Henrietta, there would have been an altogether different response.

By seven o'clock, there was still no sign of Matt. She sent him a brief text asking if he was planning to come home for dinner, but he didn't reply. Jenna made herself some toast and Marmite; she was not going to go hungry because he was being childish. And if she was being accused of seeing someone else, she needn't feel guilty about seeing Henry again either. He wasn't after a date, he was just being friendly and after the initial nervousness, she had found he was really easy to talk to and had enjoyed their meeting. Jenna pulled out her phone and looked at the thank you e-card that Henry had made. It wasn't the same as something in the post, but as cards went, it was a thoughtful thing to do. She sent him a brief email.

> *Hi Henry,*
> *You will be pleased to hear I've found your camera. If you're free next Saturday, do you want to meet at the same place, and I'll bring it over?*
> *Jenna*

Chapter Seven

When Matt had finally arrived back sometime after nine o'clock, they'd both quietly opted not to re-open the argument. Over the following days, that unofficial policy had continued, limiting discussion to household matters or non-contentious topics, but an underlying tension permeated through every conversation. In spite of the uneasy truce, in the week following camera-gate Jenna found she preferred to be at work rather than at home. She recognised that she was just ignoring the problem, but she didn't feel she had anything more to add. Matt had still made money from the transaction, and if you followed the money, it was directly traceable back to her bonus payment from Confederated Financial Solutions.

Over Saturday breakfast, Matt announced that he was going to an auction with Parry to look at another couple of storage units. Jenna wondered whether he was just saying this in order to see what response he got, and merely reiterated that as long as he could still make his share of the bills payments this month, he could spend his money how he liked. She also took the opportunity to mention that she was meeting Henry to return the camera so that there could be no further accusations of sneaking around behind his back. His reaction was wholly predictable and Jenna was relieved when he left the flat shortly afterwards.

Jenna had arranged to meet Henry at two-thirty at the same teashop in Kings Hampton. The weather today was decidedly April showers, but even the rain couldn't dampen her spirits much further. Her visit two weeks ago had seemed more like covert reconnaissance – something a bit out of the ordinary – whereas this felt more like a mopping up operation after last week's plan had fallen apart at the last hurdle. If all had gone well, there would have been no need to mention either visit. Now the mere mention of Henry's name had the power to invoke a distinctly frosty atmosphere. Jenna sighed. The sooner it was done, the better, she supposed.

The tea shop was more crowded than last week – probably because of the weather – but Henry had already found a table and waved to attract her attention. Instantly, her mood lightened and she grinned and waved back, then turned her attention to her uncooperative umbrella. She wouldn't normally have bothered with a brolly but as she was transporting an expensive camera, she had decided to take the precaution.

After she was seated and the waitress had taken their

orders, she pulled a sturdy, hessian bag onto her lap and lifted out a cardboard box.

'Well, here it is,' she said in a sing-song voice like a game show host announcing the winner. She shoved the condiments and menu to one side and pushed the box across the table. 'I hope there wasn't anything else that was meant to go with it. I did look but there wasn't anything obvious.'

Henry grabbed the box and lifted out the camera, inspecting it almost reverentially. His smile spread slowly across his face until he was beaming. He turned it over in his hands and then removed the lens cap.

'What are you doing?' asked Jenna nervously.

'Checking it's still in working order. And taking your picture.'

Jenna immediately attempted to flatten her hair, which usually went frizzy in this sort of weather despite best efforts with her brolly.

Henry put down the camera for a second. 'Stop fussing. You look absolutely fine.' He pulled a silly face and Jenna laughed nervously.

The camera clicked a few times, and at the neighbouring table, a woman sitting with a baby on her lap glanced over and smiled at them.

'Everyone's looking at us,' said Jenna in an urgent whisper.

'No, they're not!' Henry whispered with a grin.

The camera clicked a few more times and Jenna tried not to look as self-conscious as she felt. Unlike many of her friends' parents, hers hadn't been obsessed with taking pictures of their offspring and Jenna disliked seeing photos of herself. In any case, it wasn't as if she wanted reminders of her childhood, although there were one or two pictures still at her mum's. They could stay there as far as she was concerned. She didn't own a camera and took any photos she wanted on her phone, storing them on the laptop. Most of them were of Evie and the guinea pigs, or the occasional work social event.

She picked up the menu for something to do and studied it for a few moments until their orders arrived.

'And it's my treat this week,' said Henry. 'It's a thank you for all help. I've really missed this old thing.'

Henry carefully put the camera back in the box before starting on his slice of carrot cake. Jenna wondered how long she should hang around. After all, Henry had his camera back and she had no other reason to be there. But she felt guilty about the other items on his list, which she'd been unable to locate. And she was also curious about Isla.

'Henry, do you mind if I ask you something?'

He gestured with his hand. 'Be my guest.'

'What was Isla like? It's just I can't imagine packing up your stuff, going off round the world and leaving your possessions in a storage locker to be auctioned off. Especially as some of it was sentimental stuff.'

'I guess break-ups are always tough, but I'm as surprised as you are about the storage locker. She could be quite sentimental about certain things.'

Jenna thought about the pretty box with the eclectic assortment of knick-knacks. Postcards, fridge magnets, the cuddly toy puffin. They were the sort of thing you bought as a holiday souvenir, to remind you of somewhere. Maybe Isla had just decided to move on and leave the past behind. But Jenna was mindful of dragging up past hurts.

'Do you mind me asking about her? I don't want to be nosey.'

Henry smiled. 'You mean you don't want to *seem* nosey but you'd quite like to *be* nosey.' He laughed and gestured with his hand. 'It's fine, honestly. Go ahead, be nosey.'

'I wondered … how did you meet?'

'It was down to a clash of interests. I was at Avebury – I love old places full of ancient stories and legends. If you can get there early, it's not heaving with tourists either. I went to take some photos and just my luck, there was a large party of sightseers doing one of those whistle-stop tours. You know the sort of thing – trundling round the county in a coach with fifteen minutes at each stop. Isla was the person in charge and I asked how long they were going to be as I wanted to get some wide-angle shots without loads of people in the way, and we just got chatting. The next week she was doing a guided tour of the Brighton Pavilion so we arranged to meet there – have you been?'

Jenna shook her head, feeling like whatever the opposite of a culture vulture was.

'Really interesting place,' Henry enthused. 'I'd recommend a visit. Anyway, Isla quite fancied a trip without doing all the guidebook stuff for the massing hoards, and I suggested – tongue in cheek – for our next trip we ought to pick somewhere beginning with the letter C, since we'd already done Avebury and Brighton.'

'That's a brilliant idea, I'd have loved to do that!'

Jenna recalled the model of the little mermaid. 'Was it Copenhagen by any chance?'

'Yes, good guess. The thing is, I was only being semi-serious about the alphabet thing, but Isla seemed to like it, and so we carried on. We hiked, explored and photographed Dubrovnik, then Edinburgh, followed by Florence, Guernsey and the bulb fields of Holland – I got some fabulous photos there. And then…' Henry sighed. 'Then Iceland happened. You know how it goes.'

Jenna didn't actually. All she knew was that this was now an ex-relationship, but poring over the details of someone's break up was the sort of thing you might do with your best friend or sister, not with someone who was a virtual stranger, albeit a very chatty one.

The sound of Henry's voice broke into her thoughts. 'Anyway, I'm now certifiably a romance-free zone.' He paused for a second. 'So can I ask you a question now? How did you get my camera back? Not that I'm not extremely grateful, because I am, but people buy these storage units in order to make money from selling the contents. If your boyfriend simply gave the camera back to you, he's either rich or magnanimous.'

'He's certainly not rich,' replied Jenna. Matt wasn't

magnanimous either, but now wasn't the time to mention that. She scrambled around for an interesting change of subject but wasn't quick enough.

'So … was he okay about you taking it back? I don't want to be responsible for causing any problems.'

'I gave him some cash,' said Jenna, trying to be deliberately vague.

'Then I must reimburse you. How much did you give him?'

Jenna shrugged. 'It's fine.'

'No, it's not! Jenna, I feel terrible that you've been put to so much trouble to get my camera back, just because my ex-girlfriend wouldn't reply to me and couldn't be bothered to pay for storage any longer.'

'And I feel it's wrong to have to buy back your own possessions just because my'—Jenna hesitated for a second—'because Matt has acquired them.'

'But I also feel a bit guilty because I don't have any proof that it was mine in the first place.'

'You were very specific on the make and model for someone who had no proof,' laughed Jenna.

'True. And now I'm looking forward to taking some more pictures with it.' He patted the box. 'My other camera is newer, but heavier and has more kit with it, and I have lots of memories attached to this one.' He paused. 'Sorry, does that sound rather flash talking about my other camera?'

'Not if your other car is a Porsche,' replied Jenna mischievously.

Henry laughed. 'I take it you are a strictly one-camera person?'

Jenna nodded. 'And it doubles as my phone. It takes reasonable pictures, but I don't bother very often, to be honest, unless my sister needs me to take some for her, to upload on her website.'

Henry slapped his hands on the table. 'Ooh, now you've got my attention! Photos for your sister's website. Hmmm…' He pretended to think while raising his eyebrows suggestively.

Jenna couldn't help smiling. 'Would your imagination by any chance be conjuring up long legs, curvy body, pouty expression?'

'Certainly not!' said Henry quickly.

She leaned forward and wagged her finger at him. 'Good. Because you'd be nearer the mark with short, stubby legs, fat, hairy body and cute, pointy nose.'

'Does your sister know you describe her like that?'

They both burst into peals of laughter. 'My sister is tall, blonde, and beautiful,' said Jenna, still trying to stop laughing. 'And she runs a guinea pig rescue. When the residents are ready to find their forever homes, they're photographed for the website. I sometimes get to play the photographer, although I'm not very good at it. And having cute pictures helps with website donations too.'

'My sister had a pair of guinea pigs when we were children; one was ginger and white, and the other was a beautiful dark brown colour – they were super cute. I think I was more upset than she was when they died. I

74

couldn't run a rescue as I'd never want to give any away.'

'Evie's really careful about re-homing her piggies. They always do a home check to make sure that the cage is big enough, and that the environment is suitable. Some people think they're a cuddly little live-action toy thing you can buy for kids, then they get neglected when the child gets bored of the new pet. Some of the animals arrive at the rescue in a dreadful state – I've seen some shocking pictures – but most of them go on to find a new home. My sister spends most of her day cleaning out guinea pig cages or buying up half the vegetable aisle in Tesco for the animals, and she's permanently broke as there are always vet bills to settle, but she says she's happy.'

'Good for her,' said Henry approvingly. 'I'd choose happy over money any day, wouldn't you?'

Jenna didn't answer. Maybe when you had money you could afford to be choosy, but as far as she was concerned, financial security came first, second, third and last.

Henry seemed not to notice Jenna's lack of response. 'I only wish my parents thought like that too,' he continued. 'Living at home isn't all it's cracked up to be.'

'So why not move out then? Or are you broke?'

'Okay, long story very short. After Isla and I split up, I decided to go travelling again. I rented out my flat and hadn't planned on returning so soon, but circumstances changed. Anyway, I felt mean kicking the tenants out; hence the temporary dossing at the parents' place.'

'And is your flat in Haxford?'

Jenna wasn't sure whether Henry's look of horror was genuine or just for effect.

'Good grief, that's way too close to home!' He chuckled. 'My home is in Poole. The scenery is far nicer, and it's only a thirty-metre stroll to the beach.'

It was only after a few seconds that Jenna realised her mouth was open and she shut it promptly. Henry lived in Poole! By the beach! How on earth did he afford that? She might not be well travelled, but she certainly knew that beach-side properties in that part of the world made Kings Hampton look positively affordable. Imagine just opening your curtains and looking out at the sea! It felt like someone had tweaked aside a curtain she never knew existed, and given her a tiny glimpse into a different world. And one that Henry clearly took for granted.

Henry waved in a hello-I'm-trying-to-attract-your-attention sort of way. 'So, going back to the subject of my camera, if you won't allow me to pay you for it, will you allow me to take you out for dinner instead? Not as a date or anything, just as a thank you.'

He had obviously realised she'd been gawping, and heat rushed to Jenna's face. 'Really, there's no need,' said Jenna, fiddling with her serviette. She told herself she felt flustered because she hadn't expected any recompense, and it was nothing whatsoever to do with the fact that he was charming, and funny, and just great company. He had set out clearly that it wasn't a date so what was her problem? Didn't she want to see him again?

'Excuse me, Jenna Oakhurst, but you don't have a monopoly on feeling guilty, you know.' Henry threw her a challenging look. For a few seconds, neither spoke. Then Henry raised his forefinger in the air. 'Okay then, how about this for an idea. What if I offer to do a photo session for your sister? I've got a variety of old backdrops that might come in handy, and then maybe she can use the pictures to put together a calendar as a fundraiser or something. I know it's still only mid-April, but in six months or so, people will be starting to buy next year's calendar. Clearly – and this is for the avoidance of doubt – I'm not trying to cast aspersions on your own photography skills, but the offer's there.' He looked at her. His blue eyes sparkled with enthusiasm, and the corners of his mouth turned up in a hopeful expression.

Jenna didn't want anything for herself but this was different. This was for Evie. Despite Kat's warnings about meeting up with strangers, she knew they would be disappointed if she turned down an offer of help without even asking them first.

'Well, that's very generous of you. I'll certainly ask, and I'll let you know what her answer is.'

———

Although she had promised to let Henry know what Evie's answer was, she knew Evie would say yes. Anybody that offered anything for the guinea pigs was invariably met with an affirmative from those two.

On the journey home, she allowed her thoughts to meander back to their conversation and she realised how much she had enjoyed her afternoon with Henry. They had talked about everything and anything. He had made her laugh. He was interested in what she had to say. And he didn't mind being teased a bit. Matt was really prickly about that and got a bit edgy if he thought she was laughing at him.

She hardly knew Henry but he seemed genuinely keen to help, and she wondered why he was going to such trouble. Maybe, like her, he felt it was only right to do something. Offer a quid pro quo in return for all her efforts. At least he appreciated them. She had expected him to be, if not angry, then at least a little surprised that she had opened his letter to Isla but that wasn't the case. She also wondered, not for the last time, why Isla really left as Henry seemed very easy-going. Maybe, despite the box of trinkets and souvenirs, she wasn't a sentimental person at all and Jenna had just super-imposed her own values on this mystery woman.

Chapter Eight

As Jenna predicted, Evie and Kat were delighted with Henry's offer and absolutely bursting with questions about her latest meeting. Jenna suspected this was, in part, Kat's way of checking him out as a suitable friend, both for her and them.

Because of Jenna's Monday to Friday job and Sundays being open visiting at Little Paws, the piggy photoshoot was fixed for a Saturday near the end of April. In the intervening weeks, Jenna didn't have much time to think about it as both she and Matt were busy at the moment. For Jenna, there had been all the usual accounting year-end jobs for her team as well as maintaining the expenses payments for employees. Last week her least favourite member of the Sales Team, Ian Ransome, sent over receipts for a three-course meal with wine at DeLaneys – the only Michelin-starred restaurant in Haxford, as she had remarked to her colleagues. She would have loved to reject it on grounds of profligacy, but it regrettably did not breach any of the company's expenses policy.

Matt was pushing ahead with what he termed his 'new ventures'. Jenna couldn't fault him for his enthusiasm but was still reserving judgement on the financial prudency of his plans. Matt had announced over breakfast the other day that Parry had bought another three abandoned storage units and that he'd offered to help with both emptying the lock-ups and storing the contents while Parry was scouting around for a more permanent arrangement. This would mean rearranging their stuff in the garage, he had informed her.

Jenna had pointed out that nothing of hers was actually in the garage so he could move around what he liked. Unfortunately, Matt had taken her response literally, so now their lounge resembled an overflow storage locker, with a stack of brown cardboard boxes on one corner, and more than once, Jenna had stubbed her toe or tripped over an unsuspecting obstacle.

As the days went on, Matt seemed to spend the majority of his time either on the internet posting auctions and researching items, or with Parry. From time to time, Matt showed Jenna his spreadsheet of sales, but it didn't generate the enthusiastic response Matt was clearly hoping for. She didn't object to his plans in principle, and if he'd been a person she'd met casually in the pub, maybe she'd be more interested in his business ventures. However to maintain a long-term relationship, there had to be a level of trust; Jenna would never have admitted it to anyone, but the way in which he had left a paid job and leapt straight into a highly risky venture without even telling her beforehand, had seriously unsettled her.

Also in the never-admit-to-anyone box was the fact that she was looking forward to seeing Henry again. He was interesting. He had travelled, seen amazing things. Yet he was still interested in helping her sister and had become all enthused when she'd told him about the guinea pigs. People who didn't know Evie well often thought she was a bit aloof, but then, other people hadn't grown up like they did, moving from place to place, hardly having time to make friends before they were forced to move again, each time to a smaller place, or a poorer area. Jenna could still remember the pitying glances and whispered gossip between neighbours when they thought she was out of earshot. *Those poor girls*, they used to say. *As if they haven't got enough problems*.

From an early age, Jenna had worked out that the 'problems' referred to her frequent visits to (and occasional stays in) the children's hospital, and she had been determined to protect her sister from that sort of gossip, but Evie always seemed remarkably unscathed. Things happened, they moved home, her parents eventually separated. Evie adjusted, coped, rode out the waves. In the end it was her, not Evie, that had needed protection but somehow nobody noticed that, so she built her own. It was called financial security.

Jenna had more or less insisted on picking up Henry

en route to Evie's. Most people got lost trying to find the place – Jenna had often missed the turning in the early days – and in any case, he was doing them a favour and giving up his afternoon so it was the least she could do. They had arranged to meet in a pub car park halfway between Haxford and Kings Hampton and Jenna was first to arrive. As the appointed time came and went, she wondered if she had misunderstood the arrangements. At T-plus five minutes she rechecked her emails. At T-plus fifteen minutes, an elderly BMW pulled up and parked alongside her.

Even though the purpose of the expedition was purely a thank you for returning his camera, Jenna still experienced a huge surge of relief as Henry stepped out of the car, and she found herself grinning.

'Sorry I'm late. I hope I haven't kept you waiting for ages.'

'Do you want a polite answer or the painful truth?'

'Sorry, I've always been hopeless at timekeeping; I blame it on an over-reliance on the school bell during my formative years – it told you when to get up, when to go to lessons, when to go to lunch'—he flashed her a playful look—'so who needs a timepiece? When I lived at home, Mum used to move all the clocks forward ten minutes. Drove Dad batty. Shall I load the car?'

She watched as Henry transferred what seemed like enough luggage for a six-month holiday from the back of his car into hers. His jeans looked like they'd seen more than a few hiking expeditions, but the dark green sweater was a nod towards smart. He'd also had a haircut, Jenna noted.

'You don't travel light, do you?' she said as they pulled out onto the main road.

'You never know what you might need. The suitcase is full of props though, not clothes, in case you were worried. I'd like to move out but I'm not that desperate!'

'I remember you said you don't like living at home.'

'It's hard to explain without sounding ungrateful. Living at home is comfortable. Practical. Cheap, obviously, but...' He paused. 'In a nutshell, my parents had high expectations for both my sister and me. She lived up to them, I didn't. Still don't. The trouble is Dad doesn't let me forget it either. So, when someone comes along and offers me a free afternoon out of the house, doing what I enjoy most, how can I resist?'

'Except technically I didn't make the offer, you did.'

'Are you always this politely pedantic?' Henry asked with a laugh. 'I have written email evidence that you did accept my offer, you know.'

Without taking her eyes off the road, Jenna could sense that he was looking at her. 'So I did,' she said with a smile.

'So tell me all about this rescue. I really admire people who just follow their passions – how long has your sister been running it? Did she set it up by herself?'

The remainder of the journey was spent discussing Little Paws Guinea Pig Rescue. Jenna told him about Evie and Kat, where they lived, what the place looked like, how they set up as a registered charity and relied on donations and the occasional contribution from a supermarket green token scheme.

Henry was such a good listener that Jenna found herself telling him about how Evie had struggled at school, how she had felt responsible for her little sister and wanted to help her get settled in a job after she left education. It had even worked for a while, but unlike Jenna, who had been prepared to sacrifice personal preferences for financial security, Evie was not.

'So now she's happy, but broke,' said Jenna as they turned onto the gravel track lane that led up to the farmhouse.

Before they were out of the car, Evie was running towards them, her blonde ponytail swinging wildly, and the sisters hugged.

'Evie, this is Henry. You wouldn't believe how much stuff he's brought with him, just to take a few pictures.' Jenna opened the boot and lifted out a few of the smaller bags. 'We might have to clear space in the barn first.'

Henry hurried round to help Jenna. 'Hey! You don't need to carry those; I'll do the bag shifting.'

'And the reason why I shouldn't be moving bags is…?'

Evie heaved one of the holdalls from the boot. 'Let me give you a helpful tip. If your answer is anything to do with wobbly balance, Jenna might clout you.'

The first thing Henry wanted to do was look at all the guinea pigs. He was enchanted with the loud squeaking that struck up as soon as he entered the barn and he spent several minutes peering into all the hutches admiring each of the occupants. Once everything was unloaded and Henry had been introduced to Kat, the four of them discussed how best to create a studio set. Evie and Kat were naturally nervous about taking pictures outside; a scared guinea pig could make Usain Bolt look positively pedestrian, explained Evie. Being Saturday, there were several volunteers busily getting on with the cage cleaning but they cleared some space in the centre of the barn and agreed that by pushing several hay bales together they could make a flat area, which they covered with a large sheet. Around the edge, they used old fence panels and their display board to prevent any of the piggies making a sudden dash off the stage.

Henry then opened one of the suitcases and lifted out what looked like two white parasols.

'What on earth are they for?' asked Jenna. 'We're not doing a guinea pig version of *Pride and Prejudice*, are we?'

Henry laughed and lifted out two tripods with extendable legs. 'They attach to these. It's my portable lighting kit.'

Jenna watched as he attached the umbrellas to the tripods, which had light bulbs attached to the underside. He then spent a while adjusting the height, fiddling with his camera, and doing test pictures, while Evie and Kat decided which piggies they wanted to use as models.

Henry had brought along a number of cloth backdrops, including a garden scene, a woodland clearing, a prairie, a library, a theatre stage, as well as a couple of plain colours, which he explained often worked well with props.

Evie and Kat spent even longer looking at the props; they admired the mock window and a wooden bridge, the realistic-looking artificial flowers, they adored the top hat and the children's toy jeep, plus the miniature trees, a small wicker picnic basket and a selection of board games. There was also a variety of different towels and hessian tiles to use as flooring.

'So, who is going to be the first model?' asked Henry.

'We thought you could start with Oreo,' said Evie, bending over the large pen behind them and lifting up a chunky, dark brown piggy with a white patch across her back. 'She's very nice-natured, but watch the props as she does like to chew things, don't you, madam?' With Evie and Kat acting as animal handlers, Jenna adopted the role of photographer's assistant, helping to reposition the lights or the props as required by the photographer. Henry sat cross-legged on the floor and before long there was a regular blip blip from his camera as he took several pictures from a variety of angles, with each of the sets.

Then out came Lady Maud, a beige guinea pig with a white crest on her head. Jenna found what looked like a doll's throne, which they put in the background, and added a few other regal looking props and a doll's velvet cap, which they balanced gently on the guinea pig's head. After Lady Maud made it perfectly clear she didn't want anything on her head, they put it on a teddy instead and sat her next to it. Jenna then had the idea of using one of the many guinea pig books lying around the barn and propped that open in front of Lady Maud who obligingly sniffed at the pages.

As each new piggy had their turn in the spotlight, their ideas got bolder and bigger, and when Henry suggested using two piggies in the shot, Evie and Kat responded enthusiastically to the idea. Daisy and Maisie obligingly posed side by side peering through the fake window with their paws on the sill, for all the world like two old ladies having a gossip.

After each piggy had posed, they were paid their fee in cucumber treats, and Henry insisted on being allowed to help with that task. After a good hour of photography, Evie and Kat went back to the house to fetch refreshments while Henry sat with Lulu on his lap – one of a litter of three baby guinea pigs born at the rescue a few weeks ago.

'Are all baby guinea pigs this unbelievably cute?' he asked Jenna as he gazed at the black and tan piggy that wasn't much bigger than his hand.

'Yep. That's why they're so popular as children's pets, but they're classed as exotics as far as insurance and veterinary services are concerned.'

'Oops!' Henry swiftly scooped up the tiny animal in his hands. 'I think someone needed the toilet.'

Jenna laughed and grabbed an old towel from a pile and dropped it on his lap. 'Occupational hazard with guinea pigs. Sorry, we should have warned you – not all of them are good at telling you when they need a wee.'

She returned the baby to its mum in the large pen behind them while Henry dabbed at the damp patch on his jeans.

'Luckily it's nearer your knee, so no one will think you wet yourself,' said Jenna with a wry smile.

'They're old things. Probably seen worse,' said Henry, passing the towel back to Jenna who couldn't help but think back to when the same thing had happened to Matt. He had insisted on going indoors to use some hot soapy water in case it left a stain and had refused to hold another guinea pig after that.

Kat returned with a tray of mugs balanced on it and Evie was waving a tin of shortbread biscuits around. It reminded Jenna of the empty tin she'd found in Isla's box. 'A thank you present from a family who visited last week,' said Evie, pulling the lid off and passing them round. She pulled over a few plastic chairs and they all sat down while they drank their tea.

Henry was fascinated to hear about how they had started up the rescue and how people had different reasons for giving up a pet. Quite often it was because they had lost interest after finding out how much work went into looking after them. Sometimes people were left with a solitary animal and didn't want to adopt another one. Guinea pigs are sociable animals, Kat explained, so it was always nicer if they were able to live with a friend. And then there were the awful cases of neglect where guinea pigs were simply dumped in a box on the doorstep or they were called out to help rescue an animal. Evie told him about some of the appalling places from which they had recovered traumatised and often sick guinea pigs.

Henry was also shocked at how much they relied on donations to keep going. 'Well I'm delighted to be able to help with your fundraising efforts. I'll buy all my friends a copy of the calendar for Christmas.'

'Assuming we're not—'

'So, Henry, what do you do when you're not taking photographs?' said Kat quickly, shooting Evie a warning glance.

'At the moment, not very much,' he replied. 'I used to travel a lot.'

'Was that with your ex-girlfriend?'

Jenna gave Kat her best I-can't-believe-you-just-asked-that look, but Kat pretended not to notice.

If Henry was embarrassed, it certainly didn't show. 'In more recent times, yes, but before that I was travelling about either on my own or with friends.'

'You must have seen some amazing places,' said Jenna in an attempt to steer the conversation away from Isla. 'Did you take that northern lights picture?'

At this point, the inevitable question of *what northern lights picture?* resulted in the others insisting on seeing the picture, so Jenna pulled out her phone to show them.

'It's a stunning photo, Henry. You must be really good,' said Kat. 'You should sell these.'

'I do, actually, although only the best ones.'

'How do you know where to sell them?' asked Jenna,

wondering whether he had his own eBay shop like Matt did.

'I use a photography agency. I send my agent pictures from time to time and get paid for the ones they want to use. Some go on to a stock library and then I get royalties on those.'

This revelation sparked a flurry of questions about how many photos he had sold, which ones were popular, and whether he had travelled to specific places to take them. Jenna noted with relief that Evie and Kat didn't go as far as asking how much he got paid for them, although the nosey part of her almost wished they had. After their last meeting, she had looked up prices of flats in Poole with a beach view and spent half the evening admiring the luxury apartments on Sandbanks. It wasn't the real world but it was free to look.

The photography session resumed with another line up of equally cute, conscripted guinea pigs, including a mum and her pups, one of which Henry had cuddled earlier, and a tri-coloured guinea pig that looked like its fur had been styled into a series of rosettes.

'It's an Abyssinian,' explained Evie. 'His fur just grows like that. Abbys carry this dominant gene so if they breed with a smooth coated piggy, the babies might have one or more rosettes appearing.'

Henry was fascinated by the way the rosettes and the varied colours gave the piggy a real punk look.

It seemed to Jenna as though the afternoon just flew past. One moment it was two o'clock, the next it was nearly six. Evie and Kat excused themselves to go and prepare the evening veggies for the guineas while Henry finished the last couple of photos. They were using the green, prairie backdrop, which was a great contrast against the toffee-coloured guinea pig.

'She's a gorgeous looking guinea pig,' said Henry, angling the camera to get some different shots. 'I love all that long hair.' After a few more photos, he put down the camera. 'I think that's the lot for her.'

Remembering his earlier comment about being politely pedantic, Jenna refrained from saying: *Actually it's a him*. Instead, Jenna gently lifted up the piggy. 'This is Snickers, and he's got a lovely coat.'

'Can I give Snickers a quick cuddle?'

'Sure.' Jenna placed the piggy on Henry's lap. She had helped out often enough to feel almost as confident handling the guinea pigs as Evie was, although she drew the line at certain procedures. It wasn't that she was squeamish, but she hated the way some of the piggies squealed and squirmed as though they were being tortured, even if Evie was only doing toenail clipping.

Jenna did have a soft spot for Snickers though, despite his fondness for chewing holes in other people's clothes, and she reached over and gently brushed her fingers against the silky, long hair.

'He loves a bit of a massage, don't you, Snickers?' Jenna gently rubbed her fingers along his back and Snickers made a cute purring noise. She wasn't quite sure, then or afterwards, how it happened, but one minute she was stroking the guinea pig and the next, the piggy had shifted position, and her fingers were caressing a denim-clad thigh.

Mortified, Jenna yanked her hand away and stepped back quickly, wobbled for a second, then toppled backwards into a pile of boxes.

'Shit! Are you okay, Jenna?'

She must have hit something solid as there was a sharp pain in her hip, but she wasn't about to make a scene in front of Henry. Instead, she squeezed her eyes shut for a few seconds and took several deep breaths waiting for the spike of pain to ease off. People always made a fuss when she fell over; once she lost her balance in the cake aisle at the supermarket and an elderly gentleman had insisted that she remain on the floor until they had summoned the first aider, while arguing loudly with the more practical-minded shoppers who were helping her to her feet.

She opened her eyes to find Henry kneeling in front of her. He reached out his hand, hesitated, then swiftly retracted it.

'Erm … stay there for a mo. I'll go and fetch Evie.' He leapt to his feet.

'Please don't, I'm fine.' As if to prove the point, she pushed one of the boxes aside and sat up carefully and rubbed her leg for something to do. Henry held out his hand again and Jenna used it to pull herself up. He must think she was such an idiot! Her cheeks glowed with the embarrassment of the whole thing.

Henry pulled over one of the folding chairs and Jenna sat down gratefully. She wanted to apologise but she wasn't quite sure how to explain what happened, and the less she said about her hand on his thigh the better. She directed her attention to another more urgent question.

'Where's Snickers gone?'

'Don't worry, I put her home. The important thing is whether you're okay.'

'I'm fine. Really. But maybe we ought to be making a move; you're probably desperate to get away now.' She stood up and folded away the chair. 'Luckily, I only dented my dignity and a few boxes, and not your photography apparatus.'

Jenna helped Henry pack everything away and tried not to wince too often. It had been an exhausting afternoon, but hopefully there would be some good photos to show for it. Evie and Kat hugged Henry gratefully as they said their goodbyes and said he was welcome to visit whenever he liked. Henry handed out his business card with the assurance that he'd had a wonderful afternoon and had enjoyed every second of it. Jenna hoped he was excluding the brief seconds where she'd accidentally groped him.

Chapter Nine

It was a relief to be back in the car. Not solely because she was now running on empty as far as energy reserves were concerned, but also because it meant Henry was sitting further away and she couldn't accidentally grab his thigh. If it had happened to someone else, she would have found the whole episode hilarious, but it wasn't and she didn't.

'Lovely countryside round here,' said Henry, breaking into her embarrassed thoughts.

'It is,' she agreed, 'but probably a bit boring compared to what you're used to.' She guessed he was making polite conversation just to fill the awkward silence. 'For someone who's been halfway round the world, if not all the way round, Haxford must seem rather ordinary.'

'It's true that I've been lucky enough to see some fabulous places, but the landscape doesn't have to be exotic to be fascinating.'

'You can hardly compare a Scandinavian forest illuminated by the northern lights to the sky-scape in a provincial English town,' argued Jenna. 'And you need money in order to go to all these interesting places.'

'I admit it does help, but let me dispel any ideas you have about my luxury lifestyle when I'm travelling; my trip to Norway was on a working boat, not a luxury cruise ship, and I've camped in the wild and lived out of a backpack many times.'

'So why rough it if you have the money to do it in style?'

'Because sometimes it's fun. Anyway, who says I have the money to travel in style?' There was a distinct challenge in Henry's voice and Jenna instantly wished she could take back what she'd said. Why had she just tried to spoil a lovely afternoon by being combative? If Evie or Kat had said that she'd have been mortified. Jenna kept her eyes fixed firmly on the road ahead as she attempted to smooth over what was clearly a few ruffled feathers.

'Sorry. I probably added two plus two and made seven. It was because you'd mentioned you had a flat in Poole you see, and … well, I guess I just made some assumptions.' She flicked her glance over to her passenger. 'Money was the cause of all the problems in my family. I hated being the kid in school who had second-hand books, second-hand uniform. All my parents ever seemed to do was row about money and—'

Her outburst skidded to a halt. 'Sorry, you don't need to hear all this.'

Henry didn't respond immediately. She guessed he was probably embarrassed. For several seconds, neither of them spoke. Then he said, 'Do you remember about five years ago there was that little boy from Luton who disappeared while he was staying with his grandparents in Malta? There was a massive international police search and it was all over the papers for a while.'

The question baffled her. 'I think I remember reading about that. He was found in Morocco, wasn't he?'

'That's correct. He—'

'Yes, I remember now,' Jenna continued. 'Wasn't he identified months later from a photograph taken by some clueless tourist who clearly hadn't been aware of this international appeal for information?'

'That's the one.'

Jenna frowned as she tried to connect these pieces of information together. 'But … so…'

'Yes, is the short answer. I was that clueless tourist. I was mostly backpacking out in the sticks so it was only when I got home weeks later that I saw the appeal for information. Most of my pictures were of landscapes but I'd taken a few photos of people in a local market. I actually remember seeing the kid with a miserable expression on his face so I took his photo. It reminded me of my own family holidays where I was dragged round some fancy palace or ancient ruins when I'd have been a lot happier making sandcastles on a beach back home. When I saw the boy's picture in the papers it jogged my memory, so I sent in my photo just in case. It was sheer fluke that I'd taken it and pure luck that I heard about the story on my return.

'Nevertheless, all the newspapers wanted a copy of the photo and there was a reward for information leading to the safe return of the boy.' He shrugged. 'So, that was my nest egg. I invested it in property rather than shoving it in the bank and then went back to my travels. But with a better camera,' he added with a grin.

'But that's amazing. You're an unsung hero!'

Henry gestured modestly. 'I was just in the right place at the right time and I was more relieved that the little boy was returned to his family. Anyway, that's how I paid for my flat. And if it makes you feel better, I still have a small mortgage.'

Jenna was dying to hear more about Henry's past, but before she could think of what to ask that wouldn't appear appallingly nosey, Henry posed his own question.

'So now that thorny subject is out of the way, let me ask you something.' He turned his head to look at her. 'Haven't you ever wanted to just get away from everyday life for a while, see a bit of the world, see something extraordinary?'

Did she want to get away from everyday life? No one had ever asked her that question before. She liked the security of her job; that paid for her home. And travelling anywhere always seemed like it would be a lot of hassle and for what? To see things she could look at online or on Google Earth. In any case, the question was irrelevant.

'Sorry to disappoint you, but I don't have that sort of disposable income.'

'I know. But what if you didn't need money? You can find amazing sights right on your doorstep if only you know where to look.' Henry laughed. 'I can tell by the expression on your face that you're not convinced by my persuasive arguments. Okay, let me prove it to you. I will take you to somewhere scenic and just a little bit magical that is not far from here and costs absolutely nothing.'

'You don't need to do that,' Jenna said hurriedly.

'No, I don't *need* to, but I'd *like* to. Provided your boyfriend doesn't object to you taking a sightseeing trip. Maybe Haxford's attractions aren't in the same league as the temples of Angkor Wat, but you can find the amazing anywhere.'

Jenna's first priority after dropping Henry back at the pub car park was to get home and have a long soak in the bath; in an ideal world, she'd have a book and a glass of wine, like the heroines in her favourite novels did. Right now she had to make do with a cup of tea and a couple of co-codamol. As she lay back in the warm water, her thoughts returned to the events of the afternoon. Henry certainly seemed very at home behind the camera and she couldn't wait to see the results. Evie and Kat seemed to have forgotten their earlier suspicions about Henry, although to be fair, anyone who loved guinea pigs was automatically welcome at Farm Cottage.

The first time she'd taken Matt over to see her sister he had waxed lyrical about how much potential there was for developing the land, rather insensitively overlooking the fact that Evie and Kat were only renting and already concerned about what might happen in the future. He had also referred to the guinea pigs as *a bit like chunky rats but without tails*, which unfortunately Kat had overheard, and clearly wasn't the rapturous response they'd been expecting. It hadn't started things off on quite the right foot, but that was all in the past now and they got on well enough whenever he accompanied her on visits.

In contrast, Henry had rushed into the barn, exclaiming enthusiastically over all the furries, and had sat cuddling the models after each photo session. And Jenna couldn't help but notice how Evie and Kat had hugged him at the end of the afternoon. Saying goodbye to Matt was generally restricted to a brief peck on the cheek. Perhaps she might suggest that Matt made a little more effort next time they visited.

And what of her own goodbye? She had deliberately stayed in the car when Henry got out. Mostly because she was now in a lot of pain, but also because she didn't want him to feel awkward. Didn't she feel comfortable with a friendly peck on the cheek? After all he was just a friend, albeit a rather heroic one. Before she could answer her own question, Matt's voice wafted through the bathroom door.

'Your sister just rang. She needs to ask you something. Can you call her back when you've finished lounging in the bath?'

It was probably to discuss the events of the afternoon. She was sure that during their tea break, Evie had been about to say something important, and equally sure that Kat deliberately stopped her. She wondered whether it was related to the building work over the road. The last she'd heard, Evie and Kat's landlord had made it clear he would not be selling any of his land despite the offers he had received, but Jenna knew that where business was concerned, money talked. She was glad Evie still felt able to talk to her though, whatever it was she wanted to ask.

As children, they had shared a bedroom and Jenna often fell asleep listening to Evie talking about the events of the day, sharing confidences or asking her to help with something. Sometimes there wasn't anything that Jenna could do to help, but she always listened. Kat had now inherited that role to some extent but Jenna was still big sister and felt a duty of care.

Now, wearing her pyjamas and cosily wrapped up in her dressing gown, Jenna lay on the bed and called her sister back.

'Hello little sis, everything okay at your end? Matt said you needed to talk about something, and I noticed that you were going to say something—'

'What happened after Snickers finished modelling?'

That wasn't at all the question she expected. Technically, and following a strict chronology of events, the answer was *I accidentally fondled Henry*. Jenna blushed again at the memory of her hand on his warm, muscular thigh.

'The thing is,' Evie continued, 'Snickers wasn't standing at the front of his hutch waiting for supper, but he'd had a busy afternoon so we just assumed he was sleeping. It was only when we came to came to collect up the bowls that we realised he hadn't eaten anything, and then we opened the sleeping compartment and found he wasn't even in there!'

Jenna sat up. 'Has he escaped? Could he have got out of the barn, do you think?'

'It's okay, we found him in the big pen with all the girls; he was completely zonked out in one of the fleecy tunnel beds.'

'Oh.' Jenna realised instantly what must have happened.

Don't worry, I put her home…

She hadn't liked to correct Henry again, so thinking Snickers was a girl, he must have automatically assumed the piggy lived in the main girls' pen. Apart from which, there had been a slight urgency about putting him down somewhere safe.

A suspicious thought edged into her head. 'Oh heck, you don't think that he…'

'Jen, you knew he was a young, un-neutered male. I'd be surprised if he *hadn't* done anything. I thought you of all people would know what a stupid idea it was to put him in there.'

'Sorry Evie. I guess I was tired too.'

'You sound tired. You were probably on your feet for too long. Henry had you running around – you should have told him you can't do that.'

'It's one day. I'll be fine. Sorry for all the trouble.'

'Don't worry, I'll send you the bill.'

'Evie, before you go – when we were talking earlier, you started to say something and Kat abruptly changed the subject. Is everything okay?'

There was several seconds of silence before Evie responded. 'I'm sorry, I was just worried. Gerry and Paula have had an increased offer from the developers but Gerry says it's dependent on them getting planning permission and he personally doesn't think that's very likely.'

'Neither do I,' said Jenna robustly.

Jenna heard a sigh. 'I just wish he hadn't told me, that's all.'

'I know. But try not to dwell on it because it's highly unlikely that even if he wanted to accept the offer that the council would approve more building right now.'

'Really? Thanks Jen. You've cheered me up. I'm glad you know about these things.'

Jenna didn't really. She just didn't want Evie to worry about it until more facts appeared. And it might not even happen. She hoped that they were worrying unnecessarily and that any application would be turned down. She also hoped for everyone's sake that Snickers had behaved himself earlier. If he had mated with any of the females it would mean finding extra space for the potentially pregnant piggies, who could not then be rehomed until they were sure there were no babies on the way.

It was an honest mistake, so why hadn't she simply said it was Henry's fault? After all, she didn't owe him anything. She'd given him his camera back, and in return he had given up his time to help Evie and Kat, and had livened up their afternoon. And apparently that of a randy guinea pig too. But somehow it mattered to Jenna that Evie and Kat retained their good opinion of him.

Despite their different outlooks on life, she had enjoyed his company and she didn't want to contact him purely for the purposes of telling him off. As she lay on the bed, she wondered whether she would even see him again; he might easily email over the photos and that would be an end to it. Unless she took him up on his offer.

That was just to prove a point though, wasn't it? Or perhaps he felt sorry for her. Jenna hadn't travelled further than North Wales and that was to stay with Great-Aunt Mary one half-term holiday, while her parents were allegedly 'sorting things out'. She had assumed that had meant getting a permanent home, not settling a divorce.

In contrast, Henry's life was a million miles apart from hers – it was like something you read about in a magazine. He lived in a posh apartment in Poole for a start. And his parents lived in Kings Hampton. She'd checked out Harcourt Drive using online maps, and it was not the sort of place ordinary people lived. He also didn't have outstanding loans or lingering student debts like most people she knew, and he probably didn't need to check his bank account every week to make sure he wasn't going to be overdrawn.

Jenna mentally added that task to tomorrow's to-do list and shelved the more difficult question of if, and how, to respond to Henry.

Chapter Ten

The following morning, while Matt was rearranging boxes in the garage, Jenna carried out her regular checks on both her own bank account and the shared bills account. The latter had been set up when they'd moved in together, and Jenna had worked out exactly what they needed on a month-to-month basis to cover the rent and other maintenance bills, with an allowance built in to include the weekly food shop and a few other miscellaneous items. She had set up a standing order to pay across her share, but Matt preferred to make individual payments for some random reason of his own. By his own admission he wasn't as experienced at financial planning so Matt had been more than happy for her to manage their joint finances and it had continued on that basis ever since.

Reviewing the accounts gave Jenna a sense of security. Like checking the iron was switched off, or the doors were locked before you went out. These figures were her security blanket – her reassurance that all was well with the world. Even as a child, she'd often counted her meagre pocket money savings to make sure it was all still there.

Today, she started with her own bank account. The main income was her monthly salary, which had been two hundred pounds higher this month. She had been looking forward to treating herself without feeling guilty, but it couldn't be helped. She noted the corresponding payment of £220 going across to Evie, and the £650 standing order to the joint bills account. It didn't leave a lot left over but it worked. She had no idea how Matt managed his bank account; it must be more complicated now he had so many eBay sales on the go, but that was his problem. She had offered to help, but the offer had been declined.

She then logged in to their joint bills account and quickly scanned the entries. For Jenna, spotting an accounting anomaly was as easy as identifying a zebra in a donkey sanctuary, so it took all of around two seconds to spot that Matt had only transferred across £300. In case he had made the payment in two tranches she scrolled down again. No, definitely not there.

Jenna frowned. Why hadn't he mentioned this when he made the payment two days ago? Surely he would realise she would notice? Just because she preferred to avoid confrontation didn't mean he could take advantage of her. Relationships were based on trust.

If Matt had gone out to the garage he could be

there for the rest of the morning, but she wanted to straighten out this misunderstanding before it could fester. She found him at the back of the garage, where he was clearly having a reorganisation of some sort as several of the boxes now sat outside along with a number of empty, more sturdy looking cardboard packing boxes.

'Matt, do you have a minute?'

'Can it wait? I want to get this lot sorted so that I can put another batch of items up for sale this afternoon.'

'It won't take long. I just want to understand why you only paid half of the agreed amount this month. Less than half actually,' added Jenna, trying not to sound as indignant as she felt. 'When were you going to get round to telling me? Or were you hoping I might not notice?'

Matt put down the boxes he was holding. 'Of course I was going to tell you.'

'Like when you got made redundant, you mean?'

'No.' Matt rubbed his hand across the back of his neck. 'Look, I'm a bit short this month, so I was hoping you might be able to give me a loan.'

'I might have if you'd asked me, but you didn't – you just assumed the answer was yes.'

'Okay, I'm asking you now.'

'Technically you're making a statement.'

'Jenna, give it a rest will you! I'll get it back in a week or two.'

'Get it back from where?'

Matt inspected the contents of the box by his feet and

scribbled something on the flap. Jenna recognised these well-worn evasion tactics.

'Matt?'

'Yes, okay, I loaned some money to Parry. He had a bit of a cashflow situation – it's only temporary, but he's my best mate so I could hardly say no, could I?' He picked up the box and almost threw it onto a stack against the garage wall.

'So you said yes to Parry, knowing that you didn't have enough money, but you thought you'd borrow from me?'

'Finally she gets it!'

Jenna wasn't sure what infuriated her most; her effectively lending money to Parry without being asked, or Matt's assumption that this situation was perfectly okay.

'And what if I said I didn't have enough either? Do you suppose the landlord will let us pay the extra next month? Or the month after that? I'm sorry to say I don't share your faith in Parry's financial acumen.'

'Well, for your information, Parry is well on the way to setting up his own trading company.'

'Really? Is this the Haxford branch of Financial Accidents R Us?'

'But the paperwork isn't completed,' Matt continued, ignoring Jenna's comment, 'so the bank declined to extend his credit.'

'Very sensible,' muttered Jenna. She sighed. 'Well, it appears I have little choice unless we want to default on the rent this month. Just promise me you won't be doing any more unofficial loans to Parry. He's a nice enough bloke, Matt, but he's really not savvy enough to be running a company. From what I remember, the last sure-fire investment'—she made speech marks with her fingers —'turned out to be some sort of Ponzi scheme.'

'He got tricked into it,' retorted Matt. 'He realised he'd been done.'

'Only after I provided the evidence,' replied Jenna. 'The real trick is to spot the scam *before* you invest, not afterwards.'

Chapter Eleven

No matter how hard she tried to ignore it, Matt's casual disregard for their financial arrangements rankled, and over the course of the following morning Jenna found herself frowning every time the memory resurfaced. It didn't help her frame of mind at all that Sales Account Manager Ian Ransome had submitted yet another large expenses claim, and Jenna could immediately see that he had included various items that were not strictly covered under the company's expenses policy but fell into what was referred to as 'discretionary consideration'. It had been accompanied by a longwinded email pointing out that he expected to see this claim settled in full before the end of the week, totally ignoring the payroll due dates that determined when payments were actually made.

'Mr Rant is certainly living up to his name today,' Jenna observed. 'Well, he's missed the payroll deadline for this month so it will be carried forward as I'm not inclined to make special arrangements for that man.'

'Wow! You're not taking prisoners today, are you?' observed Denise.

'Do I sound rather aggressive? Sorry, it's not aimed at you. I'm just fed up of being taken for granted.'

Denise lowered her voice. 'Are we talking about our friend Mr Ranty, or someone closer to home?'

Jenna sighed. 'Matt trusts me to look after our joint account, which is lovely, but then he goes and does something stupid that he knows I will find out about.'

Jenna gave Denise the abbreviated version of yesterday's argument. 'I mean, it's fine if it's his money, and it doesn't impact on our ability to pay the rent, but this does. Or could have. For some reason he has a blind spot as far as Parry is concerned, and he can't seem to see that the bloke's a walking financial disaster.'

'A case of wake up and smell the coffee, do you think?'

'More like wake up and smell the smoke because the bank's on fire.'

Denise laughed.

'I mean, what would happen if I also assumed I could spend what I liked and not worry about paying the bills?'

'Have you actually asked him that question?'

Jenna nodded. 'Last night. He just got all huffy and said that I'd done exactly the same thing. So then I pointed out that my share of the bills account was never in doubt, so the fact I used my own bonus to buy the camera back for Henry was nothing to do with anything.

Even though it was a few weeks ago and we had a row about it at the time, I know he's still annoyed.'

'Hold on, you've lost me. Who's Henry? What camera?'

With a quick glance towards Adam's office to make sure he wasn't staring out over the department, Jenna updated Denise on how she had met the writer of the letter at the bottom of the box of treasures (as she mentally referred to it), and how she had used her bonus to buy back his camera.

There was a short pause after she finished speaking.

'So go on, tell me I'm mad then.'

'Of course you're not mad. But Adam told you to spend that bonus on yourself, didn't he?' Denise rolled her eyes. 'If you don't listen to him, you're hardly going to listen to me, but for what it's worth, I think you've got too used to putting other people before yourself. Just make sure this Henry doesn't take advantage of you too.' She smiled briefly. 'It sounds quite romantic though, doesn't it?'

Jenna immediately started shuffling the papers on her desk. 'No, no, it's nothing like that,' she said hurriedly. Very unhelpfully, the memory of her hand on Henry's warm thigh popped into her head and she felt her cheeks colour. 'We're just friends. Henry travels around a lot and photographs loads of exotic places. We have a healthy difference of opinion on how much money you need to do that sort of thing.' She gave Denise a knowing look. 'He bet that he could take me to places right here in Haxford that are'—Jenna screwed up her face as she tried to recall his exact words—'scenic and magical.' She snorted. 'The words "Haxford" and "magical" do not go together in the same sentence, so I'm looking forward to proving him wrong.'

Denise looked at her with a pensive expression. 'It's a bet, is it?'

'Absolutely.'

'And when does this bet take place?'

'Saturday.'

'So what do you win?' Denise asked.

Jenna shrugged. 'Being proved right, I guess.'

Chapter Twelve

Henry was running late again. Jenna sat in her car and glanced anxiously at her watch for the umpteenth time. Then she double checked to make sure she hadn't got the wrong date altogether. The location at least she was certain about; they had arranged to meet at the same pub car park as previously, although Henry had insisted that it was his turn to drive, which was sensible given that Jenna still had no idea where they were heading. Just somewhere that was allegedly scenic and magical. She would reserve judgement on the adjectives until later.

Jenna had only made up her mind to respond a couple of days ago, but it was her conversation with Denise that had cemented her realisation that she enjoyed Henry's easy-going company. It wasn't some illicit affair – he was a friend. He just happened to be a very good-looking friend and this was a friendly bet. Of sorts. Not a date. Nothing to cause any upset to a relationship. Not that she and Matt had much of one these days.

Matt had announced over breakfast that he was going out for the day with Parry, so he wasn't at home when she left just after lunch. He had deliberately waited to see if she made any remark, but Jenna had kept her own counsel. She didn't have anything personal against Parry; in fact, he was a thoroughly likeable bloke. The sort of person who was a generous conversationalist and didn't just drone on about his own pet hobby horses; the type of bloke who (unlike Matt) would actually notice if you'd made an effort to look presentable, and who would always be the first to get in a round of drinks if they went out anywhere. But would she trust him with someone else's money? Absolutely not! And certainly not hers.

Jenna was just about to reclassify Henry from a bit overdue to wildly late, when she saw his old BMW swing into the car park. She stepped out of the car and waved in his general direction.

Henry sprinted over. 'Sorry, I'm a bit late. Family things. My sister's decided I need to start toeing the line, whatever that means. She's like a bloody parrot. Get yourself a proper job,' he mimicked in a squeaky voice. 'You don't want to swap sisters, do you?'

Jenna laughed. 'No thanks, I'm very happy with the one I've got.'

'You're very lucky, your sister's lovely.'

Jenna experienced a momentary twinge of jealousy that took her back to her teenage years. Even at school, the boys had all loved Evie. The more she'd ignored them the more they had pestered her. Evie used to laugh about it at night, as they swapped girly confidences in the privacy of their shared bedroom. Jenna always seemed to get the wrong sort of fuss. The sort that accompanied hospital visits and long periods of convalescence. Jenna had detested it, but it came with the territory if you had the medical history she did. But that wasn't Evie's fault and they had only grown closer as they got older.

'So do I need to bring anything with me?' Jenna asked, changing the subject.

'Just yourself. I've got my camera kit.' Henry nudged his foot against the khaki rucksack at his feet.

'Not quite as much as last time then,' joked Jenna.

'We won't need any props today.' Henry squinted up at the sky. 'Should be good light though. Not too much direct sunlight.'

They drove for longer than Jenna had anticipated. She was sure that they'd already passed the outskirts of Haxford a mile or so back but didn't want to seem picky. Instead she asked about Henry's family.

'Not much to tell, really. Dad's a solicitor, Mum works from home as an indexer for a scholastic publisher, sister's also a qualified solicitor. You can imagine the riveting conversations they have over the dinner table.' He chuckled.

'And you didn't want to follow in the family footsteps?'

'No, although it wasn't for lack of trying on their part.'

'What do you mean?'

'I'm the product of ambitious parents. So naturally I was sent to the same expensive school as Dad went to, and I did exams and stuff because that's what was expected of you, but I enjoyed the sports and photography clubs far more than A level law studies.'

'So you didn't go on to university?' asked Jenna.

'Oh yes. The agreement was that they would fund my university studies provided I did an academic degree first; I would then be free decide for myself what I wanted to do. So basically I graduated with a degree in business studies and law because that was what my parents wanted. But even though I'm a disappointment in the academic department, it's my life so hey…' They turned off the B-road onto a narrow lane that meandered further into less cultivated countryside. 'Anyway, what about you – did you go to university?'

'I'd have liked to, but I needed to get a job. Priorities and all that. But fear not, I work in the financial services industry, so I can regale you with an equally boring amount of technical conversation should you so desire.'

Henry laughed. 'I'll pass on that offer. Today we are leaving behind the boring.' He slowed the car and turned off onto what looked like a track that quickly petered out into a scruffy looking parking area. There was one other car already parked up.

'So where exactly are we?' Jenna got out and looked around. A fresh breeze whipped a few strands of hair loose, and she tucked them behind her ear. 'Have you brought me to see a wood?'

'It's what's in the wood that's more interesting,' replied Henry with a smile.

It certainly wasn't the sort of dank, dense forest favoured by writers of sinister tales. If anything, it reminded her of the woods that featured in her childhood books; those safe havens where children escaped from their everyday world and which, as a reader, she had found so enchanting. As they walked the short distance towards the start of the trees, Jenna noticed a path that meandered downwards at a very gentle gradient between the trees.

'How far is it, this surprise?'

'Not too far.'

Jenna hoped that Henry's idea of *not too far* wasn't calibrated on his walking pace. If she had a pound for every time someone had used that phrase and been proved woefully wrong at her expense, she would probably be living on her own private Caribbean island by now.

There was something calming about the way sounds were deadened even just a few feet inside the edge of the trees. Apart from the occasional call of a bird that echoed overhead and the gentle crackle of twigs underfoot as they walked along the path, the only other disturbance was the distant shouts of excited children. Presumably the occupants of the other car.

Even wearing her sturdiest trainers Jenna had to walk slowly, being careful to avoid tree roots and other trip hazards, and she regretted not bringing her sticks with her. Henry matched his pace to hers and kept up a running commentary on their surroundings. The thick oak trunks, he said, were used in centuries past for ship building and construction. The hazels would produce a crop of nuts in the autumn for the animals that lived in the wood. Henry showed her how you didn't need to see the leaves in order to identify the species of tree because you could tell by the different textures and colours of the bark.

The new leaves of spring were only just beginning to unfurl, and plenty of sunlight still filtered through the canopy of branches above, although they were now sheltered from the breeze. The woodland floor was carpeted with tufts of wild grasses, ferns, and small piles of dead leaves, while tendrils of ivy snaked up the tree trunks. Here and there, wildflowers poked up out of the ground.

They hadn't gone far before Jenna noticed a couple of stone steps set into the ground, and she sighed inwardly. With nothing to hold onto, there was more than a distinct possibility of a repeat of the ungainly and unintentional pirouette she had performed in the barn. She paused as she looked around for the safest place to step down.

'Here.' Henry held his hand out, and after a moment's hesitation, she took it. His warm fingers wrapped themselves around hers and she experienced a sudden wobble that had nothing to do with her rickety sense of balance. He kept hold of her hand until they had descended the three steps.

'Thank you,' Jenna said as he gently let go of her hand.

At the next sets of steps, she took Henry's hand without hesitation.

'One more set of steps and we're at the bottom,' said Henry. Jenna turned to look back. The path snaked away between the trees but the gradient was deceptively steeper than it looked. She hoped it wouldn't be a problem getting back up again. Downward was always her preferred direction.

It seemed as though either the path was getting narrower or the undergrowth was closing in on them and she was glad that Henry had been in front of her when, as the path turned again, an over enthusiastic child cannoned straight into him.

'I'm so sorry,' the woman following behind apologised. 'They have so much energy at this age, don't they?' She ushered the human cannonball back up the path with the promise of burgers and chips if they behaved and then turned and gestured to the two children behind her. 'Stand aside so these people can get past, please.'

The two children looked to be about six or seven years old and were still shoving each other as Jenna limped slowly past, conscious that they watching her.

'Why are you walking funny?'

Jenna sighed patiently. She'd heard every variation of this question ever since she'd learned to put one foot in front of the other. Most times children were just curious, but after nearly three decades the novelty had worn off for her. 'I didn't like to eat vegetables when I was younger. I just ate lots of burgers and chips instead.' She gestured at her foot. 'That's what happens. Your leg doesn't grow fast enough.'

Henry clapped his hand to his mouth to stifle a snigger. He waited for the family to get further up the path before he turned round to look at her. 'You've just put that kid right off his burger now!'

Jenna snorted. 'That's what you get for being nosey.'

'Does that happen a lot?'

'Depends where I am, but yeah, it can do. Sometimes I tell them I'm doing secret training for the Paralympics.'

They both laughed.

The final set of steps were less even, and Henry gripped her hand firmly as he helped her down. Jenna had kept her eyes fixed on her feet and it was only as she let go of Henry's hand and looked around that she realised the path led to the edge of a clearing. It now became patently obvious what Henry had wanted her to see.

Roughly circular in shape, the space was devoid of trees, shrubs, ivy … in fact, there was virtually no flora or fauna to speak of at all. Just lots of rocks.

Scenic? She wasn't sure. Magical? Probably not. Impressive? Most definitely. On one side the rocks stood almost as if they were arranged in a row like a Viking burial field. Some were the size of a car wheel, others much bigger, all a dark grey colour. On the other side of the circular area were two single stones, both more upright.

As they got closer, Jenna could see that one was around six foot in height, roughly hewn in the same dark grey stone, now partly covered in lichen. The other stood a little further away but was clearly a different type of stone. More purpley-grey and less jagged. It was around five feet tall and domed at the top. She ran her hand over the surface of the stone and it felt strangely smooth to the touch. She instinctively jerked her hand away.

'Interesting, isn't it? This one is called the Maiden Stone. No one knows whether it's so smooth because of centuries of being touched or whether it was carved that way.'

'So how old are these things?'

'I'm not entirely sure. Certainly nowhere near the same age as those at Stonehenge, or the Rollright Stones in Oxfordshire. But legend has it that these were once people.'

'Really?' said Jenna dubiously. 'That sounds a bit made up to me.'

'Still a sceptic, I see.' Henry grinned and pointed at a couple of the flatter rocks. 'If you want to perch over there, I'll tell you the story.'

Jenna found a suitable, flat-topped rock and brushed off the loose dirt before sitting down gratefully. Henry sat on the ground in front of her, his hands clasping his bent knees.

'So – the legend of the Maiden Stone. Once upon a

time, a beautiful, young maiden lived in a cottage in these woods with her mother—'

'Why does she have to be beautiful?'

'Because it's a story. Okay then, she was reasonably pretty but she had wild hair. Happy now?'

'Where's her father? If it's a story, shouldn't he be there too?'

'Are you going to interrupt all the way through?' asked Henry with an amused expression.

'Perhaps he just buggered off when she was a child. That's what mine did.'

Henry paused his narrative, his face turned towards her. 'That must have been tough,' he said quietly.

'Sorry, I'm listening now.' Jenna pointed at her own face and smiled with her lips pressed firmly together. 'This is my non-interrupting look. Please carry on.'

Henry nodded thoughtfully. 'Okay.' He waited a few more moments before recommencing. As he talked, he stared across the clearing at the trees beyond.

'So one day this reasonably pretty maiden met a young man from the village who was gathering kindling in the wood. And she met him the day after, and the day after that. It wasn't long before they were madly in love, but when her mother heard about this she wasn't happy at all. Oh no. You see, she had plans for her daughter to marry a noble, or a prince, and forbad her to see this lowly – but moderately handsome – young peasant.'

Henry turned to look at her with an enquiring expression.

Jenna flashed a smile and gestured at her ear. 'Still listening.'

'Well, the couple were so much in love they didn't care what her mother thought, and they made plans to marry in secret. On the appointed day, they met here, according to the legend, with the local notary and a small group of villagers, who were curious to meet this girl and accompanied him to witness the happy event. They sang songs and plaited a garland of wildflowers for the bride, and carpeted the ground with sweet smelling herbs.

'Then, just as the ceremony was starting, the girl's mother appeared between the trees. The girl begged them to hurry for she knew what they did not; that her mother was a witch. But it was too late. In her fury, the witch cursed them and turned them all into stone, including her own daughter. Now no one could take her daughter away again, and she lived out the rest of her life totally alone. But thereafter, no trees or flowers ever grew on this spot, and'—Henry gestured at the row of stones—'the villagers never returned home.

'Furthermore, it's said that if any unmarried woman makes a garland of wildflowers for the maiden, she will reveal to you the true meaning of happiness.'

Henry got to his feet. 'So, while you think about that, I'm going to take a few photos. Is that okay or are you in a hurry to get back?'

Jenna was already tired, her leg was aching, and the thought of hiking back up the path was daunting. 'I'm happy to have a rest. You go ahead.'

As Henry set up his tripod and then walked around checking various things on his camera, Jenna wandered slowly over to the Maiden Stone. She reached out and touched it again. She let her fingers slide gently over the smooth rock. 'I know you're just a lump of rock, really,' she whispered. 'But it's a nice story.'

As a child, Jenna had always adored stories of magic, and witches, and fairies that lived in the trees. It had been her own private world of imagination and fantasy, which she could dip into and where there was always a joyous happy ever after, unlike real life where practicality and financial solvency turned out to be more useful concepts.

Henry walked over to the far side of the clearing and for a while she watched him at work. Whenever Jenna took a photo, she simply made sure she could see the object being photographed – usually one of Evie's guinea pigs – and tapped the screen. When photographing guinea pigs you learned to be quick as even the placid ones like Lady Maud could get antsy if the photographer took too long or there were insufficient cucumber bribes involved. However Henry seemed to spend a lot of time peering through the camera, pressing buttons and adjusting things, peering again.

She wandered back to the path. Like Henry said, the flowers grew in the wooded part but no further. There was probably a logical explanation although she couldn't think of one off the top of her head. But while he was busy she might as well pick some of them. On the way down, she hadn't paid much attention to what was growing there.

Now she could see all manner of flowers. Some she recognised, like the wild narcissi, small clumps of bluebells and the white, scented pearls of the lily of the valley. Others she couldn't name like the delicate white flowers decorated with veins of a rich plum colour, and the stars of blue flowers with butter yellow middles.

She wandered along the edge of the clearing, gathering an assortment of flowers and then tried to work out how she was going to make a garland. In fairy stories, these things were made without any thought of hints or instructions for the unpractised. Jenna tugged a long strand of small leaved ivy from one of the tree trunks and wished she'd paid more attention when Evie was showing off the Christmas wreath she had made last year at a local crafts session.

After a few failed attempts to fasten the ivy into a circular shape, she turned her attention to the flowers. As a child, she had made daisy chains and she applied the same method to the wildflowers, starting with the thickest stalks and using her fingernail to make the slit in the middle of the stem. There was even something therapeutic about sitting here, sheltered from the outside world by the blanket of trees. The legend may be made up, but the place certainly exuded a calming influence, not unlike those magic realms she had visited in her childhood imagination.

'I see you're keeping busy then?'

The sound made her jump and she dropped the flower she was holding. Henry picked it up and twirled the stem between his fingers. 'Wood sorrel if I'm not mistaken.' He passed it back to her. 'For a dyed-in-the-wool sceptic, I'm impressed with your creativity.'

Jenna pulled a face at him. 'If you're going to do something, you might as well do it properly. That's what Great-Aunt Mary used to say.'

'Hooray for Great-Aunt Mary!'

Jenna smiled at his sudden burst of enthusiasm. 'She could be a bit of a tartar at times, and there was no mucking about allowed at bedtime, but you always knew where you stood with her.'

'It sounds as though you were very fond of her.'

'I was. She died thirteen years ago and I was heartbroken.' Jenna held up her delicate garland of flowers. 'What do think? Will that do?'

'Try it on.'

'Are you sure I won't stir up any evil curses?' Jenna wagged a finger at him as she added with a teasing smile, 'If I turn into a frog you have to promise not to leave me behind.'

'I thought you didn't believe in all that sort of thing?' Henry laughed. His eyes did a sort of sparkly thing when he smiled and Jenna suddenly wondered what it would feel like to have his strong arms wrapped around her.

Henry took the garland from her and placed it gently on her head. 'It would look better if you untied your hair though.'

Unlike Evie's fine, straight hair, Jenna's shoulder length hair was thicker and wavy, which meant it didn't always stay where it was intended. She tugged out the scrunchie and stuffed it in her jeans pocket. 'Better?'

'A bit. May I?' Without waiting for an answer, Henry scooped up her hair in his hands and spent several seconds arranging it. When his fingers brushed against the sensitive part of her neck, a tingling sensation trickled down her spine and she took a sharp intake of breath.

'There. That's perfect.' Henry stepped back, picked up his camera and took a few shots from different angles. The last couple were taken close up and Jenna fidgeted self-consciously, aware of his closeness.

'That's great. Thanks for being my model for the day.'

'Ooh, do I get paid then?'

Henry laughed. 'No, you did it out of the kindness of your heart. Wasn't that generous of you?'

While he packed away his portable tripod and camera lenses, Jenna took her garland over to the Maiden Stone. She hadn't used the ivy in the garland, but it was a shame not to do something with it, so she draped it around the stone where it narrowed near the top, like a floral necklace. The stone was almost as tall as she was but she was just able to reach and spent a few seconds carefully arranging the garland on top.

'If you'd like to do anything miraculous to sort out my defunct love life, you're more than welcome,' she whispered.

Then she pulled out her phone and took a picture. Just to show Evie.

She stood for a moment in front of the stone and

listened for any strange vibes or ghostly whispers but heard nothing. 'Jenna Oakhurst, I think you've gone a bit soft in the head,' she said sternly.

As they headed out of the clearing, following the woodland path once again, Jenna looked back only once. From inside the tree line it just looked like a clearing with some random rocks strewn about. But it had felt different sitting in the peaceful surroundings of the stones. Perhaps not magical, but she'd admit to scenic.

As she'd expected, the up was far more arduous than the down. Henry had a rucksack on his back and was still making light work of the uneven path. The steps definitely hadn't seemed that steep from the other direction, and Henry held out both hands to help her up. Before long there was a definite painful twinge in her hip as she put weight on her left leg. A couple of times she winced and paused for breath. Most of the time she gritted her teeth and kept moving. It was no good complaining since there was nothing anyone could do, and she wasn't about to spend the night here.

It was kind of Henry to offer to show her the local sights, but he was clearly more used to a faster pace of life. The next time she would politely refuse. She almost laughed out loud at the idea – why would she even expect there to be a next time? Surely Henry must have realised by now that his outdoorsy camping lifestyle was not something that she indulged in very often.

By the time she got back to the car, she was not only in a lot of pain but also feeling distinctly irritable. It was her own fault; she shouldn't have agreed to go along with someone else's plans without finding out what was involved. Years of other people's *not too far*, or *just around the corner* had taught her that it was better if she was the one in charge of the logistics.

Thankfully, Henry didn't natter much on the drive back and just said he'd give her a call. She was probably a bit short with him when they said their goodbyes, but in her experience, when blokes said *I'll give you a call*, it was simply a convenient way of not having to say 'sorry, I'm not interested'. And why should he be? She wasn't his type, he was just proving a point, and besides, she was already in a relationship, even though it was currently a slightly strained one.

She had definitely overdone it today and the already stretched nerves in her leg would be reminding her of that over the forthcoming week. As it was, within forty-eight hours she had something entirely different to worry about.

Chapter Thirteen

On both Sunday and Monday morning, Jenna woke suddenly, aware that she had been having strange dreams. She didn't usually remember much about hers, but as she showered and dressed for work on Monday morning, she tried to piece together the residual fragments of the dream that floated around in her head like filaments of fine thread.

There was a faceless voice that kept giving her instructions that she couldn't understand and she recalled sitting outside and clasping a wooden box that Matt was trying to take away. It had seemed very real at the time, and over breakfast she asked Matt if she was talking to him in her sleep.

'If you were, I didn't hear you,' he replied cheerfully, heaping a generous spoonful of blackcurrant jam onto his toast. 'You know what I'm like – out for the count.'

'So what have you got planned for today?'

'I'll tell you when you get back.'

'Ooh, is it a surprise? Can't you tell me now?'

'Haven't done it yet, have I?'

'You are making about as much sense as my dream,' said Jenna, swallowing the last of her tea. 'You've got me curious now, so don't go forgetting to tell me this evening.'

Matt smiled like a cat that had spotted an extra large, unattended pot of cream on the counter. 'It won't happen. Promise. And I think you'll be impressed.'

In the past, Matt's idea of what would impress her was often some distance from the actual truth, but she supposed she ought to give him the benefit of the doubt. Early on in the relationship he had taken her to a karaoke night at the local golf club and she'd sat for a large part of the evening pretending not to be bored rigid with his strangulated rendition of various popular songs interspersed with anecdotes from his golfing pals. Even back then, she'd been making compromises, but then Matt had also invested more of his time in making the relationship work. Now he seemed to be investing in decidedly riskier waters.

Her attention was diverted from Matt's plans by the list of things to do sitting on her desk and which she'd written last thing on Friday afternoon. However it wasn't long before further distraction arrived in the form of her colleague, Denise, who had barely got her feet under her desk before she leaned over and asked in a hoarse whisper, 'So did you win the bet then? I'm dying to hear all about it!'

Jenna obligingly gave her a brief description of the afternoon, which seemed to satisfy Denise's curiosity, but she omitted the more personal details, such as how her insides went all jittery when Henry had arranged her hair. Matt had never run his fingers through her hair like that, or tucked a curl behind her ear in a way that was almost sensual, and Jenna found herself not only mentally replaying the event throughout the day but also exploring other imaginary possibilities.

It was as she drove home with her analytical brain still in operational mode that she had time to reconsider her conversations with both Denise and Matt earlier this morning, and she found there were lots of unanswered questions stacking up. Why was she suddenly so stirred up by Henry's attentions? Was she that starved of affection that she now resorted to creating imaginary scenarios? In the time that she and Matt had been a couple, she had rarely thought about whether he paid her much attention. His listening skills all but vanished when the sports channel was on, and his attention had certainly been diverted by his eBay activity, but what about before that? Without bothering to search for an answer to that one, she turned her attention to this morning. What was it that had put him in such a good mood? Recently he'd been quite grumpy when she had dropped even the smallest hint about maintaining some sort of financial security but now…

I think you'll be impressed

Those were his exact words. He knew how she felt

about his seemingly reckless investment and the corresponding reduction in his ability to pay his share of the bills. It had to be a job. A proper job! Admittedly he had been secretive about being made redundant, but she was prepared to compromise and accept that was a one-off. He had guessed – correctly – that she hadn't been happy about his new hobby. He had been talked into the idea by Parry and he must have known it wasn't viable in the long-term as a way of creating steady income. And now he had done something for her. Something to impress her.

Any relationship was based on trust and that worked both ways. She needed to trust him to do things the right way, and to be fair to him, Matt usually got there in the end. Jenna took a detour via the local supermarket to pick up a few treats. The planned frozen dinner could stay in the freezer for another day. Tonight they would have salmon en croute with minted new potatoes and fresh veg. She also added a few of Matt's favourite beers to the shopping trolley plus a bottle of Pinot Grigio. Today they would have their own little celebration and then maybe at the weekend they could go that Thai place that Matt loved.

'Sorry I'm late!' she called out as she leaned against the door to close it. Matt bounded into the hallway and took the bags from her, inspecting the contents. 'I stopped off to get a few bits and pieces. If you don't mind putting the oven on, I'll go and get changed and then you can tell me your exciting news.'

Matt had already poured them both a glass of wine

by the time Jenna reappeared ten minutes later and she took an appreciative mouthful, enjoying the crisp, fruity taste.

'So, come on then, spill the beans because I can see you're dying to tell me!'

Since she'd got in the door, Matt had hardly been able to sit still, and there was a definite air of fidgety excitement about him.

'Okay, well, first I want to say that I know you were upset about me being made redundant, and that I didn't tell you in advance I was going to buy those storage units, although to date I have made…' He picked up his phone and tapped at the screen a few times before putting it down again. 'Okay I don't have the exact figure but it's getting better each month. And I know I should have told you about loaning the cash to Parry, but last month was the only time it's meant I've been late with the bills payments.'

'You mean you've loaned money to Parry before?'

'Yeah. And he pays me back – it's no big deal.'

'So hang on—'

'But you won't need to worry for too much longer. Once we've both signed on the dotted line it'll all be open and above aboard.'

Jenna put down her wine glass. 'I'm confused. Are you and Parry having a civil partnership?'

Matt laughed. 'Bloody hell, I don't like him that much! I just don't want you to be worrying each month about whether we have enough cash to pay the bills, and I realise that me selling random stuff on eBay isn't going to give you or us enough security for the future.'

Jenna nodded in agreement. That at least sounded sensible.

'We need to think of something else.'

Alarm shot through Jenna. 'What do you mean?'

'You remember I told you that Parry and his brother Des do a lot of buying and selling of stuff? Well, they've set up a trading company and now they've invited me to join them as equal partner.'

'What!'

'Brilliant, isn't it?'

'Hang on—'

'I won't lie, the next few months could be a bit tricky so I might need you to cover the rent for a bit, but we're going to do it all properly and I'm telling you upfront so there are no nasty surprises later. I mean there'll probably be surprises,' he added with a grin, 'but they'll be all good ones. Instead of selling to eBay punters we'll be trading with business and industry.'

'But'— Jenna shook her head to clear her thoughts— 'but you need money to set up a business. What are your cashflow projections? Who's going to keep the books? You need an accountant. A memorandum of association or something similar. And probably a website. It's not that simple, Matt. I don't want to spoil your plans but I'm glad you told me before you committed yourself.'

There were several seconds of strained silence before Matt replied. 'I have committed myself,' he said in an injured tone of voice. 'I gave him my word and we're signing everything tomorrow.'

'Please don't, Matt. There are other ways of earning money that don't carry that sort of risk.'

'You don't trust me, is that it? You think because you work in finance that only you know about these things?'

'No. I'm saying that you can't afford to throw all your savings into a business venture without thinking about how that affects us. As in both of us,' she added pointedly. As in *once again you're taking me for granted*, she added silently.

'Des knows what he's doing, okay? As a limited company we'll be able to get a bank loan, and I said you wouldn't mind being a guarantor seeing as how you're so good with budgets and all that.'

'Now hold on—'

'Not that I think we'll need it for long – Des reckons within twelve months we'll be making serious amounts of cash. He's going to apply to go on *Dragon's Den*. You just wait, you're going to be proud of us, Jenna.'

Jenna rarely lost her temper but it was fraying badly at the edges right now. She wanted to scream. This trading company had no track record and Matt had little or no spare cash. Why could he not see this was a disaster waiting to happen? And as for making her proud, she had heard that empty promise before and even all those years later, she could still recall every detail of the events that followed.

This time it would be different, her father had said. He promised this would be the last time they packed everything up. No more 'adventures', as he called them. This time it would all work out perfectly. They would be proud of him. Evie was young enough to believe it too. He promised they'd soon be able to afford whatever they wanted, and Evie had gone to bed planning a garden full of baby rabbits.

Jenna hadn't understood back then what her dad had used the money for, but it didn't take long before she noticed her mum crying quietly in the evenings. She wanted desperately to help put things right, but she was completely powerless in the face of this insidious grown-up problem that she didn't understand. She did the washing up. She tidied her room every evening. She folded all her clothes neatly. And still her mum wept.

The first time the men in dark suits turned up at the front door was not long after Jenna's third surgery. She could still remember her father's words: *You go to the door when they ring, okay? And you tell them it's not convenient to come in. They won't dare barge past a disabled child.*

She'd only agreed because she thought it would help her mum. The pain had clawed at her as she hobbled to the door on her crutches, the external apparatus around her leg a clear indicator that she was incapacitated. Without flinching, she carefully repeated the words exactly as her father had instructed. The men went away again, but her success was short-lived. They had returned the following week and this time her mother had inexplicably stood back and let the men remove whatever they wanted. It was Jenna who had shouted at them, begged them to stop, but that time it made no difference. Her influence over them had evaporated.

Jenna had never minded feeling different, but she objected to being used as pawn in a game where no one explained the rules to her. By the time she left home for good, she understood much better the fine line between gambling and financial ruin, and vowed that it would never happen again. Not to her and not to Evie.

She stared at Matt. Was he really prepared to throw away his financial security for Des's promise – and a fool-hardy one at that – of some pot of gold at the end of the rainbow?

'Matt, I need you to think carefully about this. I'm sorry but Parry's financial abilities are about as good as my grasp of Norwegian.'

Matt appeared momentarily baffled. 'You don't speak Norwegian.'

'Precisely. Look, I really appreciate you want to do something different, something more exciting than fitting kitchens, but don't do this. I—'

'No! I'm fed up of being treated as though I'm a fucking imbecile and can't manage my own money. All business is a gamble, I get that, but you know what? Not everyone is a loser and I'm not your dad. You're obsessed with money. How d'you think Bill Gates got started?'

'With a sensible plan and some know-how!' Jenna shouted back. 'And you're deluded if you think you have anything in common with Bill Gates!'

For a few seconds they glared angrily at each other.

Then Matt snatched up his wallet from the table and stuffed it in his pocket. 'I've had enough of this. I'm going out.'

'We need to talk.'

'What's the point? You'll just find another ten long-winded ways to object.'

'Fine, I'll make this simple then.' Jenna's heart pounded as she looked squarely at Matt. 'Which is most important to you – me or Parry's business?'

Chapter Fourteen

Jenna watched as Matt turned and walked out, slamming the door behind him. The adrenaline coursed through her body as she sat, stunned, motionless, staring at the wreckage of their relationship. Was she hurt? Sorry? How long had their relationship been based on convenience?

When she came home from work after a long, tiring day, she often pulled on her favourite jogging bottoms that saw absolutely zero jogging, but were really warm and cosy. Had Matt become the relationship equivalent of her jogging bottoms? Were they now working towards different goals?

Before she became bogged down in picking apart differing goals, financial motivation and this evening's conflict, she needed to decide where to go. She was not prepared to stay here, wondering every day when she might be asked to dip into her savings to bail out someone

who had already put his business and his best mate's interests above hers. She promised herself many years ago that
never again would she allow anyone else's financial aspira-
tions to dictate her future. This relationship was at an end.

She picked up the phone. It would only be temporary
but Evie would help out. The phone rang for while before
cutting to voicemail. Maybe her phone was charging or
something. She looked up the number they used for
rescue enquiries and tried that instead.

*'Hi, you've reached Little Paws Guinea Pig Rescue. Sorry we
can't take your call, but please leave a message with your name and
telephone number and we'll call you back as soon as possible.'*

'Hi, Evie, it's Jenna.' Her voice wavered with emotion
and she took a deep breath before continuing. 'Can I
come over?' She automatically paused as if she expected
to hear her sister's voice. Reluctantly, she ended the call
and put the phone down on the table. As children, they
had always helped each other out and now she felt the
need to be with someone who understood her.

…I'm not your Dad. You're obsessed with money…

Memories from the past flooded to the surface and
threatened to overwhelm her. She needed to be practical.

The rental details optimistically described their place
as a two-bedroom flat although in reality, even a single
bed would have taken up a significant proportion of the
second bedroom. Consequently, it was generally used for
storage, now mostly taken up with Matt's home gym
equipment – the proceeds of another auction – plus the
overflow from the garage. It also contained Jenna's

wheeled suitcase. She'd bought it in the sales two years ago at a ridiculously cheap price, being eight centimetres too large to be classed as carry-on baggage following yet another change by the popular airlines. Not that she ever flew anywhere but it had looked useful for storing out of season clothes.

She wheeled it back into the bedroom and quickly rounded up her toiletries, enough clothes for a couple of days and some personal items. For reasons that she didn't even try to rationalise, she also took Henry's letter from the bottom of the box. He ought to have that back really; it didn't belong to her.

As she packed, she found herself comparing Henry and Matt. In many ways they were complete opposites: Matt had come from a poor, working-class family – as she had – and was prepared to take any sort of gamble to make as much money as possible. Henry clearly came from a well-to-do background but seemed uninterested in moneymaking opportunities, and had enough money to travel around indulging his interests. On paper, she had far more in common with Matt in terms of background and upbringing but there were times, Jenna decided, that rationalising things on paper just didn't work.

She found a small notebook and tore out one of the pages before scribbling a quick note to Matt saying that she'd be back for the rest of her things tomorrow. After her nose detected a warm smell, she realised the oven was still on, and quickly turned that off. She'd take her dinner with her and cook it later. When she got to Evie's, she would also compile a list of things to do, top of which was find someone to help move the rest of her possessions.

As Jenna pulled up outside the barn, she saw the door was shut. On closer inspection it was also padlocked, which was strange but not unheard of. Maybe they'd got all their jobs done for the night. The only sounds were the comforting, gentle squeaks of a few guinea pigs.

Jenna tried the front doorbell, but there was no answer and no lights on inside that she could see. Where were they? It was eight o'clock, and the evening light was beginning to fade as Jenna retreated to the car. She tried Evie's number again and this time her sister answered, although it was difficult to hear her clearly.

'Thank goodness! I was beginning to get worried about you. Nobody was in. Where are you?'

'We're in the car. We've been out on a rescue.'

'At this time of the evening?'

'Someone phoned us to report a gang of youths using guinea pigs as bait for dog fights. The poor little things were terrified, and one of them has serious injuries. We're bringing them all back for a proper assessment. Why are some people so horrible?'

Jenna could hear Kat talking in the background. 'What's Kat saying?'

'You don't want to know – it's not repeatable. You should have seen Kat though, she was brilliant. She stormed across that field like a reincarnation of Boudicca on steroids and—'

Jenna forgot her own worries for a few seconds. 'You mean you confronted them? Evie, you could have been attacked or mugged – or worse!'

'Unlikely,' replied Evie sounding totally unconcerned. 'Nobody messes with Kat. Anyway, they legged it as soon as they saw her running towards them.'

Jenna had a sudden mental image of a dark-clad, armoured warrior tossing the thugs aside like one of the Marvel Avengers.

'So where are you then?' asked Evie.

'I'm at yours. Matt and I…' Jenna's voice wavered as she rubbed her free hand against her knee. 'We've split up. And I don't know where to go. I know it's stupid, and I could go and stay in a cheap hotel or something, but—'

'No, of course you can't! You're my sister, of course I'm not going to let you go off to some crummy hotel. Stay there, we'll be back in about twenty minutes – the traffic is horrendous.'

After she'd hung up, a couple of fat tears plopped onto the phone and Jenna dashed them away as she groped in her bag for a tissue. She wasn't even sure why she was crying as she'd coped on her own before now. What it boiled down to was that men were unreliable when it really mattered. They made empty promises that never came good. Even Henry hadn't bothered to call her.

As she wiped her phone screen, she wondered

whether he'd sent the photos over to Evie yet. He might have decided that he wasn't interested in keeping in contact, but she wasn't about to allow other people to be let down in the process. She called up Henry's contact details for something to do, and before she could analyse the situation in too much detail, she hit the call button. It was answered almost immediately.

'Jenna! I'm so glad you called.'

'Are you?'

There was a pause before Henry replied. 'I meant to ring you yesterday, but…'

'It doesn't matter,' she said brusquely.

'It does to me. I feel so guilty about walking the legs off you on Saturday. I mean I'm not implying that you don't – that you can't…' His voice tailed off. 'Anyway, how are you?'

She had no idea. Hurt. Upset. Confused. Let down. Take your pick. But any of those responses would only invite more questions.

'I'm fine. I was just wondering whether you'd sent the photos over to Evie yet?' she said in as normal a voice as she could muster.

'Yes. But I didn't have a contact email for her so I sent a file transfer link to the rescue's email address. They'll have twenty-eight days to pick up the photos, but I'm happy to pop a disk in the post to her in case she can't access the link. I think she'll be really pleased with the results.'

When Jenna didn't respond, he added, 'So how are all the piggies? Are they behaving?'

She could hear the smile in his voice and she attempted to smile back. At least the guinea pigs had been popular.

'They're all fine, and all bar one has been behaving.'

Henry laughed. 'Who's been the naughty guinea pig then? Not one of our models, I hope?'

'Yes, actually. Snickers has been enjoying himself with the ladies.'

'Was that the gorgeous long-haired one? Isn't she a girl pig? Sorry, I don't know what the right terminology is.'

'It's a sow, and no, Snickers is a boar. And one that still has all his little boy bits intact.'

There was a definite pregnant pause before Henry replied. 'Er … was that my fault? I put her – sorry, him – home, didn't I? I'm such an idiot; do you know if he got up to anything?'

'It's too early to tell yet, but all the females are currently on pregnancy watch.'

'Oh gosh! I'm so sorry! How many females could he have, erm, impregnated?'

'Potentially all of them. It depends how quick he was, really. Evie said he was worn out and fast asleep when they found him.'

Henry chuckled. 'Sorry, I shouldn't laugh. Poor Snickers.'

'Poor Snickers?' said Jenna indignantly. 'He's the only

one who's had a good time. It's poor Evie and Kat who will have to find house room for anything up to seventy or even eighty babies.'

She hadn't meant to make him feel guilty, but the fact of the matter was that Henry did put him home. Though in his defence – not that he was raising any – it was Jenna's ungainly dive into the cardboard boxes that had precipitated the emergency depositing of said guinea pig somewhere safe. And that wouldn't have happened if she hadn't inadvertently stroked Henry's thigh. Even now, weeks later, that memory generated a visceral response.

Henry had very gallantly said nothing about it, but she couldn't help but wonder whether part of her perpetual embarrassment was a direct consequence of her over-active imagination, which had subsequently re-run that scene in a number of different ways and with various interesting embellishments.

It was several seconds before she registered that he had asked her a question.

'Sorry, I missed that. What did you say?'

'I was asking if I could perhaps bring over the disk in person. I clearly owe Evie and Kat an apology, and you too. How are you fixed Wednesday? Or I'm free tomorrow, if that's not too short notice?'

In her head, he was in the unreliable male category, but it didn't stop her heart doing a few extra loud thumps as they talked on the phone, nor did it dampen the strange tingling of her nerve endings that had nothing whatsoever to do with over-exertion.

'I'm busy tomorrow, I'm moving house.'

'Sorry, I think I misheard you. It sounded like you said you're moving house tomorrow.'

Henry sounded amused; Jenna wished that it was a joke. Or maybe it was; maybe her whole relationship with Matt was a joke. She put up with him and he put up with her – what sort of shit relationship was that anyway? A slow tear dribbled down her cheek as the effort of trying to sound like her world was not crumbling around her became increasingly difficult.

'Jenna?'

She willed him to carry on talking about Snickers, because that was something factual, objective.

'Has something happened?'

Jenna made a noise that may or may not have been a yes.

'Is there something I can do to help? I'm free tomorrow.'

She sniffed and wiped her face. 'Honestly, you don't have to.'

'I know. But I want to, okay? And bear in mind you'll be rescuing me from another evening of disappointment with the parents, so technically you're doing me a favour.'

A scrunching of gravel alerted her to an approaching vehicle. 'I've got to go, but I'll email you later.'

Henry almost snatched at the opportunity as he said, 'Yes, of course. Just email me the where and when. I won't be late this time either.'

Two seconds later, her car door was yanked open and

Evie flung her arms around Jenna's neck. 'Quick hugs as we've got some poorly patients to get settled. Here's the house keys if you want to let yourself in.'

Jenna gently pushed the hand away. 'If I'm going to foist myself on you, I might as well make myself useful. Give me some jobs. It will keep me from feeling sorry for myself.'

Kat unloaded four pet carriers from the back of her Volvo Estate and Jenna picked up one and followed Evie into the barn. If the cavy population of Little Paws was surprised to see the lights going back on so quickly, they didn't seem to mind in the slightest, and struck up a determined chorus of wheeking in case anyone fancied handing round extra helpings of lettuce.

'You lot don't know how spoilt you are,' said Kat as she opened the fridge, which prompted a rapid increase in squeaky decibels. 'I'm getting out the medicine box, you daft furries.'

'What can I do to help?' Jenna asked.

'If you feel up to it, could you make up two hutches for us?'

From a box in the corner, Evie lifted out a pile of newspapers, and filled two trugs with shavings and hay. Jenna had spent many weekends helping Evie with the task of cleaning out hutches and was happy to be put to work. It kept her body, if not her mind, occupied and for that she was grateful. She lined the bottom of the hutches with newspaper and added a layer of shavings, then filled one side of the hutch with hay and securely attached a bottle of fresh water to the mesh at the front.

The first pair of guinea pigs were in a very sorry condition. One was white with pink eyes, and the other a chocolate brown colour. Their fur was dull and matted, and the white one had a bald patch on her face, which was very likely to be ringworm, according to Kat.

Evie brought them over and placed them in the hutch. They immediately darted into the hay and buried themselves. 'Poor little girls. We'll let them get settled for the night and then check them over thoroughly in the morning.'

A third, rather emaciated-looking sow, soon joined them after Evie had administered some eye drops and cleaned up a bite wound.

The next hutch became home for a solitary male who was limping badly, missing patches of his chocolate brown fur (also probably ringworm) and had one ear badly torn. After the emotional evening she'd had, Jenna couldn't cope with any more trauma and burst into tears at the sight of the poor animal.

Kat gently placed her hand on Jenna's shoulder and gave her a friendly hug. 'You wait. With a bit of love and care, he'll be just fine.'

It was well past nine o'clock by the time they were finished and Jenna had brought her bags in from the car. A fuzzy, aching tiredness crept over her as she sat at the kitchen table, a significant proportion of which was covered in papers, a half-drunk can of lemonade, an unopened family size packet of crisps, Kat's thyroid pills and other unidentified items.

Using her arm as a boon, Evie swept all the table detritus to one end and placed a mug of tea in front of her sister. 'Are you hungry?'

'Not really.'

'I'm starving,' said Kat, opening the bag of crisps and munching noisily.

Jenna pointed at the carrier bag sitting next to her small suitcase. 'There's a dinner for two in there. We never got round to actually eating it.'

'Are you sure you don't mind?' Kat asked, her eyes lighting up hopefully. Within seconds the oven was on and while they waited, Evie and Kat coaxed out Jenna's explanation of Matt's second planned foray into the realms of self-employment, and how he had factored in her money without her knowledge or consent. Evie listened quietly, slipping her arm around her sister and pulling her close as Jenna spewed out the sorry tale. Kat, on the other hand, interjected volubly. Her indignation was strangely comforting, and her choice of insulting epithets confirmed Jenna's long-held suspicion that she'd never really liked Matt from the outset.

'I'm glad we're on the same team,' Jenna said with a tired smile. 'And it's good of you to give me a place to doss. If it's okay, I'll go back to the flat tomorrow and collect the rest of my things. I'll try not to fill up your house for too long.'

Evie gave her a gentle hug. 'We'll help.'

Jenna shook her head. 'You have enough to do here, and besides, Henry's already offered. Well, sort of offered. I'll email him later.'

'Henry? As in…?' Evie made camera clicking gestures with her fingers. 'When did you arrange that? I thought you came straight over here?'

'I did. But you weren't in. So … while I was waiting, I decided to call him, that's all. About the photos.'

Evie and Kat exchanged twinkly glances.

'Good idea,' Kat said resolutely. 'He looks the strong type.' She gave Jenna a knowing smile before turning her attention back to the dinner.

Chapter Fifteen

The following day, Jenna messaged Matt to say that she'd be back after work to collect her belongings. She hoped that he'd take the hint and make sure he wasn't around. During her lunch break, she typed up a list of items that belonged to her and printed off two copies so there were no misunderstandings about what she was taking. She had expected to feel more emotional about the process, but to her surprise, the overwhelming feeling this morning was one of relief.

How long had it been since she and Matt had felt like a real couple? Shared experiences? They hadn't ever been away together, both being too busy trying to remain financially solvent. Even at a more granular level, they didn't like the same films, or food. Matt would happily live off fast food given the choice, whereas she preferred fresh cooked produce. He never read books whereas she loved immersing herself in a fictional world, especially if there was a happy ever after. Was the requirement to have money and a roof over their heads the thread that had tied them together? If so, it had well and truly been severed last night.

Henry didn't seem to think that either mattered that much, but then he'd never had to worry about where he was going to live or how. She had pre-warned Evie that she'd be back a bit later this evening as she'd go straight to the flat after work, but Evie was happy to eat later on, and made Jenna promise to call her if she needed extra pairs of hands.

———

Jenna was relieved to find the flat was empty when she let herself in. More boxes had appeared from the garage since yesterday, but Matt could do what he liked from here on in. Evie had lent her a larger wheeled suitcase and Jenna had acquired a number of redundant but sturdy cardboard boxes from the Office Facilities Manager who had been only too delighted to offload some of the company's cardboard recycling.

She set to work packing up the remainder of her clothes, books and other items, before turning her attention to the airing cupboard. She was taking the towel set that had been a present from Evie one year; it had the words *Jenna's towel – hands off* printed on it. It still brought a smile to her face every time she used it.

There were also a few items in the kitchen that

belonged to her, but she had to be practical about how much she would use or could store. The bookcase in the lounge was hers though, and so was the upholstered chair in the bedroom; if she left those behind she was fairly certain they would appear on Matt's eBay shop in the near future.

The irony of asking Henry to come over and help her move things to prevent Matt selling them off, when that was precisely what had happened to his own belongings, was not lost on her, and she decided she would ask Evie and Kat if they minded her inviting him over for dinner as a thank you. Not that they were likely to have any objections; they seemed to have already made up their minds about Henry, and there were definitely some furtive looks exchanged between the pair of them over breakfast when his name popped into the conversation despite Jenna explaining that Henry was a self-declared romance-free zone. He was a friend, that was all. Just an exceptionally good-looking, often tardy, friend. Today though he arrived more or less on time, and she buzzed him in.

Henry was sporting his usual crumpled look, and the collar of his red and navy rugby shirt was clearly not even on nodding terms with the iron. Jenna would have happily offered to press it for him, but that might involve a bit too much stripping off, even though from a personal point of view, she wouldn't object in the slightest. He might be a romance-free zone but she certainly wasn't. She suppressed a giggle at the thought of a half-naked Henry standing around while she ironed his shirt.

'Hello! Mr Shifter at your service,' Henry said, rubbing his hands together. 'Where shall I start? And what's so funny?'

Even with the backseats down in Jenna's car, it was clearly obvious that it wasn't all going to fit, but Henry was more than happy to use his car as an overflow removal van. Despite his willingness to give up his evening to ferry Jenna's boxed up belongings out to the car, she felt more than a little guilty that she wasn't able to do a lot of the actual ferrying, but it was a question of practicality. She had already demonstrated her falling-over skills in Henry's presence, and that was while she was empty-handed.

While Henry was outside wedging the bookcase into his car, Jenna filled up large shopper bags with the clothes she'd already piled up on the bed, and she dragged them out to the hall to make it easier for Henry. It was as she was propping open the internal front door with one of the bags that she heard a familiar voice.

'You've decided then.'

Jenna looked up slowly to give herself time to arrange a neutral expression on her face. It was clear they had both outgrown this relationship, so she was not going to waste her effort on tears, recriminations, or debate.

'I decided last night, Matt. As did you. I'll be finished here in another ten minutes. Shall I post the keys through the door when we're done?'

'And who's "we"?'

Jenna cursed her careless use of pronouns, but before

she had time to correct herself, the outside door opened and Henry's footsteps came to an abrupt halt. Matt swung round and scowled.

It was interesting, and not a little bit weird, seeing the two of them standing face to face in front of her. For a few seconds neither spoke, and it reminded Jenna of a scene from a wildlife documentary where a new, competing male of the species strolls into already occupied territory. She half expected to hear David Attenborough's voice wafting down the hallway narrating the scene as the two protagonists eyed each other: on Matt's part with deep suspicion, on Henry's with studied interest.

'Matt, this is Henry. He's kindly offered to help me.'

'Is that the please-would-you-buy-my-camera-because-I-couldn't-be-bothered-to-get-it-back-from-my-girlfriend Henry?'

'I didn't *ask* her to buy anything,' Henry replied in a tone of voice Jenna had not heard before, one which had a distinct edge to it.

Matt turned to face her. 'So he's the new boyfriend, is he? Or is he just looking for more of his gear while I'm not around?'

'No. He's kindly offered to help if you must know.'

Henry's eyes narrowed and his chin tilted ever so slightly upwards. 'Don't talk to Jenna like that.'

'Or what?' asked Matt aggressively. Without waiting for a response, he stepped forward but Henry was quicker and raised his arm defensively. 'En garde!' he said in a play-acting voice, then turned to wink at Jenna. 'I knew those expensive fencing lessons would come in handy one day!'

Even as he turned back towards his opponent, Matt had closed the gap between them. His balled fist slammed into the side of Henry's head and sent him staggering sideways into the wall. 'I can say what I like, you posh git.'

A small shriek escaped Jenna's lips and she stared at Matt open-mouthed. 'I can't believe you just did that!'

She'd seen him hurl abuse at the referee during England Cup matches, and he'd punched a cardboard box once when he got wound up about something, the details long forgotten, but the fact that she'd lived with — shared a bed with — someone capable of doing that to another human being shocked her.

She stepped round the pile of bags to where Henry stood with his hand against his cheek. 'Are you okay?'

Henry gave a brief nod and glanced across at Matt who was now glaring at him. 'You know what?' Matt said nastily. 'You are exactly how I imagined you would be.'

Henry proffered a rueful smile. 'That's funny. I was going to say exactly the same thing to you.'

Matt spun round and marched through the hall past all the waiting bags, and a few seconds later the lounge door banged shut followed by the sound of the television.

'Did you need anything else from that room?' asked Henry, gesturing with his hand.

'Nope. I'll just do a quick look around and then we're done here.'

A few minutes later, the keys had been posted through

the door and they were heading back out to the cars. They drove in convoy over to Little Paws with Jenna in front. She drove deliberately slowly as she was very concerned as to whether Henry was even in a fit state to be behind the wheel of a car. Having already rung her sister to say she was on her way, there was a reception committee of two humans and one guinea pig waiting to greet them as they pulled up.

'I'll take Lady Maud home and then give you a hand with the unloading,' said Kat as the sisters hugged. She gave Henry a penetrating stare. 'What's happened to your eye? It almost looks like a bruise or something.'

Henry reached up and touched his cheek. 'I'm fine. I just tripped and knocked my head against something.'

'Poor you,' said Evie. 'That looks sore.'

'He's being polite,' said Jenna. 'And inaccurate. The thing he knocked his head against was Matt's fist.'

The shocked looks on Evie and Kat's faces as she told them briefly what had happened mirrored her own feelings on the subject, and Evie immediately went in search of the human first aid kit. While not as extensive as the guinea pig one, she returned with a tube of arnica cream, which she insisted on rubbing over his cheek as soon as he had sat down.

'There you go,' she said cheerfully. 'Your fur will grow back in no time.'

They laughed and after a few seconds, Henry joined in. 'Will I start squeaking for my dinner too?' he asked with a smile.

'Talking of dinner,' said Jenna. 'I – that is, we – would like to invite you over for dinner tomorrow night as a thank you for all your help, if you're free.' She looked across at her sister. 'You don't mind, do you?'

'Provided you don't mind us having to temporarily abandon you while we do piggy suppers and the usual evening medications routine.'

'That would be great! I'll bring over a CD with all the photos on it to save you messing about with the file transfer stuff.'

They all helped unload Henry's car so he could get off home. Jenna was quietly impressed that he passed her a few of the lighter bags to take in, without doing that don't-you-carry-anything-it's-all-too-heavy-for-you stuff. How many times had she heard that? Or been told to just sit and watch while other people did things because they were worried about her trying to help or falling over?

At the moment, she was more worried about Evie and Kat than herself. If the developers continued to up their offer, they could find themselves homeless. Now she was based here for the time being, she would find out exactly what the latest position was. She had noticed on the way over that dark green hoarding had been erected along what was presumably going to be the entrance to the building site on the opposite side of the road. There was nothing anyone could do now about that, but as far as their side was concerned, this was far from being a done deal.

Chapter Sixteen

Jenna left work early the following day and stopped off at the petrol station shop to buy some flowers for Evie and a bottle of wine. As an afterthought she added a few cans of beer to the basket in case Henry preferred it to wine.

It was just a thank you, Jenna insisted, as she caught Kat giving Evie an amused smile. He'd given up his evening to help out, and now they were reciprocating.

'So it's got nothing to do with the fact that he fancies you then?' asked Kat.

'No! I mean he doesn't, he's just a friend.'

Kat raised her eyebrows and smiled. 'If you say so.'

Henry had already made his position clear so if there was any attraction, it existed solely in Jenna's imagination. On several occasions she had revisited their trip to the Maiden Stone, and after mentally airbrushing out the strenuous trek through the wood, she accepted that the rest of the afternoon had certainly been different. And interesting. She recalled how Henry had arranged the flowers in her hair, and how – in the privacy of her own imaginary world – it was his lips and not his hand that had brushed gently against her neck. She would never admit it out loud but yes, perhaps it had been a little magical too.

Henry arrived fifteen minutes late bearing a bottle of prosecco for Evie and Kat, and a box of expensive-looking chocolates for Jenna.

'You haven't seen the dinner yet!' joked Kat as she gave him a friendly hug.

'Oh don't worry, I eat anything,' replied Henry jovially. 'When you're trekking round remote parts of Peru, you either eat what the locals do or you starve.'

'And what do the locals eat?' asked Jenna.

Evie and Kat stared at him, then both cried in unison, 'They eat guinea pigs!'

'Well, you'd better not admit to having done that, Mister!' said Kat grabbing his ear between her forefinger and thumb.

Henry squealed with mock terror. 'Aargh! Not the ear cleaver! I don't do violence and I've already been thumped once this week.'

'Kat!' pleaded Jenna, more than slightly embarrassed. 'Please don't torture the guest – he's brought all the guinea pig photos with him.'

While the dinner simmered in the oven – chilli con carne, Jenna confirmed for avoidance of doubt, and definitely *not* guinea pig – they fired up Jenna's laptop and reviewed the piggy pictures. Henry's skill as a photographer clearly extended to animals as well as landscapes, and despite being taken inside the barn, they were well lit and beautifully composed. They spent ages discussing the first eight pictures before Henry pointed out that there were over two hundred, and suggested they had a quick whizz through first to eliminate any they didn't like. He had already taken out the few where Evie or Kat's hand had appeared in the shot, and the many where the guinea pig had turned round, started chewing the props or otherwise declined to pose in the desired manner.

After an initial run-through, amid much discussion and heaps of praise for the quality of the pictures, they paused for dinner, which they ate at the wooden table in the large farmhouse kitchen. The chilli was served with fluffy white rice and crusty bread, and Henry was an appreciative diner, complementing Evie and Kat on their culinary skills.

'So do you cook much, Henry?' asked Evie.

Henry wrinkled his nose slightly. 'No. I like eating food, but I don't enjoy the cooking part. I try to eat out if possible.'

'But I thought you lived at home. With your parents?' said Jenna.

'I do, but…'

Jenna detected a barely audible sigh before Henry abruptly changed the subject.

'So – what I suggest is that you all take a few days to

go through the photos and whittle it down to around maybe fifteen pictures; you need twelve for the calendar itself plus a couple for the cover. I'll then arrange for the printing. One of Dad's clients runs a printing firm in Haxford so I'll try and negotiate a discount for you.'

'Do you have any idea how much it might cost?' asked Kat. 'It's not that we're not grateful or anything, but we don't have a huge reserve and—'

'No, I'm paying for it,' interrupted Jenna. 'You can treat it as part of my rent. I'm not paying anything on the other place anymore, so I'll give it to you instead.'

'I think *I* ought to be paying for it seeing as I'm the one responsible for the possible influx of baby guinea pigs,' argued Henry.

Evie laughed. 'Females don't get pregnant just by photographing them, you know. It was my dear, big sister who accidentally put Snickers back with the girlies.'

Henry threw Jenna an enquiring look. 'Well anyhow, I'll get some costs while you decide on the photos, then Jenna and I can fight it out over who pays.'

They all laughed and Evie retrieved an apple crumble from the oven.

'Wow, is that homemade as well?' asked Henry.

'Mr Sainsbury kindly made it for us,' said Kat with a smile. 'We do have a barn full of needy guinea pigs to look after, you know.'

Henry accepted Jenna's offer of the beer, and she retrieved one of the bottles from the fridge while Kat and Henry chatted about all things guinea pig. She wasn't sure

Henry really wanted an update on Chocolate's ringworm problem, but she was glad he got to see the kinder side of Kat that not everyone noticed.

Henry asked who looked after them when they went on holiday.

'We don't do holidays really, do we, Kat? Although Jenna did come over for the weekend when we stayed overnight after the wedding of one of Kat's cousins, and we roped in a few extra volunteers.' Evie smiled her thanks at her sister. 'The furries take up a lot of the day.'

'And have there been any updates from Farmer Giles?' Jenna asked.

'Is he the neighbour?' Henry grinned. 'He's not really called Giles, is he?'

'No,' said Evie. 'He's called Gerry and his wife's Paula. And they're a nice couple really—'

'Yeah. So nice, they're happy to make us homeless,' added Kat.

Evie and Kat explained how the developers were already building 150 new houses on the other side of the road and had now made an offer for Gerry's farmland, the freehold of which included their house.

Henry looked shocked. 'That's awful! I saw the large sign as I turned into your road, but surely they can't build on both sides? That's a massive overdevelopment of a rural area.'

'Yes, but it's subject to planning permission being granted. Even though nobody wants more houses round here,' she added.

Jenna didn't want to spoil the evening by stating the obvious: that unless she was very much mistaken, the granting of planning permission rarely took into account what ordinary people wanted. Starting tomorrow, she would sit Evie and Kat down and encourage them to put together a coherent plan for an objection. And now this was her home too, at least for the time being, she could legitimately add her name to the objection. In a worst-case scenario, the three of them could find somewhere together but she didn't want to even think about what would happen to all the guinea pigs. It would break her sister's heart to have to rehome them.

Henry was clearly thinking something similar. 'Look, you can say this is none of my business, but I have some knowledge of planning law. I'd be more than happy to help you put together an objection. Obviously I'm not suggesting that you don't know how to write a letter, but there are a number of rules regarding what you can and can't use as grounds for objection. For example, if your neighbour builds an extension, you can't object because it you don't like it, or it spoils your view. You have to look at the town planning guidance and try and find ways that the building work contravenes that.'

'So can we write it now?'

'Yes, you get a period of time to comment on the plans and raise any objections. After that it goes to an open planning meeting.'

'And how soon could that be?' asked Jenna.

'Usually around eight weeks from the original application,' replied Henry. 'That's where everyone gets a chance to put forward their case although you probably only get a few minutes to talk so the trick is not to waffle. Make your case based on the law, not on emotional points. But your first step is to work out your grounds for objection and then we can work out what we're going to say at any meeting.'

A flutter of panic danced around inside her. When was that planning application actually made? Could they really all be made homeless? Other than Kat's part-time job, they didn't have any other income. If they became homeless, where would they live? Would Kat's parents be delighted to have Evie, Kat, and several dozen guinea pigs moving in with them? Because if not, it would be largely down to her to support all three of them.

'I know it's hard, but try not to worry.' Henry reached across the table and placed his hand over hers, giving it a gentle squeeze and causing the hairs on her arm to leap to attention. 'It's a long way from being a done deal.'

'And in the meantime, we still have the furries to feed,' said Evie as she stood up and shoved the chair aside with her leg. While Jenna and Henry stacked the plates and cleared the table, Evie and Kat began filling several large bowls with chopped vegetables, salad and fruit.

'They eat healthier than I do,' laughed Henry. 'Is there anything guinea pigs *don't* eat?'

'There's a lot of misconceptions about what guinea pigs are allowed to eat,' Kat replied. 'Some you definitely want to feed in smaller quantities like fruits, but absolutely not any dairy stuff, cereals, grains, nuts, mushrooms—'

'Or iceberg lettuce,' chimed in Evie. 'That's why the fridge in the barn is full of romaine and other varieties.'

Jenna's offer of help was politely declined.

'Your job is to entertain the guest,' said Kat, ignoring Jenna's blushes.

'And Henry's job,' said Evie, steering her sister back towards the chair, 'is to make sure Jenna sits down. She won't tell you when she's tired or in pain.'

'I'm fine.' Jenna dismissed them with a wave. 'Go on and feed the piggies.'

Henry waited for Evie and Kat to leave before he asked, 'Do you always say that?'

'What?'

'"I'm fine", even when you're not.'

Jenna shrugged. 'Sometimes it's just easier.'

Henry chewed his lip for a few seconds. 'Look, I know I probably get over enthusiastic about things, but I want you to know that I'm sorry I wore you out last time. I wanted to show you that there were some genuinely interesting places round here, but I hold my hand up, I didn't really think all the logistics through.' His eyes fixed on hers. 'Am I forgiven?'

He really did have lovely eyes. Jenna proffered a small smile. 'There's nothing to forgive. And you were right, it was really interesting.'

'Seriously? You're not just saying that to humour me?'

'It's me who ought to be apologising to you after what

Matt did. I still can't believe he hit you. I'm glad it's not got any darker round your eye.'

'Probably thanks to Evie's prompt administration of the miracle fur regrowth cream or whatever it was she put on my face.'

Jenna chuckled. 'You know perfectly well it was arnica.'

The conversation lulled, and for a few seconds they were enveloped in a cosy quietness, punctuated only by the rhythmic ticking of the clock on the wall. It was Henry who eventually broke the silence.

'Jenna, I'm planning a photoshoot on Friday; the weather forecast looks good and I wondered if you'd like to come with me?'

Before Jenna had time to open her mouth, Henry rushed on. 'I promise there won't be any treks involved. Not. At. All. And I'll bring a picnic,' he added.

'And do you always bring a picnic when you go on photo expeditions?'

'Only when I have VIP guests.'

'So where is this photoshoot then?

'Well, that would spoil the surprise, wouldn't it?'

Jenna folded her arms and raised her eyebrows.

'Jeez, you're a tough negotiator. Okay, I'd like to take you to Northlands Abbey.'

'What, those old ruins?'

'Have you actually been there?' Henry waited for a few seconds, then smiled triumphantly. 'You haven't, have you?'

'I've driven past them.' Even to Jenna's ears that sounded feeble, and she failed to suppress the guilty smile that broke out.

'But I bet you haven't seen them at sunrise.'

Jenna blinked in surprise. 'But that's around half past five in the morning!'

'Jenna, don't you ever want to stop being serious and practical, just for one day? Give it try. Be spontaneous. What's the worst that can happen? Actually, don't answer that – just say yes.'

In the weeks since he'd first sent it to her, she had admired Henry's northern lights photograph many times. And she'd enjoyed their last trip, although the knackering element of the expedition had taken the edge off the afternoon. Matt's idea of a day out usually involved the pub or a round of golf somewhere. He'd never thought about what might interest her. Had she always just fallen in line with what he wanted to do to avoid potential conflict? What happened to that child who had daydreamed about fairy houses and happy ever afters? Why shouldn't she be allowed to enjoy herself for one day without worrying about money and security and everyday things?

She looked into Henry's smiling eyes. She wanted to experience that joy, that spontaneity for herself, and for once not vicariously through magazine pictures or other people's photos. 'Okay, I'll trust you,' she said softly.

'Is that a yes?'

Jenna nodded. She'd probably need to tell her boss

that she'd be in late that day. She immediately checked her train of thought. Why the hell shouldn't she take a day off? It wasn't what she normally did, but this new, cautiously adventurous Jenna didn't like the idea of going back to the office after a promised magical picnic experience.

'And I'll try and get the day off. I don't want to be clock watching.'

Chapter Seventeen

Jenna was one of the first in the office the following morning. She savoured the peace and quiet without the whirr of printers, the ringing of phones, and the hum of human interaction that formed the white noise backdrop to everyday office life. Within the space of around fifteen minutes or so, the trickle of arrivals would increase steadily until nine thirty, when the office should be fully staffed and the engine of business at full throttle.

Her plan was to get as many of the urgent jobs for the next two days done as quickly as possible, and then hopefully she stood a greater chance of getting the time off.

It wasn't long before her colleague Alisha arrived, and she'd barely deposited her bag and shrugged off her jacket before she blurted out her news.

'Hi, Jenna, you're in early! Guess who paid us a visit yesterday after you'd left? Only Mr Ranty.'

Jenna rolled her eyes. 'So what did he want this time? Payment of his expenses in person?'

'No, he wanted to speak to you, but we said you'd left the office for the day. He got a bit huffy about that.'

'He can huff all he likes, but we have this thing called flexi-time,' replied Jenna.

'That's what Jamie said to him. He also pointed out that you usually got in super early as well, so technically you donated free overtime to the company. And he mentioned the employee of the month thing for good measure. It was brilliant.'

Jenna smiled. Jamie was loyal if a bit over enthusiastic. 'So did Mister Ranty stomp back downstairs?'

Alisha winced. 'No, he went in to talk to Adam. We all kept our heads down after that.'

'Well, I need to speak to Adam later – I'm hoping to book a short notice day off – so I hope he hasn't put our boss in a bad mood.'

As Jenna expected, she heard the same tale from Denise, and then Jamie. Ian Ransome had no outstanding expenses to process, although he frequently grumbled about having to wait until the next payroll due date before it arrived in his bank account. However they were not her rules, and they applied to everyone.

She waited until mid-morning before knocking tentatively on Adam's open office door.

'Do you have a minute?'

Adam gestured towards his visitors' chair.

'I won't hold you up, I'm only here to ask if I can take

a day off tomorrow. I know it's short notice and I'll book it all officially through the online system, but I wanted to speak to you as I'm not sure how quickly the system notifies you about requests.'

Adam nodded. 'Efficient as always. We all have short notice requests from time to time, so that's fine, just send me a note of anything that could be urgent. There's no emergency, I hope?'

Jenna flashed a brief smile as she stood up. 'No emergencies. But thanks for asking.'

'Before you go, there's just a couple of things.'

Jenna reluctantly sat down again. She had a million items on her to-do list, which didn't include long chats with her boss.

'I had a visit from Ian Ransome yesterday.'

'Oh really? That's a coincidence. I heard that Mr Rant – I mean Ransome'—Jenna hurriedly corrected herself—'was looking for me yesterday as well. I was going to email him later this morning.'

'I'd hold that, if I were you.' Adam fiddled with his pen as he spoke. It was the same sort of fidgety, self-conscious behaviour that Matt normally exhibited when he was hiding something. 'The thing is, he's not happy about some of his expense claims.'

Jenna snorted. 'That makes two of us.'

'And he's threatening to make an official complaint.'

'What? Against the company's official expenses policy? Good luck with that.'

'No. About you.'

Jenna stiffened. 'For the avoidance of doubt, I've settled every one of his claims in accordance with the company's procedures and policies.'

'He's claiming that you've withheld amounts without reason.'

'With all due respect, Adam, that's utter rubbish! In fact—'

Adam held up his hand. 'I know. I would not have put you in charge of settling expenses if I didn't trust you. So … in the interests of keeping the peace, I have agreed that I might review a few payments but it will be as and when I get time to do so. In any case, I have no doubt that everything will be in order, and should Ian decide to make a formal complaint, you will have my full support.'

Jenna tried to keep the annoyance out of her voice as she said, 'Thank you.'

'The other thing I wanted to mention was that I've also got some leave booked. You probably already know I'm away the last week of June and first week of July. Nearer the time we'll have a catch up on any outstanding projects, but I'm happy for you to continue to manage any expenses issues. If there are any problems that you can't handle in my absence, Lester Norris will be happy to advise. Otherwise, just continue to exercise your discretion as you see fit.'

That, at least, was a vote of confidence, but the thought of Ian Ransome trotting into Adam's office to complain about her behind her back really annoyed her. There weren't many occasions when she regretted that her feet were not more cooperative, but right now she really wanted them to perform a pissed-off march back to her desk. However, falling over in the middle of the office wouldn't make her feel any better so she consoled herself with muttering instead.

'Stupid, ignorant, impatient, ranty man.' She peppered her diatribe with a few additional expletives for good measure.

'You're not talking about our favourite Sales Account Director are you?' asked Denise as Jenna plonked herself down on her chair.

'I think you mean Mr I Rantsome-more,' replied Jenna pithily. 'He's only gone and moaned to Adam. He's like a child who keeps asking the same question of different people until they get the answer they want.' Jenna banged her mouse down on the corporate blue mouse mat. 'Adam has now agreed to review'—Jenna made speech marks with her fingers—'a couple of claims just to keep him happy but why should he have to do that? It either fits within the corporate expenses policy or it doesn't.'

'Ah, but have you considered that maybe Adam will review them and decide you've been too generous and decline some of his claims,' ventured Alisha. 'That'd be funny.'

'We'd have to ask for the money back!' said Jamie with a grin.

'And we could draw lots to decide who got to write the email,' added Denise.

'Dear Mr Ransome,' said Jenna, grinning as she pretended to type on her keyboard, 'I am pleased to advise that Adam has completed a review of your last three months' expenses claims as you requested, and I am delighted – whoops! I mean sorry – to advise that you have been overpaid.' Jenna's improvisation prompted a gale of laughter from the team.

'Furthermore,' continued Denise picking up the thread, 'as you have previously expressed dissatisfaction with the company's monthly timetable for expense payments, please arrange for an immediate bank transfer to Confederated Financial Solutions.'

Even though there was no possibility of there ever being a need to reclaim anything, the idea was highly entertaining. And apparently infectious too, as Jenna heard various permutations being created and expanded upon as she opened up the company's online leave booking system to upload her day off. She noted there was a project meeting scheduled for tomorrow afternoon, so she emailed her apologies and asked if Alisha could deputise.

Jenna worked through most of her lunch break so that she could get tomorrow's urgent jobs completed or dele-gated. Even so, she didn't manage to leave until shortly before half past five, which meant that she caught the tail end of rush hour traffic. Her daily commute was a bit longer now but once out of town, it was a pleasant journey and it gave her time to think.

Mentally setting aside the usual work-related issues,

she turned her thoughts instead to tomorrow's crack-of-dawn adventure, and she considered what she might wear for an outdoor picnic at five o'clock in the morning. She also made a mental note to adjust the time on her alarm clock – pyjamas was definitely not the look she was hoping for.

Chapter Eighteen

It felt weird getting up in the dark at this time of the year, but Jenna had already laid out her clothes so getting ready only required ten minutes in the bathroom. Evie had left the keys in the kitchen so Jenna could lock the door without waking everyone, and as arranged the previous evening, Henry was waiting outside. He was wearing his usual jeans and a navy rugby shirt. It was unbuttoned at the neck and she could see the top of a white T-shirt underneath.

Without any traffic to contend with, it was not a long drive, and it seemed strange driving into Haxford without the usual line of cars backed up over the river crossing. The ruins of Northlands Abbey sat on the edge of what the locals called the Old Town; ye olde touristy part of Haxford, which, in the height of summer, was heaving with visitors. Most flocked to the triangle of streets that made up the pedestrian shopping area, dominated at one end by the magnificent Victorian building that was Pennewicks Clothing Emporium. Several of the restaurants and eateries in the Old Town boasted open air spaces with views over the river, and during the summer months, boating was popular with locals and tourists alike.

Northlands Abbey, known more colloquially as The Ruins, was situated on the south bank of the river. Jenna had never taken much interest in it – it was just something she drove past from time to time. Now she was curious, and pulled out her phone to do a quick bit of research.

'I hope that's not work,' said Henry, giving her a sideways glance.

'You hope correctly. I was actually trying to find out when the abbey was built.'

'Sometime in the early thirteenth century I think,' Henry replied. 'It was home to an order of Franciscan monks who quietly went about their business for a couple of centuries until good old King Henry VIII decided to get rid of all the monasteries.'

'It's funny to think of it being a complete building once,' mused Jenna. 'Someone's home. It must have been awful for them seeing it taken apart stone by stone.' She shivered in the dark.

While not as popular as the main riverside attractions, the abbey still saw plenty of visitors, although not usually at this time of the morning. Even though the sun was not officially up yet, the sky was already paling and there was certainly enough light for Jenna to note with disappointment that the parking seemed quite a distance from the ruins themselves. And from what she could see as she opened the car door, the ground was stony and uneven too. Brilliant. Even in daylight there was no way she'd get over there in one piece, and a wave of frustration crashed over her. She was fed up with struggling with things that other people decided were accessible, and if that meant everyone thought she was awkward or anti-social, so be it.

She needed to speak up quickly as Henry was already unloading the car, but before she could think of how to phrase it politely, Henry bounded round to the passenger side.

'As you can see, we are this side of a stony field and our picnic site is over there. So, here's the plan. I will unload the car, dump everything and then come back for you, okay? I'm the transport, so all you have to decide is which option you'd prefer. The choice is the Jane Austen swoon, or Charge of the Light Brigade.'

'So the former is…?'

Henry picked up the large rucksack in his arms.

'Right. Got it. And the other option is?

'Piggyback.'

'Piggyback?' Jenna repeated, in case she'd somehow misheard.

He laughed. 'You look highly dubious. I'll have you know I've got an NVQ in piggyback safety.' Henry hoisted the rucksack onto his shoulders and then picked up a wicker picnic basket in one hand and a large overstuffed unzipped holdall in the other. 'Give me five minutes and I'll be right back.'

As she watched him trot off like an overladen pack horse, she rummaged in the bag at her feet and pulled out a dark pink cable knit cardigan. It had been a birthday present from Evie a couple of years ago, and Evie had replaced the rather ordinary buttons with ones in the shape of hedgehogs. It didn't feel cold in the car but overnight temperatures could still be cool at the beginning of May.

Streaks of pink and orange stretched across the eastern horizon and the air was filled with the dawn tweets and calls of the birds. She inhaled sharply and relished the sweet smell of the fresh morning air as she weighed up the pros and cons of Henry's suggestion.

Henry waved as he reappeared, now unencumbered. 'So, what's it to be?'

'Jane Austen, my good man.'

Henry tugged an imaginary forelock, and Jenna giggled. 'You're not photographing this bit, are you?'

'Do I look like I have a GoPro strapped to my head? Come here. Put your arms round my neck.'

His strong arms scooped her up and he pushed the car door shut with his foot. Jenna couldn't remember ever being carried anywhere other than by her mum. Hospital didn't count. Henry felt warm and comforting; there was a scent of freshly laundered clothes, and a woody cologne that reminded her of their visit to the Maiden Stone. Her head rested against his shoulder, and she imagined his heart pumping forcefully. Hers was performing a military tattoo that had nothing whatsoever to do with physical exertion.

He was certainly strong as he wasn't panting for breath as he strode across the stony field and then down a short flight of stone steps into what was originally the inside of the building, but was now a smooth, green lawn. Along one side of the rectangular area was a series of stone stumps, about half a metre in height, that had clearly once supported soaring columns along the middle of the church. The other was the outer north wall of the church. Even stripped of its internal decoration and glass, the gothic arched windows towered above them and Jenna almost gasped as she saw them close up.

Henry put her down carefully and she reluctantly let go of his neck. A large blue tartan picnic blanket had been laid out on the short, cropped grass, to which several plum-coloured velvet covered cushions had been added. He had also brought along a camping chair. At the side was the wicker basket fastened with leather straps – she had only seen those in films! A few metres away, Henry's tripod and camera were set up. It was getting lighter by the minute and Jenna noted that her watch already said ten past five.

Henry explained that he wanted to check the light and take a few exploratory photos and then they could unpack their picnic. Jenna was happy to watch him and having arranged the large comfy cushions, settled herself on the rug.

The eastern wall of the ruined abbey church

contained a stone arch into which was set three long, narrow windows, the central one balanced by two shorter ones either side. Whether it was over time or through human intervention, much of the surrounding stonework above the window had been lost, leaving the top of the arch jutting up into open sky. It was here, Jenna guessed, that in a short while, the sun would appear, and she smiled in anticipation.

Quickly now, the streaks in the sky lightened as the sun inched over the horizon, still hidden behind a wall of stone. She had rarely taken much notice of the sunrise – the sun just came up in the morning and set in the evening – but now she watched the changing colours of the sky, the cool breeze catching her upturned cheeks.

Henry trotted back. 'Are you hungry yet? I'm famished.' Without waiting for her answer, he undid the leather buckles and unpacked the hamper. Under normal circumstances Jenna wouldn't even be awake yet, but she was more than happy to participate in an al fresco breakfast.

She wasn't sure what she'd expected to see in a picnic breakfast: a few cereal bars, some orange juice cartons maybe, possibly the odd sandwich. Certainly not the fabulous feast in front of her. There was a pot of fresh, plump strawberries, two cartons of yoghurts with dainty spoons, a selection of mini cheeses and crunchy oat biscuits, sausage rolls with lattice pastry, and several deliciously flaky croissants in a variety of flavours.

At the bottom, wrapped in a tea towel, was a bottle of

Taittinger, which Henry deftly opened and poured into two glasses.

Jenna stared open mouthed for several seconds. 'I don't know what to say. You shouldn't have gone to all this trouble.'

Henry held out one of the glasses. 'And why not?' he asked, his voice gently teasing. 'Are you enjoying yourself on this slightly chilly but hopefully interesting morning?'

'Definitely.'

Henry leapt to his feet. 'Just going to get a few more pics. This will be worth it, I promise.'

Jenna sipped her champagne, enjoying the fizz of the bubbles as it slipped down her throat. She was drinking champagne! For breakfast! At silly o'clock in the morning! And with someone who made her feel special in a way that no one had ever done before.

She watched as Henry repositioned the tripod and waited as the sun, now inching its way up the eastern wall of the old church, reached the edge of the window. Like a celestial spotlight, the first shard of light broke through, creating a misty ethereal look in the damp, morning air. Henry moved swiftly, taking photos from many different angles. He then turned towards Jenna and pointed the camera at the north wall, catching the light as it glittered against the 800-year-old stone mullions.

She'd been so engrossed in watching the changing light and the quietly magnificent architecture that she didn't notice the woman at first. She was hurrying along the north-eastern corner, almost directly across Henry's camera lens. Most likely some early morning dog-walker looking for their pooch. The woman was dressed in earthy colours with a hat or hood of some sort, which was probably how she'd blended into the background. Jenna was squinting into the sun and lost sight of her just as Henry walked back to the picnic site. The accidental photobomber clearly hadn't affected his mood as he was smiling broadly. 'Shall we eat? I've worked up an appetite.'

Henry topped up their glasses and they got stuck into their picnic. Jenna picked up one of the sausage rolls and bit into the crumbly pastry. 'Mm, these are delicious,' she said, brushing pastry crumbs from her lips. 'You are officially the world's best picnic organiser.'

'Thank you. I'll try and remember to get you to fill in a customer satisfaction survey before you leave.'

Jenna laughed. 'That sounds like my first job.'

'Wow, you worked in marketing?'

'Nah, nothing that grand. I was office junior in the policy services department. Nowadays I don't do surveys, which is just as well as my last customer was not at all satisfied.' She scowled as the recollection of the previous day made an unwelcome intrusion.

'Have you always worked at the same place?'

'Yes.' Jenna looked down and made an attempt to brush crumbs off the rug. 'Does that make me a bit boring?'

'Not at all; my parents would be thrilled with that sort of track record.'

'So you haven't yet caved in to pressure from your sister and joined the family firm?'

Henry smiled ruefully. 'I've promised I'll think about it. I'd really love to keep travelling though. And I've had a couple more photographs accepted by Shutterstock so hopefully I'll get royalties from them.'

'I'm sure you will, your photos are fabulous – you are so talented.'

'And I haven't even taken one of you yet,' said Henry, picking up his camera.

'Nooo!' Jenna wailed. 'Not that close up!'

'Okay then. How about up there?' Henry pointed to one of the stone column bases. Without waiting for Jenna's response, he pulled a small throw out of the holdall and spread it over the top.

'And I get up there how?'

'We use the tried and tested Jane Austen manoeuvre,' replied Henry with a grin. 'With your permission, of course.'

Henry lifted her onto the stone plinth as easily as he had carried her earlier this morning. He passed her the glass of champagne.

'Here you go. Now, turn to the side slightly … that's it. And angle your head this way… Perfect.' The camera clicked several times. 'You look very regal sitting up there.'

'You may address me as Princess Jenna of Oakhurst,' she replied in her best attempt at a peasant-sneering voice, which ended in a bit of a giggle. That champagne had definitely gone to her head. She had rarely drunk more than one glass of fizz and certainly not at breakfast. Perhaps she would try new things more often.

'You may lift the royal personage down now,' she announced.

Henry tugged his imaginary forelock again and lifted her carefully into his arms. Oh, that she could press a pause button right now. As he held her in his arms with the warmth of his body pressed against hers, real life faded into the background and for a few brief seconds, everything was just … heavenly.

'Is that a contented sigh or a tired sigh? I'll feel awful if I've worn you out yet again,' said Henry, anxiously scanning her face.

Jenna smiled. He really did have the most beautiful eyes, framed with golden lashes that women would pay good money for. 'No you haven't, and it's been wonderful so far. More than wonderful.'

Henry lowered her gently onto the picnic rug and after arranging the cushions under her head and shoulders, stretched out alongside her. 'I'm glad. You know, sometimes you can travel the world and see all sorts of amazing sights. But you can also visit what seems on the surface to be ordinary and everyday, which with the right setting, and the right person, can still be just as amazing.'

A companionable silence settled between them, only interrupted by the distant sound of the occasional car and the happy tweeting of birdsong.

Henry was right. It was interesting. And scenic. And totally magic. She had driven past this place so many times on the way somewhere, and never felt the urge to stop and look round properly. Now she wondered who had built this place all those centuries ago and what it had looked like? How many lives and stories could these stones reveal if they could talk? And how many other places had she not bothered to visit?

It struck her then that having the right person to go with made all the difference. Matt had never taken her anywhere where she might knacker herself, or fall down stone steps, and their trips had been selected with a view to what *she* thought she could do. What if she was limiting her own horizons? Her visit to the Maiden Stone with Henry had been tiring but it had also been interesting. Stimulating.

Henry's voice broke into her thoughts. 'You look miles away.'

Jenna smiled. 'I was remembering our last trip. I think you've proved your point.'

'Even though I wore you out?'

'That wasn't your fault.'

Henry propped himself up on his elbow and looked at her with an amused expression. 'Whose was it then? Yours?'

'Well, seeing as it's my leg that caused the problem, yes it probably was.'

Henry continued looking at her. 'You know what, you are amazing.'

'No, I'm not.'

Henry sat up. 'But you are. You don't moan about

things being unfair, or complain that you can't do things. You just get on with it. You are an in—'

'Oi!' Jenna clapped her hand over his mouth. 'Stop there, matey. I hope you're not going to say what I think you are, because if you were heading even remotely near the word inspiration, I will have to hit you over the head with this plastic plate.' Jenna reached out and grabbed the promised artefact and waggled it in front of him.

'But I'm trying to pay you a compliment!'

Jenna shook her head. 'To you it might sound like one. The trouble is that when you look at someone with a disability, the reaction often tends to be either "oh no, poor you, your life must be shit" or "thank goodness I'm not like you". Because most people can't imagine not being able to do all the things they take for granted, there's an underlying assumption that disability must be tragic. I'm not saying it's easy because that's not true either, but I'm personally not an inspiration to anyone just because I get up, dress myself and manage to get to work.'

'Point taken. So can I ask'—Henry picked a blade of grass and fiddled with it for a few seconds—'were you born with … erm … does it have a name?'

'It does. And extra points for not assuming it was some sort of car accident.' Jenna smiled wryly. 'I was born with something called fibular hemimelia. My shin bone wasn't as long as it should have been so in effect, you end up with one leg shorter than the other.' She looked at her two legs lying side by side. 'They're not too bad now, and the orthotics in my shoes help. But it means I never get to wear really nice princess shoes like my friends have.' She looked across at Henry. 'That bit is tragic – shoe envy is allowed.'

'So did you have to have a lot of operations when you were younger?'

Jenna nodded. 'Mostly to lengthen my left leg. Effectively they break the leg then bolt each side of the bone to an external fixator which holds the bone apart. As new bone grows in between, you crank it apart a bit more, quarter of a millimetre at a time, four times a day. Then it's a case of eat, sleep, repeat until the leg reaches the desired length.'

'How long does that take?'

'Usually months.'

'That must have hurt.'

'Yep. And then in between, they tinkered with my foot, ankle and all sorts of other bony stuff.'

Henry let out a low whistle. 'Bloody hell. Surely I'm allowed to say you're brave?'

Jenna threw him an I-did-warn-you look and then rapped him on the head with the plastic plate.

'I'll take that as a no. Okay how about incredible? Ow! Or awesome? Ow again!'

'You're only allowed to use the awesome word if you're talking about my boobs.'

They both laughed and Henry held up his hands in a gesture of surrender. 'Jenna Oakhurst, you should come with a government health warning.'

'Will this do instead?' Careful not to lift too many

layers of clothing and inadvertently flash said boobs at him, Jenna pulled up her thin knit sweater to show off her T-shirt underneath. Kat had bought it for her last year and she loved watching people's reactions as they read the slogan:

Legs not working efficiently.
(Everything else meets or exceeds manufacturer's specifications)

Henry burst out laughing. 'I don't care how many times you bash me over the head, that is officially amazing.' He picked up his camera. 'Do that again.'

Jenna obliged and grinned as Henry took several pictures.

'Definitely one for the album,' he said after reviewing the photo on the small screen. 'I'll call it Sunrise at Northlands Abbey plus Jenna's chest. Does that meet with your approval?'

'Plus the photobomber.'

A small furrow creased Henry's forehead. 'What photobomber?'

'The dog-walking woman wandering around earlier. She was over there.' Jenna pointed.

'I didn't see anyone. Or a dog.'

'I didn't see a dog either,' admitted Jenna. 'I just assumed she was looking for one.'

'What did this woman look like?'

Jenna did her best to describe her but really, it had

been rather difficult with the sun in her eyes to see anything that clearly.

Henry picked up one of the croissants, tore the corner off and chewed thoughtfully for a few seconds. 'I suppose it could have been the mysterious Grey Lady.'

'Seriously? Have you ever thought about writing fiction?'

'It's true!' Henry protested. 'Well, the legend exists anyway. Look it up in the library if you don't believe me, you philistine.'

Jenna helped herself to an almond croissant. 'Go on then – who is the Grey Lady?'

'According to the legend, she's the lover of one of the monks.'

'But surely they weren't allowed to have sexual relationships?'

'They weren't. But they fell deeply in love and met in secret, down by the river. Then one day he just stopped coming. She never knew that he'd been sent away to another monastery on the orders of the abbot. It is said that the woman died of grief, although it's more likely that it was one of the common diseases around in medieval times. But even in death she wouldn't abandon her lover and – if you believe the legend – she returned, again and again, searching for him, and it's said that she's still looking.' Henry paused. 'Of course it could also just have been your mystery dog-walker.'

'But you didn't see her, did you?'

'No, I didn't,' Henry admitted.

It was probably the effects of the alcohol, but Jenna felt unexpectedly touched by the story. 'Isn't it sad to think that she never knew why her lover had abandoned her? To be left always hoping that one day he would come back.' She poured the last of the champagne into the two glasses, quietly marvelling that they had finished the entire bottle, and picked up her glass. 'To her lost love,' she said, raising her glass.

'To all lost loves,' he replied as he clinked his glass against hers. Just briefly, his eyes seemed to cloud over with a look of wistfulness, but before Jenna could ask anything he posed a question of his own.

'So is Matt your lost love?'

Jenna almost choked on her champagne. 'God, no!'

'So you don't regret breaking up with him? I'd feel very guilty if it had anything to do with me.'

Jenna shook her head. She'd been thinking a lot about that relationship over the last few days. She had always assumed that she and Matt had shared the same values but looking back, she could see how her desire for money was in order to achieve financial security, permanence, stability. His dream, she now realised, was to be rich, and he was not afraid to take risks in his pursuit of wealth. She'd just allowed him to quietly steer the course of their relationship because she was frightened to rock the boat. Worried about what would happen if the relationship fell apart. Now it had, and nothing had happened. Nothing bad at any rate.

Living with Evie and Kat, she could see first-hand

how they barely had enough money to afford anything, but until this developer had appeared on the scene, they'd been content. She didn't count the mishap over Snickers, which, admittedly, was cause for concern as well as being partly her fault.

'This is where my mum would say, penny for your thoughts?'

Jenna smiled. 'Sorry, miles away again. I was thinking about my sister. Evie and Kat were so grateful that you did those pictures for them, and it will be a wonderful way to fundraise, provided the rescue is still going by Christmas. They'll be heartbroken if they have to close.' She didn't add that they'd all be homeless as well.

'What would happen to all the guinea pigs?'

Jenna made a face. 'I don't even want to think about it to be honest.'

'Well, my offer still stands; I'm happy to help in any way I can. It would be nice to be able to use my degree, although probably not in the way my parents were hoping.'

Jenna accepted his offer immediately. She didn't need to consult her sister or Kat to know what the answer was, and as they packed up the remains of the picnic, they arranged a date for Henry to come over to review all the available information.

'So, Princess Jenna, you have one more decision to make this morning. How do you want to be transported back to the car? Same two options – Jane Austen, or

Charge of the Light Brigade. You have five minutes to think while I take this lot back.'

While Henry carted the hamper and his photography equipment back to the car, Jenna reclined on the velvet cushions, arms outstretched like a bad imitation of Vitruvian Woman. The serenity of the early morning was gradually being replaced by the hum of human activity and she was glad they'd had that quiet, intimate time together. She stared up at the sky, now blue and dotted with delicate wisps of white cloud.

On any other day, she'd be getting ready to go to work about now. Worrying about spreadsheets and payroll deadline dates. Boring stuff. Now she wanted to do more than that. Going somewhere with someone who didn't mind a few extra logistics made all the difference. Whereas Matt had just avoided anything that looked like it might be problematic, Henry had – admittedly, by trial and error – created work-around solutions and it had worked brilliantly.

A female voice from behind jerked her out of her reverie. 'Excuse me, love, are you okay?'

'I'm fine, thanks,' Jenna replied with a nonchalant wave of her hand. 'I've got a part in *Casualty* as a corpse, so I'm doing a bit of practising.'

There was a sound of hurried throat clearing, some mumbled response and then quiet again, although it didn't last long.

'I saw you had a visitor while I was gone.'

Jenna sat up and locking her hands together, stretched

her arms upward. 'Just a concerned member of the public. Perhaps she thought I'd been abandoned here as a ritual sacrifice.'

Henry chuckled. 'Now who's straying into the realms of fiction? Oh, and I forgot to mention, there's a price for the return journey.'

Jenna looked up at him. 'Which is?'

Henry knelt in front of her. 'A kiss from the princess,' he said softly. 'If she will permit.'

He cupped his hand around her chin; his fingers felt warm despite the gentlest of touches, and she willed him to move closer. His lips parted in a shy smile and as hers reciprocated, he leaned forward and kissed her gently, sending sparks of excitement racing round inside her like miniature fireworks.

Then, just as quickly, the moment was over. He leapt to his feet, held out his hands and helped her up. 'So, what's it to be?'

The journey back to the car rounded off what had been a perfect morning. A hilarious piggyback charge to the car, with Henry trying to recite Tennyson's poem as he jogged along, and Jenna trying to keep hold of Henry, the cushion, and the picnic rug that was wrapped around them like a tartan cloak.

She was still smiling as they drove back to Farm Cottage, where he dropped her off with promises to return soon with a printer's proof for the calendar.

Henry emailed later that evening to make sure she wasn't lying in an exhausted heap on the sofa, and Jenna replied with a selfie of her with volunteer Val and Lady Maud with the caption: *The work of a piggy slave is never done.*

Evie and Kat had been desperate for details when she returned grinning, a little drunk, and more than a little sleepy, but Jenna swiftly skimmed over the details of the morning; she wanted to hug her precious memories in private.

Over the following days, a number of emails sped back and forth between her and Henry, and they chatted a few times on the phone. Not about anything in particular, just the cosy chit-chat of everyday life which, at Farm Cottage, was never more than a whisker away from the world of guinea pigs. Then, towards the end of the following week, Henry confirmed he had a proof copy of the calendar, which he promised to bring over on Saturday. Jenna couldn't wait.

Chapter Nineteen

'Look who's turned up!' bellowed Kat from the front yard, in a voice that would put the town crier to shame. In Jenna's opinion, given that Haxford's historic Old Town only employed the services of the town crier two or three times a year for ceremonial occasions, Kat could easily save the council some money by doing the job in exchange for a few free bales of hay.

It had only been three weeks since the photoshoot at Little Paws, and just over a week since the outing to Northlands Abbey, but in Jenna time, it had felt like several months since she'd seen Henry. More than once during the last working week, Denise or Alisha had caught her smiling at her phone; despite inducements to do so, she had refused to furnish them with any details, and thankfully Jamie had ceased waffling on about stranger danger.

'On my way!' Jenna called happily. This morning

she'd been giving Snickers a brush and tidy up as now he'd been neutered he would be ready for rehoming in a few weeks. 'Tomorrow could be your lucky day, you handsome chap!' she said as she carefully lifted him back into his cage, then made an attempt to brush off some of his long toffee-coloured hair as she headed outside.

'Sorry for the delay, I was just—'

The smile froze on her face as she stared at the dark-haired man getting out of the car.

'Hello, Jenna, how are you?'

'Matt! What are you doing here?'

Why didn't Kat warn her? Jenna glanced around, observing that Kat had already legged it.

'I came to see you. To see how you are.' Matt slowly shifted his weight from foot to foot as though he was trying discreetly to clean something off the soles of his shoes.

'I'm fine. Thanks for asking.'

There was an awkward pause as Matt continued his shoe shuffle. He never was much good at small talk.

'How's the business going?'

'Okay… Early days, you know? Parry's not as good with finance as you are.'

Hallelujah! It had certainly taken him long enough to work that out.

'Actually,' Matt continued, 'I wanted to ask what happened to the money in our bills account. I can't seem to log on and the rent's due now.'

Jenna suppressed a smile as she twigged the real purpose of the visit.

'No, you won't see anything, because I closed that account. I did email you about all this last week,' she added, patiently. 'When I moved out, I divided up what was remaining in the account and transferred your share over to your personal bank account, plus an amount from me to cover my share of the next month's rent.'

Even though she technically only owed two and half weeks, that had felt like a reasonable compromise.

'Ah…' Matt cleared his throat. 'The thing is, Jenna, I think I might be a bit tight this month, and I was hoping you could … erm…'

Jenna shook her head. 'I'm sorry, Matt, but I've given you this month's rent already. Where's it gone?'

'I had to buy some stuff for Parry. He's going to pay me back, it's just temporary.'

Jenna sighed. 'Surely you know that you won't see that money again? He's a lovely bloke, Matt, but he's hopeless with money. You know how I feel about Parry and money, but you've bailed him out over and over again. You lent him money that was needed for *our* rent, and now you're doing it again. You might be able to live like that but I can't. I'm sorry but the answer's no.'

'Can't you come back and give me another chance?'

'Let me ask you something: if I was jobless and skint, would you still want that second chance?'

'But you're not. The question's irrelevant.'

In spite of their disagreements and Matt's brief foray

into fist fighting, Jenna still felt sorry for him. He really was deluded if he believed Parry would pay him back, but she knew from experience that nothing she could say would make any difference, and she also knew how it would end.

Jenna had been thirteen when she learned what bankruptcy really meant. Being unable to pay your debts. That's what her dictionary had blandly stated, but it was far worse than that. It meant watching your mother pawn and sell every last thing of value and still it wasn't enough. It meant leaving your home and taking what you could carry to live in a single room in a hostel with your mother and sister while you were placed on somebody's waiting list. And it meant sharing a bed with your sister who cried herself to sleep because their father – who had promised her the world – had abandoned them to start over somewhere else. This time Jenna had choices and she already knew what the answer was.

'I need to sit down, Matt, and you need to leave. I'm not going to ask you to give up your buying and selling, or your new company, and that's not how I want to live.'

'So you want *him*, do you?'

A flicker of anger fizzed inside her. Henry was not going to be dragged into this discussion.

She was saved from having to respond as Kat ran out of the barn carrying one of their black, tubular folding chairs. 'We thought you might fancy a sit down,' she said airily as she opened the chair and patted the seat as if Jenna needed a clue where to place her bottom.

Clearly, both of them had been hovering somewhere well within earshot.

'Thanks, Kat. I'll be back in a minute to help.'

Kat remained standing, seemingly – or more likely deliberately – oblivious to the hint that she might want to go back to wherever she'd been hiding.

Like a silent Mexican standoff, Matt, Jenna and Kat stood looking at each other, waiting for someone to speak.

It was the sound of car tyres scrunching up the track that broke the deadlock and caused three heads to turn, and Evie to gallop out of the barn waving energetically.

'You're not flagging down a bus!' said Kat. 'I think he's seen us.'

They watched as Henry leapt out of the car and waved. The smile on his face slowly morphed into a scowl as he turned to stare at Matt.

'You again. Who have you come to punch this time?'

'Matt was just leaving,' Jenna said.

Matt bunched his fist and gestured towards Henry. 'I'm not scared of you.'

Surely he wasn't going to try that again? 'Matt, I'm not coming back. And I'm done with the loans, so just go before do you something stupid.'

Kat grabbed the now unoccupied folding chair and holding it in front of her, marched towards Matt like a determined lion tamer. 'You heard her.'

Matt edged backwards with his hands in the air. 'Right. I get the message. I'll leave you to enjoy your visitor then.'

Jenna watched as he drove away. She had loved him. In the beginning. But not now. Love was more than just being housemates or helpmates, it was a mutual concern for the other person. It was being thoughtful and considerate, and above all it was a relationship based on absolute trust. Once those foundations were undermined, the rest rapidly disappeared into a sinkhole of suspicion and disillusionment.

'I'm obviously not the first visitor of the day,' observed Henry.

'But you're the first welcome one,' replied Jenna warmly, giving him a hug.

'And you brought us a present!' added Evie.

Henry rummaged in his rucksack and handed over a sturdy, white board envelope to Jenna with a big grin. 'There you go.'

Evie and Kat crowded round Jenna as she opened the envelope and pulled out a glossy printed A3-size calendar with a picture of Snickers on the front, looking obligingly straight into the camera lens with his best *where are my treats, humans?* expression.

Every picture was admired and discussed. Every setting was different and so well suited to each animal. The one of Lady Maud on a (familiar looking) large, velvet cushion ought to be framed and hung up in the barn, declared Evie.

Jenna looked at Henry and the memories of being swept up in his arms came flooding back. 'It's absolutely brilliant. You are brilliant.' She knew she was grinning like an idiot but she couldn't help it.

'So now all you need to decide is how many you want to order; I can get them printed in a matter of days. I've had a word with the printers and we can do a second print run if you want to start off cautious.'

They spent a good part of the morning sitting round the table in the farmhouse kitchen discussing how they were going to sell them and at what price, aided by a plate of Evie's visitors' biscuits. The rescue website was the most obvious starting point but they all agreed to use their social media accounts as additional signposting.

'And I can use the For Sale and Wanted board on my company's intranet,' said Jenna. 'It will be something different for people to look at; it's usually full of car adverts, or I'm-moving-house-and-need-to-sell-off-these-items posts.'

'And while we're all here, I know it's not as exciting as the calendar proof, but I've printed off the details of the planning application for you from the council website.' Henry pulled another envelope from his rucksack.' You may have already received a letter but it's useful to have another copy.'

'A letter from the council arrived a couple of weeks ago, but…' Evie shrugged. 'We didn't know what to write. Even I know you can't just reply saying "no, thank you".'

Henry smiled. 'Sadly not. But you can object to the over-development of the area and the destruction of wildlife habitat etcetera.' He extracted several papers from the envelope and spread them out in front of Evie and Jenna. 'The planning meeting is fixed for the 15th of June so you've plenty of time. It says somewhere on this page'—he pointed at one of the sheets in front of him—'when the window for objection letters closes.'

Before he left, Henry asked for visiting rights to the barn and paid particular attention to Snickers.

'Do you think he realises he no longer has all his equipment?' Henry asked.

Kat jabbed his shoulder with her forefinger. 'Snickers has caused enough mayhem, thank you. He needs to live a very quiet life from now on.'

'It will be sad though, won't it, when he goes off to his new home.' Henry stroked the piggy nose pressed up against the mesh of the hutch. 'I'll miss this little character.'

A strangled sob came from somewhere and Jenna looked round.

'Oh, Evie!'

Her sister was sitting on one of the hay bales and cuddling Theodore, one of their permanent residents who was unable to be rehomed due to longstanding health issues. Tears were trickling down her cheeks and dropping onto his black and white fur.

'He won't have anywhere to go if we close,' she sobbed. 'He's old and won't get adopted. And no one else will love him as much as I do.'

Kat dropped to her knees on the dusty floor and gripped Evie's hand. 'We're not packing up without a bloody fight! If they try and chuck us out they've got to get past me first. And they can take down their stupid, fucking sign as well, or else I'm going to go over there and do it for them.'

Henry reached into his pocket and produced a clean white, folded handkerchief, which he passed to Evie.

Who carried a handkerchief these days?

Jenna mouthed a thank you, and mentally added another point to Henry's already high scoreboard as she sat down next to her sister.

'We love him too, Evie, and I promise you, I won't let this happen. Don't ask me how, because I don't know yet, but we're a team and I'm always here for you. Now we have the details of the planning application, we'll start to write our objection together.'

'But we should have started it weeks ago. And the letter asked if we wanted to speak at the meeting and I'm no good at that sort of thing,' said Evie in a shaky voice, holding Theodore so she could rub her cheek against his soft fur.

'There's plenty of time to decide about who's going to speak,' said Henry. 'Just get your objection lodged first.'

'You see,' said Jenna, giving her sister a gentle shake. 'There's a plan already. We'll brainstorm a list of the relevant points and then I'll draft the letter for you.'

Chapter Twenty

Henry had been as good as his word and had delivered the initial print run of calendars a speedy six days later. Over lasagne and an end-of-the-week bottle of red wine, they had also reviewed Jenna's first draft of the objection letter to which he had added a few helpful suggestions. Jenna had tried to maintain a positive attitude for her sister's sake, but it was a relief to actually be able to do something positive, rather than just talk about what ifs.

She had decided Monday morning was a good time to add her message to Confederated Financial Solutions' For Sale and Wanted board, which was probably the most visited part of the intranet. After the weekend, most people liked to ease themselves gently into the working week, so any excuse to peruse new and interesting adverts was always a popular Monday morning diversion

Now all she had to do was upload her advert, which she'd jotted down yesterday.

For Sale – guinea pig calendars – £12
Buy next year's calendars early! All animal lovers will adore
these gorgeous photos, and all proceeds go to Little Paws
Guinea Pig Rescue in Haxford.

Underneath she added:

Little Paws is currently under threat of relocation following
a planning application from developers. Every calendar sold
helps provide a secure future for all the guinea pigs.

She didn't add *and all the little ones that are probably on the way as a result of Snickers' have-it-away day* as no one was quite sure yet how far his exploits had impacted on the female population of Little Paws.

The relocation bit was artistic licence as there was no Plan B. Not yet at any rate. Other rescues might take in some of the guinea pigs but what if they were already full? And what would happen to the permanent residents? That alternative was not something she wanted to contemplate right now.

It wasn't long before she received her first enquiry from a colleague in the new business department, followed by confirmation of a sale. Jenna promised to pop down with the calendar at lunchtime. She'd brought half a dozen calendars in to work with her, which were currently stored in the bottom drawer of her desk. As always, her colleagues were eager to discuss anything that didn't involve accounting projects or expenses claims, and as she ate her cheese and pickle sandwich she showed off Henry's wonderful photos, careful to avoid any pickle leaking out over the merchandise.

'And to think that all this came about because you tried to track down the owner of the camera,' said Denise. 'You must be thrilled with these pictures. My granddaughter loves guinea pigs so I'll definitely buy one off you.'

'My favourite is the one on the front,' said Jamie. 'He looks wicked with all that long hair.'

'How do you know if it's a he?' asked Alisha.

Jamie shrugged. 'He just looks up for anything.'

'You don't know how accurate that is,' joked Jenna. 'Anyway, I'm off downstairs to deliver this calendar to Kara. Back in a sec.'

She could feel she'd been sitting down for too long, so a gentle stroll down to the first floor was a welcome break. The lift lobby was a cocoon of quiet, punctuated only by the occasional ping of the lift doors as they opened.

Jenna spotted the new poster immediately. For reasons unknown, the Human Resources department, who managed the company's health insurance policies, had recently started producing short bulletins and posters encouraging staff to keep healthy and active, and they'd clearly decided that the lift was an ideal place where they could guarantee a captive audience.

Take the stairs and look after your heart!
Burn calories – Get fit – Keep healthy!

It seemed rather pointless putting the poster in the lift when you'd only spot it once you'd decided to take the lift in the first place. Plus it totally ignored the fact that at least one of their employees was not able to do the suggested energetic activities. Jenna was therefore amused to see someone had already scrawled underneath:

If you're having a heart attack on the stairs, please
complain to the HR team on extension 2342.

You couldn't put up anything in this place without some amateur graffiti artist whipping out their Bic biro.

The lift opened on the first floor to reveal two employees chatting right in front of the door to the sales area. She guessed that the tall, curly-haired man with his hand on the doorplate must be one of the sales staff, although his name was unknown. However the same could not be said of the person standing next to him. If she'd been looking up instead of where her feet were going, she might have had time to pretend she was heading into the ladies' loo, but if she turned away now it would seem churlish. And anyway, Mr Ranty was hardly going to start complaining about his expenses in front of his colleague.

His colleague smiled. 'Hello! We don't normally see you down here.'

'Just delivering a calendar for someone.'

'Yes, I saw your advert this morning,' Mr Ransome said in an annoyingly pompous voice. 'I'm not sure it's appropriate to be making political statements on the company's official notice board.'

'Well, I'm intrigued now,' said his colleague. 'What political statements have I missed?'

'I'm selling calendars on behalf of a guinea pig rescue,' replied Jenna. 'I can't see how that's at all political since rodents are not eligible to vote.'

'She has a point there, Ian!' His colleague laughed as he headed off towards the stairs with a wave of his hand. 'Catch you later.'

'You know perfectly well what I mean,' Ian Ransome said in a low voice. 'You're already treading a fine line.'

'I've no idea what you're talking about,' replied Jenna, refusing to lower her voice as though they were discussing something illicit.

'I'm referring to the length of time it takes you to settle my expenses. I shouldn't have to justify what's on my form every month. Your predecessor never had any problems.'

Jenna almost trembled with the effort of holding back her indignation. Some people just couldn't accept the rules were the rules, and it really grated when they tried to make exceptions for themselves. She should really ignore him, but that supercilious, smug look pushed the wrong button.

She smiled sweetly. 'Adam informed me of your

discussion. But unfortunately it doesn't change the company's expenses policy. Nor the timescale for making payments.'

She clamped her tongue between her teeth to prevent herself from saying something else she might regret later, although any notion of regret seemed not only risible but highly unlikely.

She was still seething as she returned to her desk ten minutes later. 'You'll never guess who I bumped into downstairs.'

'George Clooney?' asked Denise hopefully.

'No. Mr Ranty. He had the cheek to lecture me about posting political statements on the For Sale and Wanted board.'

'Because you're selling a calendar? That's mental,' Jamie said, pulling a silly face and crossing his eyes.

'And hypocritical,' added Alisha. 'My mum's friend, Gloria, lives in the same road as him. She says every time there's an election he puts up one of those boards on a stick in his own front garden, and then he shoves loads of leaflets through everyone's letter boxes as well. Apparently, during last year's local council elections, Gloria got so fed up with his campaigning that she posted hers back through his letterbox with a note saying she didn't want any more junk mail thank you.

'And,' she continued, warming to her theme, 'he's really tight-fisted too. Gloria told Mum and everyone else at the mums, bums and tums class that at the Haxford Charter Fair last year he was seen haggling with the ladies on the WI cake stall to negotiate a discount.'

Alisha's revelations were greeted with a raucous outburst of laughter.

'And to think he's so generous with the company's money,' said Denise in tones of mocking admiration. She pointed at her screen. 'And here's another load of expenses, including dinner for an unspecified number of people, plus first-class return tickets to Birmingham and Edinburgh. There'll be more complaints when he doesn't get the full travel costs reimbursed.'

'Not my problem; Adam can argue about that,' said Jenna with a careless flick of her hand.

Over dinner that evening, Jenna advised Evie and Kat that she'd sold her first calendar already and had had several expressions of interest from other colleagues. She also regaled them with the brief exchange she'd had with Mr Ransome, after filling them in briefly on his past activities. Kat's volley of outrage and expletives went a long way to helping mollify her frustrations, and encouraged by her audience, Kat proceeded to set out imaginative ways to solve the problem on a more permanent basis, mostly involving some form of bodily harm.

Evie was quiet and Jenna knew Kat was, in part, trying to be outrageous simply to distract her from the worry that now hung over all of them. After various revisions, a letter setting out their objections to the proposed planning application had been sent off and now all they could do was wait until the council planning meeting on the 15th of June, and hope that enough people in the area had also lodged objections.

Seeing the drawings on the council website with a residential housing development directly over their house, the barn and surrounding land had been a depressing experience for all three of them, but it also strengthened Jenna's resolve. As Henry had said, this was not a done deal by any stretch.

Chapter Twenty-One

Thank you, big sis!

J enna smiled at the text message, which was accompanied by some smiley faces and what emoji designers decided was a suitable representation of a guinea pig face. Over the last couple of days she had taken to printing out photos of various piggies after adding captions to the picture, and enlisted Kat's help to hide them around the barn and house for Evie to find. The latest one was of the rescued white guinea pig, now named Snowflake, with the words *Loving the new home* in a speech bubble, and underneath: *but how do you ring for room service?*

The photos on her camera might not be as professional as the ones Henry had taken, but having mastered the art of editing them on her phone, it amused her as much as it entertained her sister. Jamie had been very keen to help think up captions, and had become self-appointed copywriter for 'Operation Cheer Up Jenna's Sister'.

'She loved the Snowflake one,' said Jenna as she locked her computer and opened her lunchbox. 'You're on a roll now!'

'So who's next? Can we have that ginger dude again?'

Jenna smiled. 'Snickers is rapidly building himself something of a fan club in Haxford. Yes okay, I'm sure I've got some suitable photos, so we'll do one of him next. Let me finish my lunch and I'll ping some pics over for you.'

By the time Jenna had eaten her lunch, emailed Jamie with a couple of photos and replied to a couple of messages it was time to start work again, but within seconds she noticed a new email had appeared in her inbox.

'Ha! Well, thanks for confirming what I already knew.'

'Have you won employee of the month again?' asked Jamie.

'That was Jenna's sarcastic voice if I'm not mistaken,' replied Denise. 'Anything you'd like to share with your hard-working colleagues who'd be interested in a bit of exciting news?'

Alisha's head came up. 'Someone say exciting news?'

Jenna gave her colleague a tight smile. 'Apparently our

esteemed manager has reviewed the details I sent to him last week. He can find nothing wrong with the expenses paid to his friend, Mr Ransome. Although to be fair, he wasn't expecting to, he just got nagged into it.'

'So who gets to tell Mr Ranty the good news then?' asked Alisha. 'I'd love to be a fly on the wall when he gets the email. He'll probably march straight back upstairs.'

'Tin hats at the ready then,' said Denise.

It was galling though that Adam had even had to review the expense claims in the first place, and a low-level resentment simmered in Jenna throughout the after-noon. Maybe she would talk to Henry. It was all well and good Kat offering to disembowel someone, but she wanted sensible counsel and Henry had a business brain on him. After finishing for the day she pulled out her phone.

Are you around this evening? I need to talk to you.

The reply came back promptly.

Any time after 7:30. Living at home means dinner happens at 6:30 no matter what! Parents!!

He had added a few exasperated emojis for good measure.

Jenna smiled sympathetically but she wouldn't have minded having a fixed timetable when she was still living at home, instead of having to remind her mum that it was hours past teatime. While her stays in hospital were never exactly a bundle of laughs, at least she knew when the next meal was arriving.

After her dad had left for good, she'd assumed her mum would recover her spirits but somehow that never happened. It was as if she had been so worn down over the years that she no longer had the energy to be cheerful, or to remember the little things they had done before. It was Jenna who had reminded her to buy a cake for Evie's thirteenth birthday and Jenna who saved up her Saturday wages to buy the presents.

———————

Evie and Kat were preparing evening veggies for the piggies and immediately waved away her offer of help when she said she was going to ring Henry. She therefore retreated to the small living room and settled herself on the squashy sofa.

Jenna rang on the dot of seven-thirty.

'Punctual as always,' joked Henry.

'No comment,' she replied airily. Henry's timekeeping was by now something of a joke between them but it was something that bothered her less these days.

'Is everything okay? You had me worried when I saw your text. It's not my mate Snickers up to his old tricks?'

'No.' Jenna managed to raise a smile. 'I've just had a tiring day at work and I wanted to hear your voice.' Her own faltered as she spoke, and she held the phone close as though it could bring him nearer to her.

'Jenna, what's happened? Do you want me to come over?'

Yes! I need you to hold me and tell me I'm not an unreasonable person!

His warm, sensual voice was comforting; she closed her eyes and imagined him lying next to her.

'I just wanted to talk to you.'

'I'm listening.'

With a few hesitations and a pause to find a tissue, Jenna spilled out the details of her email this afternoon and what had led up to it. 'And my boss has been fine about it but…' She sighed. 'Sometimes I'm just fed up with it. Maybe I've been there too long. Got stuck in a rut or something. I know some people probably think I'm a bit of a jobsworth but this isn't some sort of discretionary arrangement; there's a written policy on what you can legitimately claim as an employee expense. And how to go about doing it. The man doesn't even send in the correct information to support his claims.'

'Can you give me an example?'

Jenna sat up. 'He scans restaurant receipts and just calls it client entertainment without saying who it is he's taking out – it could be any old person. And it's never some average-priced place, it's always some expensive, fine dining restaurant,' she added bitterly. 'The best Matt and I ever managed was the occasional meal at the Thai restaurant just off Brewer Street, and we considered that to be a real treat.' She paused. 'Sorry, it must sound like a load of sour grapes to you but it's not. It's just…'

She sighed inwardly. Just what? Growing up learning to scrimp and save while your father gambled away everything? Having to work hard to make sure you would never end up homeless again? Watching your boyfriend leap gleefully into some guaranteed failure of a moneymaking scheme that clearly took precedence over your relationship?

And now this. Why did people who were in a position of power and money just want more, and sod everyone else? It was like those developers; they didn't care about the people they made homeless while they were busy making money for themselves.

'That was a very big sigh.'

'It wasn't meant to have escaped, sorry.'

'Why should you be? Princess Jenna of Oakhurst, you apologise to no one!'

Memories of a magical morning came flooding back: the cool morning air, the stillness, the picnic, and best of all – his kiss. She longed to be picked up in his arms again even though she knew it had only been for practical reasons.

She rubbed her face with her free hand. 'You're a first-class cheerer upper, Henry Somner.'

'I haven't really done anything.'

'But you listened. And you believe me.'

'I do. And I haven't finished yet. Stick Friday in your diary because I'm taking you out in the evening.'

'You don't need to, I wasn't fishing.'

'I know. But I'd like to take you out anyway.'

'Where are we going?'

Henry chuckled. 'I'm not allowed to surprise you, am I?'

'Not just yet.'

'Okay, I'd like to take you to The Old Bookbinder's Arms. It's a pub conveniently only five miles or so from you.'

'And is this part of my education of local places I've never heard of?'

'Absolutely. Too many people just rock up to their local boozer or pizza parlour without exploring the hidden gems we have just a little further off the beaten track. Plus I think you still need a bit of convincing.'

If it meant meeting up with Henry, Jenna would happily take any amount of convincing.

The following day, she did a quick online review of the pub to check for proximity of parking and step access. There was also a newspaper article about the re-opening of the pub from few years back. The pub had apparently seen better days, as her mum was fond of saying, and had been bought by Steve and Shannon Bothwell, a couple from East London. It described how Shannon had fallen in love with the name of the pub and become inspired to transform it. Not only did she sink her savings into firstly buying the pub and then completely overhauling it, she also had to convince her partner that her vision was financially viable. According to the article, it took some persuading and a huge bank loan.

She had to work hard to win me over, he was quoted as saying, *but over the years I have learned to trust Shannon's judgement and look at the results!*

It hadn't been all plain sailing though, and the article went on to describe how a year after opening they were struggling with repayments on the loan and the business nearly went under. It must have taken some guts to continue.

Jenna studied the pictures on the pub website. From the outside it didn't look anything special, but the photos of the interior looked amazing. Someone had clearly taken a lot of time and care over the decoration and she couldn't wait to see it all for herself.

She marvelled at how different her response was to that of a few months ago. She had admired Henry's photo of the northern lights for what it was: a well composed photograph of a stunning landscape. Now, she wanted to see places for herself, like that childhood adventurer who had relished each new storybook world with its own customs and characters. She had Henry to thank for that, and was almost counting the hours until she could see him again.

She also helped out as much as she could in the barn and was definitely getting very attached to the cavy residents. Last week one of the sows from their recent rescue had died despite everyone's best efforts, and Jenna had cried as she collected a few wildflowers to mark the guinea pig burial site.

Now more than ever she was desperate to keep busy. With the slightest relaxation, her attention would inexorably slide like matter being sucked into a black hole towards the planning meeting, now only three weeks away, and the currently unanswered question of who was best placed to represent them.

Chapter Twenty-Two

While Jenna was happy living at Farm Cottage, the downside of the lodger arrangement was that the majority of her possessions were no longer as accessible as they had been. The bed in the junk-cum-storage room was the only clue that anyone actually slept in there, and it competed for space along with a purple armchair that had belonged to Kat's gran, a pine chest of drawers, which was missing the bottom drawer, an old bookcase full of children's stories, several boxes that had 'Kat's stuff' written on the side and a number of miscellaneous articles including a zoo of cuddly toys.

Jenna's suitcase and bags had reduced the floor space even further, in between which she had wedged a small portable clothes rail for her office wear. At some point she ought to do some sorting out before she tripped over something, but this evening she had other things to think about as she was meeting Henry later and urgently needed something to wear. She also urgently needed some pills to stop the twinges in her hip turning into a full-blown pain tsunami.

She rummaged in one of the bags searching for something suitable. The last two trips hadn't involved any dress code but this was a nice-looking pub and her clothes were mostly boring office wear.

'It's not the Queen's garden party, you know,' said Evie, hovering in the doorway.

'I know, I know. I just don't want to look shabby. It's not a scruffy pub.'

Evie crossed the room and wrapped her arms around her sister, giving her a gentle hug. 'Henry's interested in you, silly, not what you're wearing. Anyway, you never look shabby.'

'Thanks, sis.' Jenna lowered herself carefully onto the bed. 'He is lovely, isn't he?'

'Yes! Good grief, it's taken you long enough to work that out.'

'Don't you think it's all a bit too good to be true? The scam warnings we give out to customers always say, if it seems too good to be true it generally is.'

'Henry's not a scam.'

Jenna nodded. 'True. But everyone has bad points or annoying habits, don't they? So what are Henry's? Apart from his timekeeping of course.'

'Well, there you are then!' declared Evie triumphantly. 'Happy now? Stop waffling and get a move on or else you're the one who's going to be late.' She reached into one of the bags and held up a pale blue top. 'Here you go.'

When Jenna didn't move, Evie peered at her. 'Are you up to going out tonight? You look a bit wrecked, sis. I'm sure Henry won't mind rearranging.'

Jenna took a couple of deep breaths and hauled herself off the bed. 'I'm fine. You know I don't like people fussing around.'

'I'm not people, I'm your family!' protested Evie. 'I'm allowed to fuss. I'll fetch your pills and some water.'

Whether it was the tablets, or anticipation, or a combination of both, by the time Jenna was in the car she was feeling more lively. The pub was not far from the train station and situated down a side street. She had already noted from her earlier online investigation that there were only a few customer spaces in the small car park at the side of the pub. It would therefore be pot luck whether she could get an on-street parking space and if not, she'd have to ring Henry and cancel as there was no way she'd manage the walk from the nearest public car park.

She slowed down, determined not to miss the turning for the customer parking and then almost did an emergency stop. Henry was standing in the road directly outside the pub, in the only gap in a long line of parked cars stretching in both directions, holding a large notice like the ones chauffeurs took to airports when they were collecting people. The sign read:

Parking Reserved for JENNA OAKHURST

Jenna grinned and waved before executing a perfect reverse parking manoeuvre into the vacant parking space.

'Impressed?' asked Henry as she locked the car.

'Genius idea! How long had you been waiting?'

'About twenty minutes. Maybe thirty. I know you like to be early so I didn't want to take any chances.'

'But this road is full of cars, and technically you can't actually reserve a space. Didn't you have loads of people getting arsey about trying to park here?'

'I certainly did. However most folk didn't fancy running over someone just to get a parking space.' Henry's eyes twinkled and the corners of his mouth twitched. 'In any case, everyone else got shown the B side.' He turned the sign around. On the back it said:

Danger! Possible sinkhole. Avoid this space!

Jenna laughed. 'Definitely gold medal for accessibility.'

'Can I leave my sign in your car? I parked the other end of the road and I don't want to carry it round with me.' Henry waited until Jenna had locked the car for the second time and then offered his arm. 'So, may I escort you to your seat?'

If the outside of The Old Bookbinder's Arms resembled every other Victorian pub in the area, the inside certainly did not, and Jenna gasped as she stared around her.

The ceiling was garlanded with what looked like pages

of paperback books, all strung together like paper tinsel. Behind the bar a large cuddly toy in the shape of a white rabbit was perched on a stool; he was wearing a red waistcoat, from which a gold pocket watch was dangling, and the sign above his head said: *Oh dear! Oh dear! I shall be late!*

On the shelf above the spirit bottles, a large blue corduroy caterpillar peered down on customers, and at the end of the bar there was a large, green, ceramic teapot from which a toy dormouse peeked. Every spare inch of wall was covered in posters and framed prints of both pictures and quotations from *Alice in Wonderland*.

'It's amazing,' exclaimed Jenna as they made their way over to one of the tables at the other side of the bar.

The decor even extended to the tables, it seemed, and the paper placemats were styled as giant playing cards. On the wall above their table, the photo frame contained the words to the poem, *How Doth the Little Crocodile*, and a variety of different sized keys hung from the screens separating the tables.

Even the menu had made a nod to the theme and was decorated in the corners with red and white roses to match the artificial red and white rose bushes that were dotted throughout the pub in terracotta pots.

'Okay,' she conceded after they had given their order to the waitress, 'I am officially impressed.'

'With the pub, or with me?' asked Henry with a cheeky grin.

Jenna smiled. 'Both.' She looked around. 'It must have taken them ages to do all this.'

'It does. They have a new theme each year, so on or around the 15th of January, they hold a charity auction to sell off all the props. Then they close for the following two weeks to allow for any necessary redecoration and the changing of all the pictures and props for the forthcoming year. It's an incredible achievement when you think that they nearly lost everything.'

Jenna couldn't imagine the faith and dedication required to set up a business in the current financial climate, but she applauded their ingenuity. 'It's such a brilliant idea! Who decides the theme for the next year?'

'The couple who run the pub. However, there's a suggestions box for customers.' Henry pointed in the direction of the bar. 'The only stipulation is that it has to be a well-known book.'

Jenna's imagination whirred into action. 'Imagine doing *The House at Pooh Corner*! Or *Gulliver's Travels*!'

'Good ideas – you should submit them. Children's stories and fairy tales are well suited.'

'Evie would probably vote for *Animal Farm* or *The Tales of Olga Da Polga*.'

Henry's brow furrowed. 'Who on earth writes a character called Olga Da Polga?'

'I thought you knew everything,' Jenna teased. 'It's a book by Michael Bond; he wrote a series of children's stories all about a guinea pig called—'

'Olga da Polga,' they both said in unison, and then grinned at each other.

The waitress bustled over with food and rather hurriedly plonked the plates down in front of them.

'Enjoy!' was the only conversation she offered. Or maybe it was an order.

Henry raised his eyebrows. 'Not what you'd call the chatty sort then.'

Jenna prodded her fish pie to let some of the steam escape. 'Well, it's a whole heap better than being called love or dear, I can tell you.'

'That happens a lot, does it?'

'More if I'm tired, or if I'm using my sticks.'

For a few minutes the business of eating occupied both of them. The fish pie was clearly homemade and topped with fluffy mashed potato. Henry had ordered rib-eye steak and chips with a side salad, and was tucking in with gusto.

'You look like you're enjoying that,' observed Jenna.

'It's a real treat. We don't get any meat or fish at home since Mum started on this eight-week vegetarian cookery course. And it's accompanied by a lecture every evening on how humans are ruining the environment with intensive farming and over-fishing.' Henry pulled out his phone and took a few photos of both meals. 'In case I need to remind Mum what proper food looks like,' he said with a grin.

'Well, I suppose it's only for eight weeks. Then she might move on to something else.'

'Yeah, probably back to the usual topic of what are you going to do with your life, Henry Somners.' He stabbed a chip with his fork. 'It's getting tedious to be honest; it even sounds like the title of some boring music hall song!'

Henry affected a George Formby accent as he sang, 'Wha' are you going to do wi' your life, Henry Somners?'

Jenna laughed. 'And what's your answer?'

'I don't want to go on living with my parents for a start. I should give my tenants notice and then I can head back down to Poole, but...' He left the sentence unfinished. 'The thing is, I don't like letting people down and I promised they could stay until September, and anyway, summer is an expensive time to travel. So I'm making what my sister calls a "Henry compromise" and doing neither, while subjecting myself to the possibly well-intentioned but rather repetitive suggestions from my family.'

'And what do they think you should do?'

'Settle down and be more like my perfect sister. Although, to be fair, that's more Dad's line than Mum's. Sadly for him I don't want to be a lawyer.' His lips curled into a lop-sided smile. 'I'm sure that's why my parents called me Henry though – it sounded more like a lawyer's name.'

'It's better than ending up with a name because your useless father couldn't read his wife's handwriting. Mum told me years later she wanted to call me Joanna, but Dad misread the note she scribbled for him in hospital.'

Henry snorted and pinched his lips together, and his eyes crinkled at the corners.

'Are you laughing, Mr Somners?'

Henry shook his head and made a *definitely not* sort of noise.

'So come on then, what's she like, this perfect sister of yours?'

'Natalie studied hard at school, got a first-class degree in law, joined Pater's law firm, la, la, la.' He made a dismissive gesture with his hand. 'And now she's bragging about having acquired an important new client in her own right, which she clearly thinks entitles her to stick her pennyworth into the discussion. I just tune out, to be honest.' He speared another chip. 'I did the degree course out of parental pressure more than anything else, but I'm not cut out for a regular nine-to-five job.'

'You must think I'm very boring having worked in the same place for twelve years. And I haven't been anywhere further than North Wales.' It sounded terrible saying it out loud. Even Jamie on a junior administrator salary had got as far as Ibiza.

'Is that because you're not interested or because of...'

'I can see you're trying to think of a polite way of asking about accessible travel,' said Jenna. 'To be honest, it's probably mostly me. Growing up, we didn't have money for holidays. I got used to having different priorities, and after I moved in with Matt we were always saving up for something. Matt never showed much interest in holidays other than the odd weekend somewhere near a golf course, which wasn't really my thing. Accessible travel comes with a load of logistics and most people don't want all that hassle.' She smiled ruefully. 'Can't say I blame them really.'

'So where would you go? If these logistics were sorted, I mean.'

Jenna had never really bothered much with what ifs. As the waitress cleared their plates away and took orders for desserts, she tried to think about where she'd like to go.

'I'm not as adventurous as you, so nowhere too far to start with – I've never flown anywhere. But Paris sounds lovely.'

'Plus you can get there on the Eurostar so there's no airport hassle.'

'Well, when I find someone who's prepared to trundle along at two miles a fortnight, I'll bear that in mind.'

'What about me?'

'You?'

Henry pretended to look offended. 'Ye-es. What's wrong with that, O sceptical looking person?'

'You go hiking. Exploring. Bear Grylls type holidays. The only Grylls experiences I do are the cheese on toast sort.'

'I can do cheese on toast holidays. We'll have hot chocolate at one of the fabulous pavement cafes. Have your portrait done in Montmartre, go up the Eiffel Tower, sit in the Luxembourg Gardens and watch the world go by – whatever you fancy.'

Jenna fancied all of it. A picture rapidly expanded in her mind's eye of a beautiful park on a sun-drenched afternoon, admiring the city skyline from the top of the Eifel Tower, then visiting one of Paris's famous Patisseries. Maybe it wasn't the logistics that had held her back, but the choice of companion. Matt would never have countenanced travelling anywhere where the locals didn't speak enough English for him to order his pub grub, but Jenna suddenly became fired up with the idea of exploring a different country with someone who was happy to go at her pace. She had been quite good at French when she was at school – it would be fun to try it out on real French people instead of just Miss Patterson who'd taught the GCSE class and spoke French with a distinct Somerset accent.

'You're smiling – does that mean yes?'

Henry had proved he could be trusted. He understood what she could and couldn't manage to do. And yes, she really did want to see the world!

Jenna nodded. 'I'd love to.'

The waitress returned with Jenna's ice cream sundae and a plate of cheese and biscuits for Henry.

'Although,' she added mischievously, 'we are not at all compatible on dessert choices. That'—she pointed to Henry's plate—'is a supper snack, not a dessert.'

'Good,' replied Henry sampling the Stilton. 'It means there's no danger of you nicking it then.'

Over desserts and coffee, they talked about trips on the Seine, visits to museums, and reminisced about French lessons at school. By the time the bill arrived, they even had a provisional date arranged for the first weekend in

July, and Jenna was fired up with enthusiasm for her overseas adventure.

The bill was presented in a scaled down replica of a top hat, complete with 10/6 on the side, and Henry snatched it up before Jenna could look. 'It's my treat,' he argued. 'I'm cheering you up.'

'I'm cheered up thanks, but I still have to pay my share.'

'Why?'

'You paid for everything at the picnic. It's only fair.' Jenna reached out her hand but Henry teasingly held the paper out of her reach.

'Please?'

Henry lowered his arm and let Jenna take the bill, which they settled equally.

'I think I still have a lot to learn about you, Jenna Oakhurst,' said Henry, holding open the door for her as they stepped back outside.

Jenna smiled apologetically. 'Old habits die hard.'

'So can you tell me – just for future information – under what circumstances am I allowed to pay for your meal?'

'You think I'm being stubborn, don't you?'

'Yes,' laughed Henry. 'But go on…'

'Okay, well, if it was for instance sandwiches or … something like that.'

'Or a cake? Does that qualify?'

'Yes.' Jenna elbowed him. 'Stop quizzing me!'

'Just figuring you out, that's all.'

Jenna looked up at his face. She loved his quirky lop-sided smile, and that swept back hair, which on anyone else would make their forehead look too big but on him it somehow just looked cute.

'Well, it's been—'

Jenna got no further before Henry gently wrapped his arms around her and pressed his warm lips against her cheek. 'Yes it has,' he whispered.

Jenna turned her head so that her lips gently slid over his, and they danced seductively over each other for several blissful seconds.

The sensation of his warm breath against her face and the pressure of his lips remained like permanent imprints on her skin, and Jenna drove home feeling as though she was almost floating. First thing tomorrow she'd check her work calendar. Adam would be away but she'd only need to book one day off at most. Then she really would have something to look forward to.

Chapter Twenty-Three

Having fixed a date for the trip, there was now the challenge of brushing up her schoolgirl French, which had lain dormant since her last GCSE exam. She had read online that French people liked tourists to make an effort, so as soon as possible she would get some phrase books out of the library. In the meantime, having found a useful website with some French conversations, she used her lunch hours to do a bit of online practice.

Even though there was a constant background chatter of voices, telephones and printers in the open-plan office, she was mindful of distracting her colleagues, but they all seemed eager to get involved. Over the following days her colleagues became familiar with Madame Lafayette and her trips around the town, and they especially enjoyed the ongoing discussions with cafe owner Pierre on the unpredictability of the weather in Brittany. The fact that only Alisha had actually been to France in no way dampened anyone's opinions on French cuisine, and what Pierre should have done when the market ran out of fish one morning.

On the plus side, Jenna reckoned that if fish was on the menu, she'd now stand a good chance of holding a reasonable conversation.

As they counted down the days to the meeting on the 15th of June, now only two and half weeks away, all three residents at Farm Cottage employed different strategies to keep themselves busy.

While Jenna was busy with her French phrasebooks from the library, Evie was throwing her efforts into looking after the guinea pigs and coordinating the volunteers. Now every Sunday when the visitors arrived, all the piggies were brushed, their cages smartened up, and she had even prepared a little home-printed leaflet entitled: *Tips for Caring for Your Cavy*.

Kat's modus operandi was to keep busy with plans for the population expansion and studiously ignore any reference to the approaching deadline. The average gestation period for guinea pigs was anything between sixty and seventy days, but without a scan, she had explained to the volunteers, it would be hard to tell how many pregnant mummies they had until around three weeks before they actually arrived. Space was getting tight anyway, Kat argued, since they couldn't currently re-home those females on pregnancy watch, so either way they could do with some more room. That meant clearing out some of the junk in the barn, or building some sort of extension.

Without any additional finance, option A was the only viable choice, so most evenings Kat had been busy stacking up bales of hay, making better use of the storage space under the row of wooden hutches, and dismantling an old wardrobe that even fifty years ago had probably seen better days.

Jenna had also noticed on her way home the previous evening a few changes to the large board advertising the new homes, which were now starting to be built on the opposite side of the road. Over the words *Coming Soon!*, some person or persons unknown had added an interesting blue spray paint design which, if you peered at it for long enough, could have said FUB OFK. Even more interestingly, no one on this side of the road had yet commented on the impromptu street art.

Jenna was determined to understand the planning process and Henry was becoming an invaluable source of information as well as a welcome and frequent visitor. Today being Saturday, they were all in the barn and Jenna was quizzing him about how the planning meeting would be conducted. The cage cleaning volunteers had finished for the afternoon and Jenna was sitting at the table brushing a couple of the more well-behaved long-haired piggies, while Henry was supplying the treats, which ensured their continued compliance.

'So do we have to actually do anything at the meeting?' Jenna asked.

Henry shook his head. 'Not unless you want to.

There's usually a form or an email address for applying to speak, but the process can vary from council to council.'

'From what I've read, we have to respond by email if we want to speak at the meeting, and we'd only have three minutes.'

'Three minutes!' exclaimed Kat, as she stacked a large pile of donated newspapers. 'That's ridiculous! I'm very happy to do it but I can't fit a whole speech into three measly minutes!'

'You could cut it down by at least a minute if you took out any swear words,' said Evie with a cheeky grin.

There was an outbreak of sniggering at the table as Jenna and Henry deliberately avoided catching each other's eye.

'For avoidance of doubt,' added Henry, trying hard not to laugh, 'you're not allowed to insult the councillors either.'

The guinea pig currently on the stylist's towel gave a loud squeak.

'You see!' said Evie, pointing. 'Primrose agrees with Henry.'

'Well you can be spokesperson instead then,' retorted Kat, her voice heavy with mock indignation.

'Oh gosh, no, I couldn't. I mean, I do care, it's our home and of course I want to help, but…' Evie chewed at one of her fingernails.

Jenna was torn. She wanted to be involved, but her strength lay in preparation and documentation, not standing up in front of loads of people and making speeches, even three-minute ones. 'Would I be right in thinking that it would probably help our cause if someone was able to speak at the meeting?'

'I'm not an expert,' replied Henry, 'but I'm sure you're right.'

'Right.' Jenna pressed her lips together for a few seconds. 'Well—'

'So here's a suggestion,' Henry continued. 'I am happy to be spokesperson for Little Paws—'

'Really?' Jenna stared at him.

'Henry, you're our hero!' said Evie, giving him a spontaneous round of applause.

Henry smiled and held up his hand. 'But there is a condition.'

The applause ceased as suddenly as it had started.

'I would like to be allowed to formally adopt my old friend Snickers. I've grown rather attached to the rascal.'

If Jenna hadn't been so worried about Primrose doing a runner, she would have hugged Henry on the spot. Instead it was Kat who threw her arms around him and to everyone's surprise, kissed him on the cheek. 'We would be delighted. And we'll even waive the adoption fee.'

'No, no, I want to do it all properly. The only thing is I can't house him at my parents – Mum has allergies and things – but I'll pay you rent to keep him here.'

For reasons she couldn't articulate even to herself, Jenna was thrilled that Snickers was staying at the rescue. Despite the accidental groping incident, not to mention all the trouble he had caused Evie and Kat, she would have been really upset to see him go.

The appointment of Henry as official spokesman for Little Paws also led to an immediate easing of tension at Farm Cottage, and Evie in particular seemed more like her old self. It was as if there was some tacit agreement that, having acknowledged that he was their best option as spokesperson, there was now some chance of success, or at least a significant reduction in the likelihood of failure.

Chapter Twenty-Four

If Jenna had assumed her throwaway remark about Henry being allowed to pay for sandwiches and a cake had been discarded and long forgotten, she was mistaken. It had clearly been mentally filed away for future use, and three days ago Henry had invited all of them for an afternoon tea on Sunday as his treat. It was to rally the troops he said, and do a last minute run through of everything in preparation for Tuesday's planning meeting. It would mean only having half an open day for the rescue, but Evie and Kat had readily agreed.

With the all-important meeting now only days away, it was as if they were all desperate to talk about something – anything – that didn't involve planning applications, and thus over the last couple of days they had kept up an almost continual conversation about the forthcoming outing as if no one wanted the discussion to lapse, for fear of it being replaced by what had now become the unofficial elephant in the room.

After the last of the Sunday morning visitors had departed and the barn had been tidied, Evie and Kat left instructions with Val to make sure the hay racks were filled up and water bottles checked while they were out. Val and her daughter were regular volunteers, knew the ropes and were happy to mind the fort while the three of them turned their attention to the serious business of what they might wear for their afternoon treat. Jenna normally wore trousers to work, more out of habit and practicality than anything else. Repeated surgeries had left their mark and despite her determination not to be bothered, she rarely showed off what she called her battle scars.

Today, though, she selected her favourite summer dress, which had last seen service at a friend's engagement party the previous summer. It was a bit crumpled, but nothing a quick run over with an iron couldn't fix. As she entered the kitchen, Jenna was amused to see Kat already wrestling with the ironing board, which was clearly an unfamiliar piece of equipment.

'It's not the Queen's garden party,' laughed Evie as Kat swore at the hot iron, which was creating more creases than it was ironing out.

'Don't worry, she says that to me too,' said Jenna as she waited for Kat to finish.

'But it's still DeLaneys.' Kat brandished the hot iron

246

with an air of dangerous abandon. 'DeLaneys! Who gets to bloody well go there!'

'We do!' chorused Jenna and Evie.

Eventually clothes were pressed either to everyone's satisfaction (Jenna and Evie) or the best of their ability (Kat), and they bundled into Kat's car.

DeLaneys was situated on the edge of Haxford's Old Town on the site of the old Victorian brewery buildings, which had been vacated after the war for newer and less expensive premises. The Victorian brick facade had changed little over the last century, but inside was a different matter. The architects had completely modernised the interior while retaining the sense of space and proportions of the original building.

Unlike The Old Bookbinder's Arms with its cosy nooks and decorated screens, the spacious ground floor of DeLaneys sparkled as the cleverly positioned spotlights bounced light off the polished fixtures and fittings. The ground floor was dominated by a semi-circular bar lined by elegant chrome stools, and at three o'clock in the afternoon, most were already occupied. Afternoon tea at DeLaneys was a feature of the tourist trail and the room was already full of excited chatter.

The original central columns supporting the building were covering in a marble effect cladding, and at each end of the room a large, glazed pot held a tree laden with pink blossom. As they followed the waiter to their table, Evie reached up and touched the leaves.

'It looks so real!' she whispered to Jenna.

The tables radiated out from the bar to the end wall against which banquette seating, tastefully upholstered in a dark teal colour, provided a comfortable alternative to the modern looking chairs.

To satisfy their curiosity, all three of them tried out the banquette and the chairs. Jenna opted for the banquette and Evie sat next to her until Kat, attempting to be discreet and using finger-pointing gestures, indicated that she should sit on the other chair.

Before they'd had a chance to peruse the menu, Henry was waving and making his way over, and he sat down next to Jenna, folding his long legs under the table. The warm, woody scent of his cologne was at once familiar and exciting, and memories of the accidental hand-on-thigh incident came rushing back.

This afternoon his legs were clad in light-coloured trousers, and instead of his trademark rugby shirt he was wearing a dark blue collared shirt with a small orange leaf design. The top buttons were undone and Jenna noticed the inside of the shirt was overprinted with some sort of pattern, although he'd probably have to disrobe further in order for her to work out what the pattern was. The buttons were all different but coordinated colours, and it was clearly from some upmarket shop.

'Have I spilt something?' asked Henry. 'You seem fascinated by my shirt.'

'It's … unusual.'

'Birthday present from Mum last year. It doesn't get much of an outing, to be honest, but I wanted to make an effort.' He gestured to Evie and Kat. 'And you ladies scrub up beautifully.' He turned to Jenna with a smile. 'Am I allowed to say that?'

'Yes, you are,' said Evie decisively. 'Ignore anything my sister says.'

Four afternoon teas were ordered and Henry waited until their waiter had retreated before he said, 'So, has Jenna told you her interesting news?'

'What interesting news?' demanded Kat a little too loudly, causing heads at the nearby table to turn round.

'I've finally persuaded Jenna to travel further afield than Haxford, and we're going away for a weekend.'

'Ooh, where to?' asked Evie.

'To Paris,' Jenna replied, blushing furiously with a mixture of embarrassment at the sudden public announcement and excitement at the prospect of the trip. 'On the Eurostar,' she added.

'And when is this dirty weekend away?' asked Kat.

'It's not a dirty weekend away!' protested Jenna. 'It's sightseeing, and culture, and…'

Henry gave them a cheeky wink. 'And the rest is private,' he said, slipping his arm around Jenna's waist. The warmth from his hand seeped through her dress until it was as if it was resting on her bare skin. As Evie prattled on about Paris, Jenna wondered whether they would have a twin or a double room, and what it would be like to watch him undress. Her fantasy had just reached a critical point when the waiter returned bearing two three-tiered silver cake stands, which he placed in the centre of the table. Jenna pressed the pause button on her imagination – the rest could be enjoyed at her leisure later on.

In the meantime, everyone's attention had turned to the feast in front of them. On the bottom tier of the cake stand there was an array of dainty looking sandwiches, cut into triangles. The middle tier held a selection of plain and fruit scones, a pot of strawberry jam and another of thick clotted cream. On the top there was a mouth-watering selection of mini cakes and pastries. Jenna had only ever seen anything like it in a magazine.

They dived into the sandwiches, which were as delicious and varied as they looked. Soon the conversation became a stream of recommendations and urgent exhortations.

'Mmm, you must try the smoked salmon one!'

'Ooh, I've never eaten a carrot and raisin sandwich before!'

'Is this one goat's cheese and walnut? It's amazing!'

After the sandwiches were polished off, they paused for a discussion over whether to try the scones first or the cakes. Then, having voted for scones next, the conversation diverted into a debate over whether you put the cream or the jam on first.

'Whichever way you can get the most on it,' answered Kat, busily piling jam onto the scone.

Jenna watched in fascination as Kat added a huge

dollop of clotted cream and turned the scone into a scale model of a Giza pyramid.

'You've got cream on your nose,' laughed Henry as Kat bit into it.

'Lady Maud eats like that,' said Evie. 'If you give her a piece of tomato there's red juice all over her face and whiskers in under five seconds.'

There was another outburst of good-natured laughter around the table and Kat joined in.

After the laughter subsided, Jenna tapped the side of her teacup with her cake fork.

'You're not going to make a speech, are you?' asked Evie. 'It's not the Oscars, you know.'

'I just feel it's appropriate to say a proper thank you to Henry for organising this afternoon. We're all having a wonderful time.' She raised her teacup in salute. 'Thank you very much, Henry. And although I don't really do public speaking, I do have an announcement to make,' she continued. They all stared back at her with a look of anxious anticipation.

'I'm going to nick that big chocolate-y thing,' she finished in a huge rush before grabbing it off the top tier of the cake stand.

'Bravo!' Henry gave her a quick round of applause. 'Best bit of public speaking I've heard in years. Too many people waffle on for too long. You have to know when to bale out.'

Over the cakes and pastries, Henry asked how calendar sales were going and Evie and Kat gave him an update. Jenna confirmed that she had already sold twelve in the last week but was hoping demand might pick up over the summer. Jamie had already announced his intention to purchase one for each of his relatives as Christmas presents, thus removing the worry of any last-minute Christmas shopping.

After the final pastry had been savoured and the last sips of tea drunk, they had a quick run through of arrangements for Tuesday while they waited for the bill. As no one knew exactly where in the town hall the meeting was being held, they agreed to meet in the entrance, at twenty to two.

Henry may have been an experienced backpacker and traveller, but he was clearly an experienced diner as well, and with a discreet gesture to the serving staff, the bill was brought over to their table. It arrived on a plate, together with four small chocolate truffles dusted in cocoa powder and sitting in miniature cake cases.

Jenna and Henry simultaneously made a grab for the bill. 'Oh no you don't!' said Henry, winning the tussle. 'I have it on good authority that I'm allowed to buy you sandwiches and cake so this is *my* treat.'

'But I was referring to *a* cake or *a* sandwich, not a whole banquet!' Having caught a glimpse of the bill before it was whisked away, she felt more than a little guilty at the amount Henry was putting on his credit card. Something else about that bill was nagging at her, but annoyingly she couldn't put her finger on it. It didn't look right somehow, but she would figure it out later.

'Henry, are you sure I can't make a contribution? Or pay for my sister at least?'

'No, it's absolutely my treat.'

'Thank you. But can I keep the bill afterwards?'

Henry laughed. 'Anything to keep you happy.' He offered his arm to Jenna and they strolled out of the restaurant smiling their thanks to the staff.

'That was wonderful,' said Evie. 'I feel like a real celebrity now.'

'I feel like I've been a bit of a pig,' said Jenna, resting her hand on her stomach. 'It was all lovely though.'

'I am officially stuffed,' announced Kat. 'And I now know why all the guinea pigs decide they need to have a long snooze after lunch.'

Chapter Twenty-Five

The 15th of June dawned bright and sunny and stayed that way. Jenna had already booked the afternoon off so that she could accompany the others. It was the least she could do in the circumstances as she was aware of how stressful the last few weeks had been for her sister. She also wanted to show her appreciation for everything Henry had done. Together they had submitted their request to speak at the meeting, and Henry had cut through all the jargon to hone a brilliant and concise three-minute speech, the main points of which he had confirmed first thing this morning via a brief email.

She left the office buoyed by lots of good luck messages from her colleagues, and with assurances from Jamie that she would blow the opposition out of the water.

The planning meeting was scheduled to start at two o'clock and their case was second on the agenda according to the details Jenna had checked online last night. In the interests of watching how the proceedings went, Jenna had suggested they aim to arrive shortly before the start of the meeting. She had also read up a bit on the building itself, just to prove to Henry that she wasn't a complete ignoramus when it came to her home town.

According to Wikipedia, Haxford's original town hall was built in the sixteenth century, but was pulled down in 1875 to make way for a more modern design. This new Victorian redbrick building had a symmetrical frontage dominated in the centre by a tower, at the base of which a stone-arched porch guided visitors inside. The stonework continued inside and decorated arches framed a wide flight of stone steps that dominated the centre of the entrance hall. An arrowed sign indicated that the function rooms were all upstairs.

Even the ceiling was ornately decorated in carved plasterwork and around the walls elaborate shields or coats of arms hung in rows sitting incongruously next to a very modern display board.

On the left of the stone staircase there was a small gift shop. Despite her nerves, Jenna smiled. There were few places in this part of Haxford where you could avoid the tourist trail. Maybe after the meeting was over, she would buy a commemorative postcard.

'It's like being inside Hogwarts!' said Evie in a loud whisper.

In the corner nearest the door, a smartly dressed

middle-aged man sat behind a chunky looking wooden desk that could have come straight out of Gringotts Bank. With no idea of where the meeting was being held, Jenna asked for directions and then in the absence of anywhere else to sit, perched on the rather uncomfortable stone staircase.

'You would think,' announced Kat in a loud voice and looking pointedly at the man standing behind the desk, 'that somewhere this posh would have places for people to sit down.'

The man at the desk looked at her, as did everyone else who happened to be standing within the catchment area of Kat's stentorian voice. 'There's a waiting area round the corner,' he mumbled, pointing vaguely to the right of the staircase.

Kat stared at him. 'Well, we want to wait here,' she pointed at her feet. 'You don't look like you're using your chair at the moment.'

The man's face reddened as he wheeled his office chair round and Jenna sat down gratefully and hoped Henry wasn't going to be too late. She had suggested they arrived at twenty to two so he was technically only five minutes late, but the jitters inside her were gradually ramping up. She looked at her watch again, and then checked her phone for messages. By ten to two there was still no sign of him; her mouth was dry and her stomach felt like it was tied up in knots.

'Where is he?' asked Evie in an agitated voice.

'He's usually late,' replied Jenna, attempting to sound calmer than she felt. 'He's probably got parking problems – you know what it's like around here. Maybe we should go in and tell him we'll save him a seat.' She quickly sent a text and then reconfirmed the directions to the council chamber while Kat returned the chair.

Several people were also walking in the same direction and they were greeted at the doorway by an official who informed them that those speaking should sit in the front two rows, visitors behind.

The council chamber looked like the set of a 1970s television courtroom drama. The main part of the wood panelled room was taken up with several rows of chairs. At the back, there was a group of people with notebooks, and Jenna wondered whether they were reporters. At the other end, a long table stood on a dais around which there were a dozen or more people seated. She guessed they were the committee who would make all the decisions. On the wall immediately behind them was a screen showing what looked like the title page of a presentation.

They needed to save a chair for Henry, so after a hurried discussion, Jenna found a seat in the second row so that Evie and Kat could sit directly behind her. She still felt conspicuous and she looked around nervously as she checked her watch again. It was five to two – where the hell was he? She swivelled round to reassure herself that Evie and Kat were still there. To try and stop herself from panicking, she focused on watching the people filling up the public seating area – clearly attending planning meetings was more popular than she had supposed. As she scanned the crowds, she almost choked in shock. What the hell was *he* doing there? She would have recognised that pompous idiot anywhere. She recalled what Alisha had said about local council elections, but she hadn't put two and two together. He sat down four or five rows back and she lost sight of him.

She felt a prod from behind. 'Jen, what are we going to do? He's not here yet.'

'I know.' She shivered despite the stuffiness of the room. Clearly council funds did not extend to implementing air conditioning. The feeling of increasing agitation now mingled with annoyance – why couldn't Henry turn up on time? Surely he would have made a special effort knowing how important this was?

A wooden thud announced that the doors were closed and simultaneously the person sitting in the centre of the group at the councillor's table called the meeting to order.

'Councillors, ladies and gentlemen, can we run through a few housekeeping items? Firstly I'd like to ask all of you to put your mobile phones and other devices on silent.'

Jenna did as she was asked, then quickly tapped out another text:

WHERE THE HELL ARE YOU??!!

After the chairman wrapped up the general points of

order and asked for approval of the previous minutes of meeting, he then introduced the first item on the agenda, and the Principal Planning Officer gave everyone a quick overview of the application. It was the conversion of a large Edwardian house on what was now a busy main road – not the best location for a family home – and the recommendation was for approval of this development. Jenna watched as supporters of this development explained why this was beneficial, although she paid significantly more attention to how the objectors put their case forward. The screen behind changed to show a map of where the house was situated. After explanations, discussions and questions there was a show of hands and the application was approved.

Jenna heard the doors open again and she swivelled round to watch as several people exited, then a number of people edged quietly into the room. She could see a mop of dark blonde hair and for a brief second, relief washed over her. But that wasn't his face, it was someone much older. Her heart was thumping so loudly now that she wondered whether the person sitting to her left could actually hear it.

'What do we do?' she whispered urgently to Evie and Kat. 'There's no message – nothing!' Her insides churned unpleasantly.

'You can do it,' whispered Evie. 'You're just as good as Henry. Probably loads better.'

Jenna admired Evie's coping strategy. Or maybe it was blind faith. Either way she wished she could borrow it as her own coping mechanism was on the verge of total collapse.

The chairman was speaking again. 'Item two on the agenda is the proposed extension to the housing development along Nethercott Lane. A supplemental report has already been circulated to councillors and I trust you have all read this.' Jenna reluctantly stopped staring at the doors and looked at the screen, now showing a map of a very familiar part of Haxford.

'The application will be introduced by Principal Planning Officer Declan Halliday. There are two objectors to this proposal.'

'Thank you, Chair, councillors. This proposal is an extension to the current development situated on the eastern part of Haxford, indicated here on the map. It is a redevelopment of agricultural land…'

Jenna let the words wash over her as she tried to marshal her thoughts. Unless Henry made a sudden, last-minute appearance, someone else would need to speak on their behalf. She quietly pulled her phone from her bag and found the email from Henry summarising their objections.

It was a struggle to maintain her attention on the proceedings as she tried to simultaneously memorise the main points of their objections. It was like listening to two televisions broadcasting different programmes that both required her attention.

'The extended development will comprise a further

sixty residential properties, each with two allocated parking spaces as well as…'

- *Overdevelopment of the area*
- *Insufficient schools and services in the area*

'…Provision of housing is in accordance with the Haxford Local Area Plan…'

- *Reduction in trees*
- *Protection of hedgerows*

'…External consultants have confirmed that the increase in road vehicles is within acceptable limits and no additional work is required to ensure…'

- *Inadequate provision for increased traffic*
- *Conservation area – protection of barn owls 1981 Wildlife and Countryside Act*
- *Bats*

Bats? What did that mean? Jenna read the email again and again, desperate to dredge up every last bit of information from their previous discussions, while searching for an explanation as to why Henry had failed to turn up. That hurt more than anything.

The concluding words, 'I therefore recommend approval of this application', landed dully on her ears.

There followed seemingly endless questions from the councillors. One person asked about affordable housing and didn't appear totally happy with the answer. Another queried the green credentials of the developer and received a long waffling response. Surely those councillors wouldn't vote in favour of the developer? How many did she need to convince? She checked for messages at least every thirty seconds until suddenly there was no more time to fret.

'We will now here from the objectors: May Dickinson on behalf of the Haxford Environmental Protection Group and Henry Somners on behalf of the Little Paws Guinea Pig Rescue. You will each have three minutes to make your presentation.'

A dark-haired woman with a chunky beaded necklace in liquorice allsorts colours stood up. Jenna made a mental note of where she stood and how she addressed the councillors. She spoke eloquently on the impact of the development on the local ecology. She explained how the felling of trees would further damage the habitat of protected species in the area, and how the already catastrophic decline in hedgehog numbers would fall further with the increase in traffic along Nethercott Road. Jenna heard a muted clap from behind her as the woman sat down again.

'And now can we hear from Henry Somners please.'

Jenna's feet felt like they had been glued to the floor. Everything sounded as though it was coming from much further away and she felt a gentle nudge from behind.

Slowly she stood. She was now thinking literally as well as metaphorically on her feet.

With her heart hammering, she made her way slowly and carefully to the front where May had stood a few minutes before.

'Chairman, councillors, I regret that Henry Somners has been taken ill and I have stepped in at short notice. I trust this is acceptable.'

Before anyone had a chance to reply or question this change in procedure, Jenna launched into her speech. Afterwards she could remember very little of what she had said, only the enormous sense of relief when it was at an end and that no one had any questions for her.

At least it was over and she could do no more. Evie and Kat gave her encouraging smiles and thumbs-up signs as she sat back down.

'We will now hear from the supporters. Firstly, Natalie Somners from Somners & Ashurst Legal Services.'

'I assume that's no relation to our absent objector?' asked one of the councillors, followed by a ripple of laughter.

The name hit Jenna like an audible shock wave. Natalie Somners. Surely that wasn't … it couldn't be … could it? Her thoughts scrambled and for several seconds she felt like her laptop did when the screen froze and that stupid little circle just went round and round without displaying anything helpful.

As the woman talked through her very businesslike

presentation, Jenna struggled to try and remember anything Henry had said about his sister.

Natalie … got a first-class degree in law… joined Pater's law firm … acquired an important new client…

Was this developer her important new client? Was this why Henry had backed out so suddenly? Another more sinister thought presented itself: Was Henry just pretending to help them in order to help his sister? The threat of tears prickled behind her eyes and she took several deep breaths. How well did she really know him?

He could have warned her but he didn't. He must have known when he sent that last email so what did that say about him? At the very least he could have messaged to say he wasn't coming. Or even just sorry. She looked again at her phone. There was nothing.

If this application was approved, in three months' time she, Evie, and Kat could be moving out, leaving a barn full of guinea pigs and three humans with no home. The thoughts turned over in her head again and again in a repeating cycle, but they made no more sense on the twentieth iteration than they did on the first. A slow swirl of anger was building inside her. How dare he treat her like that! How bloody dare he! She had trusted him and this is how he repaid that trust. Was their afternoon tea at DeLaneys just his way of saying sorry it's all over?

Dimly, she became aware that the presentations were also over and the chairman was speaking again.

'Thank you, supporters and objectors. Councillors, we now need to move towards a resolution. Can I have a show of hands please for this application?' A flurry of hands appeared. 'And against? Thank you. The application has been approved eight votes to three. There will now be a five-minute interval to allow those who wish to do so to leave the chamber.'

There was an immediate hum of muted conversations and the sound of chairs being scraped back.

Jenna didn't move. She had hoped that maybe there would be enough opposition to defer a vote. Henry had mentioned the possibility of some sort of adjournment while the councillors carried out a site visit. Now of course it was clearly obvious where he got this information from and it certainly wasn't his degree in business study and law.

She felt her arm being tugged. 'Come on, sis. Let's go home.'

Slowly, they filed out of the chamber and Jenna observed the small group of reporters sitting at the back, now busily writing up her failure. One of them gave her a sympathetic smile as she passed. She didn't want their sympathy. Or their gushing prose.

In the corridor, people were standing around chatting – presumably carrying out a quick post-mortem. Jenna recognised the other objector, May Dickinson, who waved and hurried over. 'I'm so sorry that this has been approved, it is an absolute disaster for the local area.'

'Not as sorry as we are,' replied Kat. 'We're going to lose our home.'

'And we have a barn full of pregnant guinea pigs,' added Evie.

'Oh you poor girls! So is it you three that run the rescue?'

As Evie and Kat launched into a potted history of Little Paws, Jenna spotted another familiar face. She even looked like Henry – same mouth, same blonde hair, although hers was styled into a neat bob. She was talking to a couple of important-looking men in dark pin stripe suits, but Jenna wasn't fazed by corporate window dressing.

'Back in a mo,' she murmured to Evie, and before she could change her mind, she made her way over to the other group. She grimaced as her hip reminded her that she needed to get home and rest, however there was something even more urgent that she needed to do first.

She tapped the woman lightly on the arm. 'Excuse me, sorry to interrupt but you're Henry's sister, aren't you?'

Natalie turned round with a look of surprise, rapidly replaced by a sympathetic smile. Jenna had had enough of those for one afternoon, although if it were possible to tell from their brief three-second introduction, it seemed genuine.

'Yes, I am.'

'I'm—'

'I know who you are. And I can guess why you're asking.'

Jenna decided to ditch the small talk. 'Did you tell him not to come today?'

'My brother needs to work out where his priorities lie,' she replied, sidestepping the question. 'And I'm sorry to say this because I know he's let you down, but there's something you should know about Henry: he's not cut out for commitment. Not to his family or a relationship. He's got form and he's done this before.'

'I know about Isla.'

'There have been others.' She gave Jenna a look that felt both like scrutiny and pity. 'He's probably done you a favour.'

Jenna felt cheated. Like when you watched a magic trick and then found out how they did it. It was no longer magic, it was a carefully crafted deceit.

Jenna looked over at Evie and pointed to the exit. Evie nodded and gave her a thumbs-up. As Jenna limped painfully back towards the entrance hall Natalie's words crashed around inside her head. She wished she could run; she wanted to run and keep on running because then she wouldn't have to think about the hurt and the anger bottled up inside her, or the pain in her heart that drowned out the pain in her leg and which felt like something inside was tearing apart. Maybe it was.

Maybe that something was the fragile daydream that she'd been carefully nurturing for the past couple of months. She had finally begun to believe that she didn't have to settle for a Mr Practical, and that sometimes, miraculously, fairy tales really did come true and happy ever afters really did happen.

'Stupid, stupid, stupid,' she muttered. She had allowed herself to fall headlong into Henry's romantic dream world believing – mistakenly – that it was for real. Even if Natalie had ordered him to stay away, he could easily have sent a message. Or even defied her. But he didn't. Was this what happened to Isla? Did she take off around the world to bury her heart and her hurt and start again?'

When they got back home, Jenna shut herself in her room and lay on the bed. Only then, after taking some painkillers and clutching an armful of Evie's cuddly toys, did she let her silent tears fall. In one fell swoop she had lost an ally, a friend and yes, she had fallen in love with him too. Now she was just another statistic for Natalie to add to the list. Why was it that almost every man in her life had let her down? First her father, then Matt, and now Henry. He didn't deserve her tears, he really didn't, but they fell anyway.

It was some time later that she got up, washed her face and went in search of her sister. At least Evie had Kat to console her, but aside from the emotional support, they all needed to address the practicalities of their situation because maybe not next week or next month, but some-time towards the end of the summer their rental agreement would be terminated and they needed to be prepared.

Jenna found both of them in the barn. Evie was filling up containers from an open bale of hay; her red-rimmed eyes and hollow expression mirroring Jenna's own feelings. She had half expected to see Kat out in the yard energetically destroying something with a sledgehammer, but she was sitting quietly at the wooden table with Oreo on her lap, stroking her soft brown fur. Fat tears rolled down her cheeks and Jenna stared, dumbfounded. Kat never cried. Not ever. Not even at the end of *Marley and Me*, which had her and Evie sobbing into a pile of tissues.

It was as if the fight had gone out of her and Evie was clearly as shocked as she was.

'Oh Kat!' Jenna gave her a hug, careful not to spook the piggy sitting happily munching on a sprig of mint. 'I don't know what to say.'

'She's pregnant,' said Kat in a wobbly voice. 'You can feel the babies.'

Jenna sat down next to her and rubbed Oreo gently behind her ears. 'Congratulations, mummy pig,' she said softly.

'There's probably more on the way. We'll have to check all the females. And we'll need new pens for the males once they're weaned.' Kat sniffed, wiped her face with her hand and looked around. 'How are we going to rehome all these animals if we're forced to move out?'

Before Jenna could think of a response, Evie answered for her. 'Don't worry, Kat, Jenna will think of something, won't you? She always has a plan and she understands about finance and stuff.' Evie brushed the loose hay from her T-shirt and put her arms around her sister. 'Tell us what we're going to do, sis.'

Seeing Kat's distress rekindled Jenna's own, and a couple of hot tears trickled down her face as she leaned over and stroked Oreo gently.

She didn't have a plan. Or a strategy. And now they were on their own. But she knew what she wanted to do, even if currently she had no idea how to go about it.

'We fight back,' she said decisively.

Chapter Twenty-Six

It seemed intuitively wrong that applicants had a right to appeal against a planning decision should they require it, but objectors did not. Therefore, as Jenna explained over breakfast the following day, any further objecting would have to be done outside of the town hall. For avoidance of doubt, she added, that did not mean literally outside the town hall with placards and slogans.

Jenna had spent a large part of the night lying wide awake going over the events of the previous afternoon. Henry's non-appearance meant they had been at disadvantage from the outset, as it was he who had knowledge of the planning laws and had the experience of public speaking. Had he backed down out of deference to his family? Had he been secretly helping his family? However she tried to rationalise what had happened, everything seemed to come back to Henry.

There's something you should know … he's not cut out for commitment.

The bottom line was that Jenna had placed her trust in someone and they had let her down. Jenna could cope with business decisions. But Henry was a whole different matter. Did the last few weeks mean nothing? Was she not even entitled to an explanation? The obvious answer was that she had just been an amusement to Henry. What was it he had said to her?

Let me prove it to you. I will take you to somewhere scenic and just a little bit magical that is not far from here and costs absolutely nothing…

So that magical sunrise breakfast at Northlands Abbey, and their dinner at The Old Bookbinder's Arms, were just part of a bet? Maybe when you had that sort of money, and you were between trips and wanted a bit of entertainment, you could afford to just chuck it around like that. But he had kissed her and made her feel special. And being stupid, she had believed all of it.

He's got form and he's done this before.

How many times? Did the others feel as hurt as she did right now? The unanswered questions were still playing in a loop as she drove to work the following morning dosed up with caffeine.

'Let that be a lesson, Jenna Oakhurst,' she said as she turned into the staff car park. 'You should know that happy ever after only happens in books.'

She relished the opportunity to throw herself into

something that could keep her mind occupied elsewhere for several hours. Unfortunately, her colleagues were not so easily distracted and were eager to get chapter and verse on the whole afternoon. To their disappointment, however, they got one very short chapter.

'We lost.'

'And? Can't you appeal?' demanded Denise indignantly.

'No.'

'So what will you do?'

'I'm going to make as much noise about this as possible,' replied Jenna, chucking her pen onto her keyboard.

'Actually,' Jamie said, joining in the discussion, 'what you need is a social media account. Use that cool dude on the front of the calendar.'

You had to hand it to Jamie, he was a trier. 'I don't think Snickers knows how to use social media but I'll pass on the suggestion. In the meantime, what I need is a fundraising page. I just need to find out how to make one.'

'I can show you how to do that. I set one up earlier this year for a mate who was doing a birthday fundraiser. Hey, do you think you'll be allowed to advertise it at work?'

'You mean make a donation and you get your expenses paid faster?' asked Jenna with a wry smile. 'Somehow, I doubt that's within the rules, although I'd love to see what happened if we gave it a try. I reckon even Mr Ranty might fancy making a donation to that scheme.'

'He could start with this month's expenses,' said Alisha, pointing at the screen. 'Another client entertainment for unknown persons. And at DeLaneys too.'

The mere mention of DeLaneys flicked a nerve. 'Let's have a look at how much he's spent this time, shall we?' Jenna got up and stood behind Denise so that she could look at her screen. Something was niggling at her again.

'Could you print it out for me?'

As Jenna stared at the piece of A4 paper Denise retrieved from the printer, images of the previous Sunday sprang to mind like snippets of a film: Henry's blue shirt, which she had admired so much and had fantasised about removing, Henry laughing at Kat's table manners, Jenna trying to grab the receipt out of Henry's hand. Somehow knowing that their afternoon at DeLaney's was probably one big Henry-designed apology took all the sparkle out of the event.

Hang on; she backed up the film in her head. The scanned copy of the receipt in front of her didn't look the same as the one she'd wrestled off Henry, she was sure of it. She frowned. Shouldn't receipts from the same restaurant look identical? She'd seen the piece of paper that confirmed their bill with her own eyes, but this was a scanned copy. Could it somehow be forged? And if so, did that mean all the previous expenses were also forgeries? Jenna spent the next hour looking back through Ian Ransome's previous expenses and printed out the receipts from five meals at DeLaneys within the last twelve months.

She experienced a sudden surge of indignation. Why was it she spent her life trying to do things the right way, even when that was not always the easiest option, when clearly most other people didn't? Maybe they justified it to themselves in some small way, or maybe they thought they were owed something. Either way she was determined to find out the truth and she would go back to DeLaneys and make some enquiries. Tonight though she had a more urgent task.

Jenna hadn't shared her plan with anybody. She didn't want to raise anyone's hopes just yet as nothing might come it. She got the idea last night after mentally going over every detail of the planning meeting. At the back of the council chamber there had been an area set aside for press reporters and she'd seen at least two people scribbling in notebooks. Guessing that they were reporters for the local paper, she started with the *Haxford & Kings Hampton Gazette*.

At least her business skills didn't let her down as she composed an email setting out their current position, the arguments against the planning decision and – the crucial human interest element – how she and her sister would become homeless just as dozens of baby guinea pigs were being born at the rescue. It wouldn't change the outcome of the planning decision, but if it raised awareness and helped Evie and Kat to rehome all the piggies it would be worth it.

In the end she sent her story to not only two local papers but also several of the tabloid press publications too. 'Nothing ventured and all that,' she said to no one in particular as she pressed send on the last email. Now they just had to sit tight and wait.

Chapter Twenty-Seven

Even though she knew it could easily be several days before anyone from the papers responded, it didn't stop Jenna checking her phone as soon as she woke the following morning. It was to ascertain whether any acknowledgement had been sent, she told herself, and nothing whatsoever to do with needing to see a certain person's name in her email inbox. Or a text. Or any other form of electronic message. She was owed an apology if nothing else.

It had been forty hours now and still nothing. Almost two whole days. Her phone had been left on day and night just in case he messaged or rang, and as she had done the previous night, she had lain in bed and conjured up every possible logical reason or ludicrous possibility for Henry's absence. Each time she came back to the most obvious answer: he didn't want to be involved anymore. Not with Little Paws nor with her.

It was as she was doing a final scroll through her phone before she left for work that the accident happened. She reached for her handbag with her other hand and somehow overbalanced. Her foot snagged on the protruding leg of her clothes rail, and she yelped as she crashed onto the carpet, causing Kat to come running in with her toothbrush sticking out of her mouth.

'Wha' az akkend?' Kat gargled. She rushed over to help Jenna up. 'Are u ogay?'

Jenna winced as, leaning on Kat, she hobbled back towards the bed and sat down. 'Bugger, I think I've sprained my ankle.' She gently prodded it with her fingers. 'Ouch.'

Kat lifted her legs up onto the bed. 'U eed u zit sill.'

'And you need to finish brushing your teeth instead of dribbling toothpaste everywhere,' replied Jenna, waving away her helper and grabbing a tissue to wipe the frothy dribble off her trousers. She was dressed for work but it was rapidly becoming clear that even her crutches weren't going to be much help today.

After twenty minutes of waiting, punctuated by testing out her ankle every couple of minutes, Jenna was forced to concede defeat and rang work. Alisha assured her that everything would still be there when she returned and promised to send her boss the appropriate notification.

'Now what am I going to do?' said Jenna grumpily as she closed her phone. Almost immediately she opened it again to check for messages. Why was she doing this? She was angry with herself now, as well as Henry, all fuelled by the pain in her ankle. She didn't even have work to keep her mind occupied.

After ten minutes in front of the television, she complained that she was fed up, so with Evie's help, she hobbled outside. The area immediately in front of the entrance to the barn was sheltered and Evie brought out a chair. To keep her foot up, Evie created a makeshift footrest with a towel thrown over a sack of shavings and Kat fetched an ice pack to help reduce any swelling.

'I only need a tin can and I could go begging,' grumbled Jenna.

'Well you're not going to get much passing trade there,' Evie said. 'You'll be more visible if you sit further out.'

'I don't want to be more visible, thank you, I want to do something useful.'

'Good. I'll get you our invoice folder and chequebook, and you can sort it out and settle any outstanding bills. You might want to check first before you pay any large ones though, I'm not sure how much money we have in the account. Oh, and Val and Dorothy are volunteering later this afternoon so you'll have some different company.'

Val was lovely and very chatty once you got her onto certain topics, but it was still going to be a long day.

Throughout the morning, Jenna received regular *Are you okay?* checks from the workers in the barn, which were well meant but made her feel even more of an invalid.

It was nearing lunchtime when Evie came running out holding a set of keys.

'Jen, we've been called out to do a rescue in Cotlington. I think you ought to come with us.'

'I'm not dangerous when unattended, Evie. I'll be fine.'

Evie seemed unconvinced, but after bringing out a small table with Jenna's library books, a bottle of water and a small packet of digestive biscuits, she headed off with Kat in the car, which they'd loaded with small animal carry boxes.

Jenna checked her watch, then took a couple of paracetamol and closed her eyes for a few minutes. There was a continual background noise from the construction site opposite, which she attempted to blot out as she thought about what she wanted to do with her life. Henry had shown her that there was more to life than just work. Did she want to spend the next twenty-plus years doing the same thing in the same place? If she changed jobs, what did she want to do anyway? She wasn't qualified to do anything else and starting again was not a challenge she relished.

She didn't realise she had dozed off until the sound of footsteps scrunching up the track on the gravel caused her to jerk awake. She must have snoozed for longer than she thought. However there was no sign of Kat's battered old Volvo, only someone who clearly hadn't been intending to announce their presence. He was holding an envelope and it suddenly occurred to her that maybe this was some sort of belated apology.

Did she even want to accept his apology? Or his excuses, whatever they were? In spite of everything that had happened, her heart still jumped at the sight of him.

Before she could decide how to respond, Henry had walked over to where she sat. It wasn't his usual confident stride, it was the slow step of someone who hadn't noticed anyone sitting outside until it was too late to retreat, and now didn't know what to say.

'Jenna.' Henry paused as if he expected her to respond. When she didn't, he added, 'I … er … didn't expect to see you here.'

'That's obvious,' she replied in a neutral voice that hopefully didn't belie the turmoil within. 'Where's the car?'

Henry pointed back towards the road. 'I didn't think anyone would want to see me after…' He ran his hand through his hair as he glanced around. 'Anyway, I promised Evie I'd make a contribution towards Snickers' upkeep.' He held out the envelope. 'I didn't want to put cash in the post.'

So there was no apology. In fact, on the surface it seemed as though he hadn't come to see her at all.

'So you thought you'd come over while I was at work.'

'The thing is, Jenna, I didn't know what to do. I didn't want to… That is, I—'

'Didn't want to see me,' finished Jenna. 'Funnily enough I got that message loud and clear on Tuesday, thanks.' She spoke firmly and loudly. If she let her voice waver, she knew tears wouldn't be far behind.

'No, that's not what I mean at all. I felt—'

'Please don't bother trying to explain – it's quite obvious how you feel. And your sister kindly filled in the missing details. It was a bit of a shock seeing her at the meeting, I can tell you. She told me all about Isla.'

'Oh?'

'Isla didn't end it, did she? You finished with her, didn't you?'

'Yes,' admitted Henry in a subdued voice.

'So I was just … what? Some sort of challenge? I bet you I can show you some magical, scenic places that you've never been to before?'

'No—'

'An interesting interlude to fill up your boring life before you jet off round the world again?'

'No!' He stopped. 'Okay, in the beginning it might have—'

'Thanks.'

'But not later on. I don't know how to explain. I'm trying to be honest.' He waved his arms agitatedly as he spoke. 'It got complicated. I didn't mean to fall in love with you.'

'How very romantic,' said Jenna sarcastically. 'Thanks for your honesty.' She almost relished the pain in her ankle as her irritation spilled over into anger. 'Sorry, Henry, but you have no idea what love means. And I'll give you a really big hint: it doesn't mean simply throwing your money around on a few nice dates and it sure as hell doesn't mean promising something and then buggering off without any explanation.'

'I know I let you all down. I'm really sorry. I was in an impossible situation and—'

'You know what, I don't need this.' Jenna's heart pounded and she drew several angry breaths as all the hurt of the last few days spilled out. 'The time for saying sorry was before the planning meeting, not the day after, or the day after that, and not because you got spotted sneaking up to the front door. I need people in my life I can rely on – who I can trust. Who aren't going to let me down time after time—' She blinked furiously. There was no way she was going to cry in front of him while she couldn't even walk away. 'Please just go.'

Henry looked at her for a few seconds, as though he was trying to decide whether to say something, then nodded slowly, turned and strode down the drive without looking back.

'And we lost the case!' Jenna yelled at his retreating figure. 'Snickers is going to be bloody homeless like the rest of us!'

She wanted to tear something up and throw it in the air in tiny pieces. Or stamp up and down in the yard. Or engage in what Kat referred to as organised destruction therapy.

His version of the break-up with Isla was a fabrication. If that was a lie, what else was made up? Whatever it was he was looking for, it wasn't her. She needed certainty and security – now more than ever – and she felt cheated. He had given her some wonderful experiences and precious memories that now felt tarnished, like objects rescued from a fire – objects that had once been treasured possessions but had now been altered by tragic circumstances and could never be the same again.

When Evie and Kat returned an hour later, Jenna handed over the five twenty-pound notes. Thankfully they accepted Jenna's explanation that it arrived in the post and didn't ask for any evidence; anything else would involve far too many questions, as well as admitting that Henry had conned all of them with his charming ways and romantic dreams, while hers lay silently in tatters.

Later on that evening, in the privacy of her overcrowded room, Jenna opened up the spotty box with the flip over lid that still contained all Isla's treasures. This was where it all started, with her insistence on tracking down Isla. And look what it had led to. In some strange way she was pleased to think that her instincts hadn't let her down though – these *had* been someone's treasures, not random knick knacks.

Jenna lifted out the part-completed cross-stitch project again. Across the top Isla had stitched numbers and letters of the alphabet. In one of the rectangular blocks there was a representation of the Danish flag, and in another there was a couple of tulips. After a quick count of the marked-out rectangles, Jenna knew she was right, and now she understood what this meant; Isla was stitching an A to Z of all the places she had visited with Henry. Far from being bored of him or their travels together, it was the other way round, and after he'd finished with her, she couldn't complete it. She probably wanted to get away, much as Jenna did now, and putting everything into storage was her way of dealing with the past.

'I understand how you feel,' she said miserably as she ran her fingers over the coloured stitches. 'I loved and lost him too.'

Much as she didn't want to admit it, maybe Natalie Somners was right and her brother wasn't the settling down sort. Jenna hoped that Isla had found someone decent to be with. Maybe that was why she had been happy to stop paying for the storage unit: it wasn't a financial consideration or an accidental oversight as Jenna had previously supposed, it had been her way of letting go and moving on.

Chapter Twenty-Eight

One of the downsides of the various surgeries she'd had in the past was that everything took a lot longer to heal, although it didn't stop her testing her ankle out on a daily basis. To keep herself busy, Jenna had been looking around for somewhere to rent that might suit them. She had long suspected that Evie and Kat might have been paying rather a cheap rent because Farm Cottage was out in the sticks, but she was disappointed to be proved more than right. There were hardly any decent properties within their budget, and certainly none that would allow them to keep many, if any, of the guinea pigs. The last affordable place she had looked at online was an ugly second-floor flat in need of modernisation, situated in a concrete block near to the railway station. The best you could say about it was that it had good transport links.

Wherever possible, Jenna tried to help out in the

barn, even if it was just holding guinea pigs while the others did cage cleaning. The piggies that Evie and Kat had rescued the previous week still needed syringe feeding and Jenna was becoming very adept at encouraging them to eat. She couldn't bring herself to cuddle Snickers anymore though; he was Henry's guinea pig, and bound up with too many painful memories of happier times.

At least Snickers was earning his keep with his rental money making a contribution towards the food bill. That and Jamie's efforts. During this period of enforced recuperation, she had emailed him with some information about the rescue, and why they needed additional funds. She thanked him again for volunteering his help and told him to do whatever he thought was best. Thankfully Jamie seemed to know what he was doing as the day before he had emailed back with a link to the page he'd set up via Go Fund Me. She had sent over various pictures to choose from but unsurprisingly, given his previous remarks, he'd chosen one of Snickers with what Evie called his begging for pea flakes look, although Jenna knew all guinea pigs quickly learned to perfect that routine.

Over breakfast Kat announced that they had received their first donation on the site, and that sales of calendars were also slowly increasing. There was one further announcement later that day, which Jenna saved until dinnertime. As they sat around the non-cluttered end of the kitchen table, she told them her news.

'Evie, leave the plates, I've got something to tell you both.'

Evie immediately put down the stack of crockery and sat down again, her eyes fixed anxiously on her sister.

'Don't look so worried, little sis. The first thing is that I'm going back to work tomorrow—'

'I don't think that's a good idea, Jen, you need to give it more time.'

Jenna shook her head. 'Sorry. I love you both to bits, but I need to get back to work. It's my boss Adam's last day in the office before a two-week holiday. And there's something I need to look into, so I might be a bit late back.'

'Phew!' said Kat. 'I wasn't sure what you were going to say. I thought you might have been up to something.'

'Why did you think that?'

Kat shrugged. 'You've been very quiet. I guessed that was because of him.' She put some emphasis on the last word, which conveyed both sadness and a bitter feeling of betrayal, which was felt to varying degrees by all of them.

'You have a plan, don't you!' said Evie, her eyes lighting up.

'I don't know yet if it will work but, yes, I had an idea. I wanted to wait until I heard back before I said anything, and they replied this afternoon.'

'Who's they?'

Jenna proceeded to explain how she had contacted various newspapers with the story of how they were going to be made homeless with a barn full of guinea pigs about to give birth.

'To be honest, I think the reporter sounded more concerned about the homeless guinea pigs than the homeless humans, but hey, it's free publicity. They're sending out a reporter on Saturday.'

'We're going to be in the papers?'

'Yes, hopefully.'

'With all the piggies?'

Jenna grinned. 'Yep.'

'Brilliant!' said Evie clapping her hands together.

'Bugger,' said Kat. 'We'd better start tidying up.'

Chapter Twenty-Nine

Jenna returned to work the following day with the help of her crutches and her colleagues. It felt good to be back in some sort of routine after the unscheduled chaos and enforced recuperation of the previous week. Jenna thanked Jamie for his help in setting up the crowdfunding page, which her team all immediately logged into and admired. Jenna wasn't sure whether this was out of concern for the guinea pigs, admiration for Jamie's IT skills or the opportunity to legitimately do something other than work for ten minutes, but she happily joined in.

She was pleased to see she had more enquiries about calendars and spent a large part of the morning catching up with emails – both calendar and accounting related – departmental gossip and the latest on Ian Ransome's expenses. She made sure that the details she had printed out before the ankle accident were in her bag as she was planning to follow that up. It might be absolutely nothing, in which case she'd only be wasting an hour, but that was a sacrifice she was prepared to make.

Jenna arrived at DeLaneys just after five-thirty. Her ankle was achy, and looking rather puffy, but she was here now and this wouldn't take long. The afternoon tea service had finished and several serving staff was busily preparing tables for the early evening diners. She sat down on the nearest seat and a dark-haired waiter carrying a tray full of wine glasses hurried over.

'I'm sorry, madam, but the restaurant doesn't open until seven. Do you want to wait and have a drink at the bar, or would you like to reserve a table for later?'

'Neither, actually. I'd like to talk to someone about your receipts.'

'Receipts? You have a question about your bill?'

'Perhaps I can show you.' Jenna pulled out of her bag the print outs of all the scanned receipts that had been submitted as expenses claims, together with the receipt she had kept from their afternoon tea, which now seemed like a lifetime ago despite being only eleven days. It brought back memories of the happy occasion and it took all of her resolve to keep focused on the task in hand.

'This,' she pointed at Henry's receipt, 'is from a couple of weeks ago. So why does it look different from these?' She gestured at the scanned prints spread across the table. 'They've been submitted to my company as expenses and I'm just curious as to why they look different.'

The waiter examined the papers for a few minutes and then beckoned another member of staff over. In the end, it didn't take long to get to the bottom of the mystery, and Jenna left the restaurant with a triumphant grin and a feeling of vindication. The question was what to do with this new information. Adam was away now for two weeks so for the moment Jenna was happy to take her time and do some thinking.

Chapter Thirty

The newspaper article appeared the following week in the *Haxford & Kings Hampton Gazette* as well as several other local papers. It described how the rescue was being forced to close following the council's approval of the new housing development, despite local opposition. Several of the guinea pigs had already given birth and there was a picture of Jenna and Evie holding two of Oreo's adorably cute three-day-old dark brown and white babies in their cupped hands.

It was fair to say the journalist had been very taken with the tale of how, single-pawed, Snickers had managed to impregnate so many of the females when a visitor accidentally returned him to the wrong cage, and there was also a picture of the handsome tinker, now spearheading the rescue's efforts to fundraise.

The tale of Snickers and his antics in the midst of this David and Goliath battle clearly had human interest appeal, and a couple of the tabloid papers had also run the story online.

Everyone knew that it wouldn't change the outcome of the planning approval, but they noticed an immediate upturn in donations and interest in adopting a baby guinea pig. Despite the Sunday-only visiting arrangements, people now started turning up at various times just to see the babies, which Kat turned into an opportunity to sell extra calendars.

Jenna had assumed that people's attention would be focused solely on the guinea pigs, but she soon discovered that this was not the case. Several people at work came over to speak to her in the days following the publication, and handed her an envelope with a donation towards the upkeep of the animals, or stopped her to ask about the planning application.

Jamie had enthusiastically joined in the cause, printing out a picture of Snickers and pinning it to the desk divider, declaring it was far more interesting to look at than the corporate stuff that got handed out. Within a few days a strapline saying 'PLEASE DONATE' had been added underneath.

Even with additional volunteers, Evie and Kat were still being kept very busy with more pregnant guinea pigs giving birth so Jenna had volunteered to take over the piggy food shopping as this was something useful she could do on her own, and although her ankle was much improved, the trolley helpfully doubled as a mobile crutch.

The supermarket was also less busy in the evenings so

she could take her time without being tutted at by impatient shoppers. Jenna loved looking at what other people were buying and this evening most people were clearly shopping for families by the looks of their trolleys piled high with all manner of food items, fizzy drinks, packs of nappies and cartons of milk. She smiled as she looked down at hers, which was already full of various types of lettuces, plus broccoli, tomatoes, celery and multipacks of red, green and yellow peppers, to which she added a dozen cucumbers.

'Excuse me, but you're one of the guinea pig ladies, aren't you? I recognise you from the picture in the paper.'

Jenna turned round to see a woman with grey, shoulder-length hair held back with a thin purple hairband. She looked to be in her late sixties, Jenna guessed, and she was wearing bright-coloured trousers with a floral design that could have come straight from the pages of a Mary Quant fashion show.

'Yes, although it's my sister and her partner that run the rescue. I'm just living there for the moment.'

'They should never have started building those houses along that road; it's not the right place for that sort of development. And it's a crying shame, cutting down all those trees as well. I bet anything you like someone's greasing palms somewhere.' The woman nodded enthusiastically as she spoke. 'It's those councillors who should be paying for all your guinea pigs, not you, you poor love.' She patted Jenna's hand, and Jenna was tempted to woof politely in response.

As she drove home, she wondered why people mistakenly thought it might be comforting to be patted by a complete stranger. It was something she had experienced many times previously, but it still felt a bit strange, and nearly always happened if she was using her crutches. It was one of life's big misapprehensions that anyone in possession of a mobility aid must be in want of assistance.

Last year Evie and Kat had had a table at the Haxford Charter Fair and she had been browsing round the various stalls. Even with the help of her sticks, the ground was unhelpfully uneven and after an unexpected wobble, someone had rushed over and asked in a very slow, childlike voice whether she could fetch anyone for her. Jenna had simply smiled back and said, 'yes, thanks, Tom Hiddleston would be lovely'.

Despite the unhelpful hand-patting thing, the woman's reference to councillors had reminded her that she hadn't done anything yet about the Ian Ransome problem. Adam wasn't back for a week yet and she frowned as she recalled his words.

If there are any problems that you can't handle in my absence, Lester Norris will be happy to advise. Otherwise, just continue to exercise your discretion as you see fit.

Could she handle this problem? She wasn't sure yet, but in any case, it would be useful to do a bit more fact-finding. And it wouldn't do her career any harm either if she managed to get to the bottom of whatever had been going on.

Chapter Thirty-One

At exactly three o'clock on Friday afternoon Jenna made her way down to the Sales Department. She had booked the appointment earlier today and left the subject matter vague, just adding the word 'Meeting' for the appropriate slot on Friday 2nd July. He was already waiting for her in the meeting room and Jenna took a seat on the opposite side of the table.

Ian Ransome looked at his watch. 'I can give you precisely ten minutes, and then I have to be somewhere else.'

'That's fine, I'll get straight to the point then. I know you've been submitting doctored receipts for meals at DeLaneys. I've only looked into the last twelve months, but now I'm wondering what else I might find if I look a bit harder.'

'Right, just stop there. That's—'

'That's dishonest, that's what it is,' Jenna interjected

calmly. 'Or perhaps we should call it "fraud", which is probably how your boss and mine would describe it.' She opened the file she'd brought with her. 'Here is a receipt from DeLaneys from my visit there a few weeks ago.' She pointed at the relevant piece of paper, which still had the crease in it from where she had attempted to wrest it from Henry. 'And here are a couple of yours. If you look at the layout, you'll see that the logo is in a different place and the font is slightly different. Interestingly, I was informed by the staff at DeLaneys that they introduced a new computer system well over a year ago now, which is when these layout changes occurred.'

Ian Ransome sat back in his chair as though trying to put as much physical distance between them as possible. He blinked rapidly and his hands clutched the edge of the table. Jenna watched as the colour drained from his face. There was no smug expression now. She waited to see how he tried to weasel his way out of this one, or whether he would apply his usual blustering tactics.

'What do you want me to say?'

Jenna coughed as though a drink had gone down the wrong way. 'Sorry? I've just presented you with what looks like evidence of fraud and you don't want to explain this?' Jenna scooped up her papers and stuffed them back in the folder. She'd had her fill of people who did bizarre things and then refused to explain themselves. 'Fine. I just thought you might want to. I'll discuss it with Adam – he's back next week.'

'No, please wait!'

For almost a minute they simply sat in silence. When he finally spoke, Ian Ransome's voice was devoid of its usual arrogance, and there was a hint of a sigh as he said, 'It's ironic, really. You're probably the one person in this organisation that would even notice something was amiss, but the person who would least understand.'

'Why? Why wouldn't I understand?'

'Well, look at you.' He waved a dismissive hand but kept his gaze fixed on the window behind her. 'Young, professional woman. Good at her job. Probably never had to be responsible for keeping your family together when everything falls apart. You don't get blamed when things go wrong that are outside your control, or you're faced with impossible choices.'

Jenna's natural response was to vigorously refute these erroneous assumptions, but instead she remained silent. There was no point in arguing with people who only saw one point of view. Neither of them spoke for several seconds. Finally he said in a quiet voice, 'I suppose you might as well know – it won't make any difference now anyway.' There was another long pause before he said, 'I wanted to help my son.'

He took a long intake of breath. 'I blame all the advertising, really. Encouraging you to have a little flutter – a bit of excitement – as though it's perfectly innocent. We didn't even know he was gambling online until he had run up over ten thousand pounds of debt. At nineteen years of age! My wife and I were naive, I suppose; we thought we could just talk to him and it would stop.'

Jenna shook her head. 'It doesn't,' she said softly.

'And then it got worse. He lost his job. We paid off his debts and thought that without any money he couldn't gamble, but it all went on credit cards. He was online half the night and racking up more debts as we slept. Every time we tried to talk to him there were arguments, lies, shouting. Every time I bailed him out, he promised it wouldn't start again. And it did.

'Then it was my wife's birthday. After everything that had happened, I wanted her to have one evening away from it all so even though I didn't really have that sort of money I took her to DeLaneys and … well, I just added it to my expenses.' He rubbed his thumb nail as he spoke. 'No one questioned it. I suppose that's where I got the idea from. Small amounts here and there. No one looked at my sales record against the total expenses.'

He ran his hand through his greying hair as he spoke. 'I told myself I was doing it for my son. There's a long waiting list for places in rehab so now that he has a reserved place we've decided to pay privately and I'm in the process of taking out an additional mortgage to cover the ongoing costs.'

'And your son wants to do this?' asked Jenna.

Ian nodded cautiously. 'He knows he needs help. He says he wants to go away and sort himself out.' He reached into his pocket and pulled out his phone. After scrolling through a few pages, he held it out to show Jenna. 'That's Daniel on his eighteenth birthday.'

The picture had been taken in a garden decked out

for a party. Balloons and bunting were draped along the fence and Daniel was grinning broadly while balancing several brightly wrapped presents in his arms. It must be a bittersweet memory for his parents now, knowing what came after, and Jenna smiled sympathetically. With any luck, there might still be a happy ending of some sort, but at a massive financial and emotional cost. One that might be dependent on what she did next.

She knew the rules; in her job the reporting requirements were clear and it was her job to ensure that rules were adhered to. But if she reported her findings to Adam, Ian would certainly lose his job, and who would re-employ someone sacked for gross misconduct? The mortgage offer would fall through and his son would end up on some waiting list for help that may or may not come too late. Did she have the right to tear this family apart knowing what had happened to her own, just to prove that she was competent at her job? And could she live with her own conscience?

A sick feeling lodged itself in the pit of her stomach as long-buried memories surfaced. How different could it have been if someone had helped her family?

'You know what? My friend Kat would say there's enough shit in this world without adding to it. And she's right.' She pulled out the receipts and papers from her folder and pushed them across the table. 'Take them.'

Ian reached out and gathered the receipts. 'I suppose these are copies?'

'No, that's all there is. But there's a condition.'

His body tensed and his eyes fixed on hers. 'This expenses stuff – it has to stop. For good.'

A jumble of emotions registered on Ian Ransome's face. 'I … I don't know what to say. I thought…' He inhaled sharply. 'Yes, of course it will. And – thank you.'

Jenna got to her feet. 'You were wrong by the way. About me. You said, and I think your exact words were, "probably never had to be responsible for keeping your family together when everything falls apart".' She looked down for a brief second. 'My father gambled. For years. It wasn't just the money. We lost our family possessions, the car, the house. It ruined my childhood and my family. When my mum couldn't take it anymore, they divorced and he moved away. When I left school, I had to get a job instead of going to university so I could support my mum and my sister. I never saw him again and I was angry with him for making me feel like he didn't care about us.

'Before he leaves, tell Daniel how much you care about him. Tell him you love him. Children need to hear that.' She closed the door quietly behind her.

Chapter Thirty-Two

'You look very thoughtful,' remarked Denise as Jenna returned to her desk. 'Nothing to do with Henry, is it? I haven't heard much about that saga recently.'

Alisha's head swivelled round. 'Ooh, have you heard from him? The story sort of fizzled out.'

Jenna's thoughts were still elsewhere. 'Henry? Yes, it did, rather.' Right now, she had enough on her plate without adding thoughts of Henry. She hadn't heard anything from him since the day he'd come over with Snickers' advance rent payment. She had been angry and told him to go; now she wondered whether he gave in too easily. Why didn't he stand his ground? Offer up an explanation for what happened? Or even just grovel and apologise? He did none of those things and Jenna had been left in a no man's land of unanswered questions and a minefield of painful reminders.

Even driving to and from work, she could hardly avoid seeing the tall, majestic stone arches of the abbey ruins out of the car passenger window. The trouble was that she no longer saw a pile of stonework, elegant pillars and glass-less windows, she saw in her mind, like some sort of Pavlovian reaction, a wicker hamper, a velvet cushion, a smiling handsome face and a memory of a stolen kiss.

Jenna closed down her computer. 'Okay team, I'm going to call it a day. If anyone asks, I'll make up the hours next week.'

Jenna drove home via the slightly longer route that took her through the centre of town. It was a boring commute, but staring at the traffic backed up along the Haxford Road was preferable to driving past Northlands Abbey with its constant reminder of what she had lost. It also gave her time to think. She needed to live in the present, not dwell in the past, and move on like Isla had. She had lived most of her life with a plan, backed up with rational, reasoned decision making. But sometimes things happened without ever finding out the reason why, and she had to find a way to accept that. The trouble was she wasn't sure she wanted to. She had tried hard to banish Henry from her thoughts but the more time that elapsed, the harder it became.

She was greeted at the rescue by volunteer Val waving from the open barn door.

'Two more babies!' she shouted excitedly.

Ignoring the fact that she was still in her work attire, Jenna followed Val into the barn and headed over to the big pen where Evie was busy replacing water bottles. 'Who's the mum?'

'It's Dolly,' said Evie, carefully lifting up one side of a wooden hut. Snuggled up against mum were two small babies, both with toffee coloured hair. 'There was a third, but he was DOA.'

Jenna knew that meant dead on arrival. She marvelled at how matter of fact her sister could be about such things. The only time she had seen that happen for herself was three years ago with a piggy who was already pregnant when she was given to the rescue. Ten days later she had had four pups, but two had been stillborn. Jenna had been moved to tears at the sight of the tiny little scraps of life that for some unknown reason had not survived.

'How many is that so far?'

'Twenty-nine babies, and five more mums ready to go any day,' answered Kat, striding into the barn with an armful of washed food bowls. 'I suppose we ought to be grateful Snickers didn't manage to get round to all of them.'

Val laughed and they all turned to look at the instigator of this baby boom who was standing at the front of his hutch looking curious and – if it were possible for a guinea pig – inordinately pleased with himself. Henry's piggy. Another image that brought back so many memories, in particular the day of the photoshoot, the day she accidentally stroked Henry's leg.

'Now Snickers can't cause any more trouble, it's time

he found himself a nice girlfriend,' Kat added. 'I'm sure Henry wouldn't mind adopting another piggy.'

'Kat!' said Evie in a strained whisper.

'It's okay, I can cope with hearing his name,' said Jenna. 'In fact, I've been doing some thinking.' Jenna opened the door to Snickers' hutch and he wheeked loudly then nuzzled her hand, searching for treats. He might be responsible for the rapid population increase at Little Paws, but it wasn't his fault that Henry didn't want to see them – or him – anymore.

'Come here, Mr Noisy.' Jenna scooped him up, ignoring the wisps of hay and shavings that came with him and cradled him in her arms while he continued his search for treats. Jenna sat down carefully on the least dusty wooden chair. 'I'm going to email Henry this evening.'

'What!'

'I'm not angry now, but I just need to understand what happened. It helps with … things…'

'Do you think that's a good idea?' asked Val carefully.

'I don't know, but I've got to try.'

No one stated the obvious: that there was a strong possibility he wouldn't reply at all.

Jenna planted a kiss on Snickers head. 'Time to go home, handsome boy. You're fidgeting.'

She brushed off all the loose hay. 'Shall I go in and start dinner?'

'Good idea,' said Kat. 'Oh, and there's some post for you. It's on the kitchen table.'

'It allegedly got left in the van by mistake,' Evie added. 'I don't know if it's because it's not our usual postie this week, but he did say it wasn't his fault it's a bit delayed.'

'Your trouble is you're too nice,' replied Kat. 'That mumbled excuse did not constitute an apology.'

Jenna smiled at Kat's indignation. 'It's probably more invitations to take out a credit card, or updates from the local council that Matt has forwarded without even looking at them. Going in the recycling bin one or two days later is hardly going to matter.'

'No, it's not a letter, it's a bigger thing,' said Evie.

'But what if it *had* been something really urgent?' Kat continued doggedly down indignation avenue. 'Or donations?'

Jenna left them debating the shortcomings of their replacement postman. Since the newspaper articles, there had been a steady influx of post at Little Paws, and their regular postman often brought with him a few sticks of celery or a couple of carrots as treats for the guinea pigs. Locals had also donated fresh vegetables, hay bales and even a few spare cages, which would come in useful when they had to separate the males. Sometimes the post was just a letter of support, with or without a donation, but there had been a few letters from local businesses offering to help out with pet supplies or equipment.

Without question, their favourites were all the letters from children, many of whom had drawn pictures of the guinea pigs in all manner of colours and with varying degrees of anatomical accuracy. The artwork was pinned up around the barn like colourful bunting.

Jenna quickly spotted the sturdy, gusseted cardboard folder sitting next to the box of cornflakes and an opened bag of crisps. Evie nearly always forgot to roll down the packets, and Jenna helped herself to a few crisps and then wiped her hands before tugging off the perforated strip of cardboard sealing the package. Inside was what looked like a thin, hardback book with a glossy cover, and as Jenna removed it, she gasped.

The front cover was a photo she had seen many times before: the strangely brilliant lights of the aurora borealis, dancing above a silhouette of trees. However this time someone had added a title in white lettering and a fancy font:

WHAT LOVE REALLY MEANS

Something twisted inside her as she read the words, and the angry exchange she had with Henry came back with perfect recall:

I didn't mean to fall in love with you.

You have no idea what love means!

A thousand questions spun round inside her. In spite of everything, she still longed to feel his arms around her again, his lips on hers, his strong, lean body pressed against her wobbly one.

Jenna had thought she knew what love was at the age

of fifteen. There had been this boy who occasionally helped out at the greengrocer's during her tenure as Saturday girl. Over several months, she had become infatuated with this muscled Adonis who lifted the heavy crates of fruit and veg with ease and gave her cheeky winks as he walked past the till. That was until the evening she saw him outside on the pavement, snogging a girl in stiletto heels and gold hooped earrings. After that, she stopped smiling at him, and ignored him altogether. One evening she confided in her mother and spilled out this tale of base treachery.

Her mother had smiled sadly, almost sympathetically, but her advice had been baffling. Love, she said, wasn't just about admiring people and being admired in return. That was lust. Or vanity. She said love ran deeper than that and you could still love someone without loving what they have done. To Jenna that hadn't made any sense. Not when that someone had gambled away your savings, your security, your home.

She had not had any contact with her father after he'd moved out, and instead had thrown her energy into supporting her mother and sister. She'd needed to be strong for them. But to love someone despite everything they had done to hurt you, the way her mother had loved her father? That was a different kind of strong altogether, and she had never measured herself against that yardstick.

The volume on her lap was one of those digital photo

books that she'd seen advertised online, but never had enough pictures to put in one nor any inclination to make one. Jenna hesitantly opened the book, and was immediately jolted out of her past into someone else's.

Chapter Thirty-Three

The Beginning

Once upon a time, a young man fell madly in love with a beautiful girl called Amelie.

What? Was that a typo? Shouldn't that say Isla? A flicker of jealousy rose within Jenna, and she waited for a few moments to tamp it down. If Henry thought this was important for her to know, then she would read it.

They were both in the final year of university and after a few months the young man was sure that this was it. That indefinable 'it' that meant forever. One day he decided to confide in her; she was the woman of his dreams and they were meant to be together. He went down on one knee and proposed to her.

Amelie turned him down. She said she was not ready for marriage, to be tied down to one person forever. But the young man was not deterred, because he adored this wild, spirited girl. He was convinced she loved him as much as he loved her and that one day soon she would say yes. As they approached the final weeks of university, he planned a wonderful celebration for when their exams were finally over.

But life is not a fairy tale and it doesn't always have a happy ever after. One morning he awoke to hear the news that Amelie had died. She had taken her own life. She had been seeing counsellors for many months. The stress of exams and being away from her family in France had been difficult, they said. Everyone accepted this sad outcome. No one pointed the finger at the young man, but he felt a weight of guilt that no exam success could eradicate. His love had driven her away. Love was dangerous.

He packed up his things and flew to the other side of world. Over the years, he grew to love his nomadic lifestyle, never staying in more than one place for too long, occasionally returning home. Along the way he met friends, travelling companions. A brave few tried to form closer attachments but they always failed. He thought he was safe. He had created an impenetrable shell that the rest of the world could not break through.

Until he met someone that did…

Jenna turned the page and stared at a photo of herself. It was taken in The Cup and Saucer teashop in Kings Hampton the day she returned his camera. There were several other photos of her looking slightly apprehensive, one with her hand on her head as she had tried (clearly unsuccessfully) to flatten the frizz.

What I Learned in Kings Hampton

Sometimes doing what you believe is right may have consequences. Choosing a course of action that is right for one person may not be right for everyone else. Sometimes it involves putting yourself out to help a stranger, where there may be an emotional as well as a financial cost.

Jenna thought back to that day. How easily she had chatted to him, how they'd forged a connection that afternoon that had stayed with her even after a relatively short period of time. She had felt straight away, on reading the letter, that she wanted to meet Henry, and despite knowing that Matt would be annoyed, and that it would cost her her bonus, she still felt compelled to carry out her plan. And knowing what she did now about what happened afterwards, she would gladly do it all over again.

She turned another page and a broad smile stretched across her face.

What I Learned at Little Paws Guinea Pig Rescue

There followed several pages of photos, both of the humans and the guinea pigs. Some of the posed shots she recognised from the calendar, others were candid shots. There was a picture of Evie and Kat together, holding Daisy and Maisie and grinning at the camera. Unlike her, they weren't worried about frizzy hair, or the stray bits of hay that were part and parcel of life with a barn full of guinea pigs. Jenna wasn't used to seeing photos of herself, especially when the pictures were taken without warning, but the one of her cradling Snickers caught her attention. Henry's photo had caught the edge of a smile as she looked down at her charge, and somehow she could feel the emotion in the picture.

If you truly care about someone or something, it is done without seeking a reward, and given freely. Love is not expecting someone to feel the same way in return, and it is not conditional. It can be expensive to pursue your dreams but when you find what makes you happy, never ever compromise.

That was what she had done with Matt. She had compromised. Traded excitement and adventure for financial security and routine. Henry had pursued his dreams – travelled the globe – and had the financial means to do so, but she wondered whether it had made him happy.

What I Learned at The Maiden Stone

The decisions you make in life will not always have the approval of your family. Sometimes you have to make difficult choices in the name of love and staying together may not be the easy option. Love is holding fast to your faith in each other and not letting your family divide you in life, or in death.

Some of the photos of the wooded glade were sepia-toned, which lent an air of aged mystery to them. There were smaller colour photos of the different woodland flowers, and a double page spread of the whole glade, with the semicircle of stones around the two standing stones at the front. There was also one of the Maiden Stone, garlanded with Jenna's flowers and a necklace of ivy, and a photo, clearly take with a good zoom lens, of Jenna perching on one of the flat stones. She was looking down and obviously concentrating on joining up the flowers she had picked.

On another page, was a picture of Jenna wearing the garland she had made. Her lips were parted in a broad smile and her loose hair almost floated around her shoulders. Henry had spent several seconds arranging it, and staring at the photo stirred up a memory of his fingers brushing lightly against her neck. It didn't look like her, not the Jenna who stared back in the mirror each morning when she brushed her hair and put on her makeup. If she was being fanciful, she might almost say she looked like a wood nymph who had paused for a moment to rest on the fallen stone with a knowing, playful smile on her face as though she realised the photographer was hiding close by.

Each page of the book brought back so many memories, and Jenna marvelled – not for the first time – at Henry's skills as a photographer. If anyone else had taken photos there in that flickering light, they would have come out either over-exposed or far too dark.

She flipped over the page and gazed in awe at yet another set of beautiful pictures.

What I Learned at Northlands Abbey

Love is not simply caring for someone; it is having the faith to keep that love even when separated by distance and time. Love is accepting the past and learning to live with it. When you find the person who is right for you, no obstacles, physical or otherwise, will keep you apart.

The photos followed a strict chronological order, the first few having been taken before sunrise. The photos captured the calm tranquillity of that morning, and there were several shots of the pink streaked sky above the ruined stone wall. As the light increased and the sky gradually morphed into its usual blue colour, the photos reflected the peace and ruined grandeur of the place. The piece de resistance was the photo of the eastern arch of the abbey, with the first rays of the sun streaking over the stones. Without doubt, that belonged in a guidebook or a travel website, and she hoped he would be paid for that one.

There were several images of their picnic, together with pictures taken – again, presumably with a zoom lens – of Jenna sitting in front of the picnic basket, holding her glass of champagne.

Jenna sighed. Forget the milk and cornflakes combo, this was the way to do breakfast, and she would remember that day forever.

The best photos of her were saved for last. For someone who was very critical of themselves in photos, she was secretly pleased to see one particular photo. It was taken while she was sitting on the stone plinth holding her glass of champagne, her body angled slightly away from the camera but with her head turned so she smiled straight into the lens.

Looking at that smile brought back every feeling that she had tried to ignore over the last few weeks. That right there was the Henry effect. That wanting to be with him, longing to speak to him five minutes after saying goodbye.

You can still love someone without loving what they have done...

'I think I understand now, Mum,' she said, placing the book on the table for a second. A small tear trickled down her cheek and she wiped it away before it could splash onto the open book. 'I'm sorry I didn't understand at the time.'

As she studied the last photo from Northlands Abbey, Jenna couldn't help but smile. It was the photo of her brazenly holding up her top so that Henry could see her T-shirt.

He had added a caption underneath, which read: *The World's Best T-Shirt (according to Jenna Oakhurst)*

This book must have taken ages to put together and the background of each page had a plain colour or textured pattern chosen to suit each section. In some cases Henry had used his own photos, fading them out to use as a background. She meant what she said earlier about contacting him and now she had an urgent reason to do so after she'd finished looking at this wonderful book.

Jenna picked it up and began reading again.

What I Learned at The Old Bookbinder's Arms

It takes courage and resilience to pursue your dreams. Holding on to your vision in spite of financial obstacles takes an enormous degree of self-belief. Sometimes the obstacles in our path may not be obvious to others, and we take for granted the things that we ourselves can easily do. But sometimes those difficulties can be overcome by simply finding an alternative solution. Take the path less travelled. The journey may be slower but the scenery will undoubtedly be worth the trip.

The final pages of photographs were taken at the pub. Mostly of the fabulous *Alice in Wonderland* decor but there was also a picture of Jenna waving a fork full of mashed potato around and one of Henry's enormous steak. In addition, there were several inside shots of areas she didn't actually remember seeing, like the one of the pink flamingos and various giant playing cards. Henry definitely hadn't taken his camera with him, and he'd only used his phone to take pictures of the food as far as she could recall, so the most obvious answer was that he went back and took these additional pictures afterwards.

She marvelled at this book he had made especially for her; no one had ever gone to that much trouble to give her something so personal. Why hadn't he got in touch, or come round in person to deliver it? Probably because her last words to him were spoken in anger at being let down without explanation or apology. Even though she'd had good reason, she regretted it all the same.

The very last page was headed *The End* and it was all text. Jenna wasn't sure she wanted to read it. Not everyone wore their hearts on their sleeve like Kat did, or had learned to cope with changes like Evie. Sometimes they hid their insecurities and fears, and sometimes a picture could say far more than words could. Maybe she had been too quick to judge. A stealthy feeling of guilt crept over her as she steeled herself to read the last page:

The End

Jenna, I hope these pictures bring back memories of happier times. After Amelie, I was scared to fall in love with anyone but it happened anyway. The last few months with you have been the happiest of my life. I'm going to Paris now, just like we talked about, and I've bought a ticket for you but whether you choose to come is up to you. I'm catching the train to London on Thursday 1st July. If you want to come on another adventure and see some magical romantic sites, meet me outside Haxford Station at half past four on Thursday. I'll be waiting for your answer.

Jenna did a quick mental calculation. Shit, that was yesterday!

'No!' she wailed. 'No, no, no, we need to talk!' Dropping the book on the table Jenna snatched up her phone. She swiftly called Henry's number but disappointingly it went straight to voicemail. What should she say? She needed to think first. Quickly she cancelled the call and opened up her emails instead.

Your wonderful book was delayed and only arrived today. I still want to go with you and—

And what? He left yesterday. He would have assumed that her silence meant she didn't want to see him. Didn't want to go. And what if he didn't have internet access and didn't read her email? Or didn't want to reply? She needed to know where he was staying in Paris, and if she couldn't find out from Henry, there was only one other obvious solution. She left the phone and hurried into the bedroom to find the spotty box, which was buried under several bags of clothes. Dimly, she heard the kitchen door bang open and Kat's voice shouting, 'So when's dinner then? I'm starving!' There was a pause followed by, 'Oh, is that your package?'

After excavating the box from under a mountain of bags, Jenna quickly pulled out the letter; the start of everything. Address memorised, she headed back to the kitchen to grab her bag and car keys.

'Jenna, just so you know—'

'Sorry, no time to chat. Forgot dinner. More sorrys. You and Evie eat, I'll be back later – I've got something urgent to do first.'

Chapter Thirty-Four

She knew the way to Kings Hampton, but traffic was irritatingly slow as she headed back into town. Logically speaking, there was no rush at all since Henry had left yesterday, but logic had nothing whatsoever to do with this. She tapped her hand impatiently on the steering wheel and prayed that someone was in. She belatedly realised she'd left her phone on the kitchen table, but even without the help of an online map she found the place without too much trouble thanks to a passing dog-walker.

Harcourt Drive was a tree-lined cul-de-sac, populated with large, detached houses. They looked relatively new, built sometime in the last ten years or so, and most had expensive looking cars parked on the driveways. Number twenty-four was tucked into a corner plot and Jenna pulled up outside. There were no obvious rules about parking round here – she'd half expected to see a sign saying *No Riff Raff* – but put up her blue badge just as a precaution.

She rang the doorbell and waited, listening for signs of activity within. She was debating whether it would be rude to ring again when the door opened to reveal a familiar, smartly dressed woman. From the slightly astonished look on her face, Natalie clearly recognised her too.

Before Natalie had a chance to say anything, Jenna got in first.

'Hi. I know Henry left yesterday but I need to know where he's staying, or how to contact him. It's urgent,' she added as Natalie seemed disinclined to respond.

Natalie pinched her lips together, suddenly reminding Jenna of Denise when she was trying to think of how to say something slightly harsh in a more diplomatic way.

'I wouldn't advise going chasing after my brother. He's always been his own person. I'm not saying this to be horrible, but as I told you before, he's—'

'Yes, I know. As I told you, I know about Isla.' Frustration coiled inside her. Every minute that she wasted here meant that Henry was going further and further away from her. 'Please, just tell me how I can contact him.'

'You tried calling him?'

'Yes, his phone's off.'

Natalie took a step backwards. 'You'd better come in. I'll call Mum.'

The doorstep seemed abnormally high, or maybe she was just abnormally tired. Either way the sudden jolt of pain as she stepped forward caused her to lose her balance. A familiar prickling, burning pain shot through her hip and she gripped the door for several seconds and screwed her face up as she took some deep breaths.

It was a different, more kindly voice that asked, 'Are you okay?'

Jenna nodded, and opened her eyes to see a woman, whom she guessed was Henry's mother, dressed in colourful shorts and a white, V-necked T-shirt. Her long hair was held back by a patterned headscarf and she smiled encouragingly as she held out her hand. Jenna allowed herself to be helped into a large airy room and sank gratefully onto an upholstered chair while her unwitting hosts bustled away to organise some refreshments despite Jenna's protests that she didn't need hospitality.

By way of a distraction from the pain, Jenna studied her surroundings. The room was furnished in tasteful, neutral shades, with the main splash of colour coming from a small potted palm, sitting in what looked like some fake gold cauldron thing and various scatter cushions on the sofa. Either side of a central fireplace were built in bookshelves, and she longed to go over and have a sneaky look. On one wall was a large, framed modern art print; then she noticed it was signed underneath and wondered if it was actually an original.

There were also several photos adorning the walls and sitting on the small unit that stood near the window. Mostly were family shots all the way from first school pictures to university graduations. She looked at the one of Henry wearing a gown and mortarboard, flanked by his parents who were beaming with pride. Henry's expression was more guarded though, and the smile didn't quite reach the corners of his eyes.

'Here you go,' said his mother, appearing in the doorway carrying a tray, which she put on the coffee table. 'Sorry we weren't properly introduced'—she held out her hand—'I'm Celia, Henry's mother. Natalie tells me you run a guinea pig rescue. Henry mentioned that he'd adopted one.'

'Yes, he has,' said Jenna, ignoring the other inaccuracies and desperate to get to the point of her visit. 'Sorry to intrude on your evening like this but I needed to find out where he's gone. And when he's due back. I was going to go with him you see, and…' Her voice started to resonate with emotion. 'Well … there's been some misunderstandings and … things,' she added lamely. How could she explain that she felt let down, sad, confused and desperate all at the same time?

'You're talking about the planning meeting,' said Celia, putting a small table next to Jenna and handing her a cup of tea. 'Yes, I'm afraid my husband laid down the law on that one – Nat's first major client. Henry hadn't told us anything about his involvement; it was only because he was busy tapping away on his phone at the breakfast table that we asked what he was doing, and then of course it all came out, and Natalie was furious. My husband made it clear that as long as he lived in this house he had to respect his family. Poor Henry, he was in an impossible position; he and Nat aren't close anyway so he had no idea about whom she was representing.' She wrung her hands together delicately. 'My husband understands business very well, but he doesn't understand our son. Has never understood, really.' She sighed. 'Something happened while he was at university and—'

'He's told me about Amelie,' Jenna blurted out.

Celia raised an expressive eyebrow. 'Then you must be special. He begged me never to tell Natalie.' She picked up her cup and took a sip before continuing. 'Henry has always been measured up against his older sister, but he couldn't face being coerced into an office job just to keep his father happy. He needed some space, he wanted to get away, so I gave him the money to travel.' She sighed. 'You just want your children to be happy, don't you? It doesn't matter whether they have a fancy job title. And of course he's now financially independent and he earns good money from his photos.' There was more than a hint of pride in her voice.

Neither of Jenna's parents had ever asked whether she was happy. And without the means to get away, she had just retreated to her books and their exciting fantasy worlds.

With a sudden clarity of insight, Jenna realised how the knowledge that he had let her down through something out of his control might have triggered earlier memories. 'Mrs Somners, I think he's just scared of getting close to people and hurting them, but he needs to stop running away because I can't run as fast as he does. I wish he'd been able to talk to me about this before he upped and went, but I'm not giving up without trying.'

Celia looked at her watch. 'Well, technically, he hasn't upped and gone anywhere yet.'

'What do you mean?'

'He went to London yesterday and was planning to do a few things. You know Henry, he doesn't tell me much about his itinerary, and he rarely has his phone on when he's travelling, but I know he's taking the Eurostar tonight.'

Chapter Thirty-Five

A raid-the-fridge supper was in progress with Val when Jenna burst back into the kitchen.

'Where've you been!' cried Evie.

'We were worried about you after we read Henry's—'

'Kat!'

'What? She left the book open on the table. It's so romantic.' She swayed and clasped her hands together in a very un-Kat-like gesture.

'I went to see Henry's mother. He hasn't left yet so there's still time.'

'Time for what?' asked Evie. 'You're over him, aren't you?'

'Of course she isn't,' said Kat. 'Just look at her.'

'But Jen, I thought you said—'

'I know, I know. But it feels wrong just letting him go. I'm sorry, I have to do this. I need to see him and it might be my last chance. His train leaves tonight at half past eight.'

Jenna hobbled into the bedroom followed by the others. She grabbed her small wheelie holdall and deftly chucked in a T-shirt, underwear, hairbrush and makeup bag.

'Jen, it's already nearly half past six – you might have to wait ages for a train. Are you sure you want to do this?'

'Never been surer of anything,' she replied, wincing as she knelt on the carpet and pulled out the metal document box with her financial paperwork in.

Evie knelt beside her. 'Tell me what you're looking for and I can help.'

'My passport.'

Evie stared at her. 'You're going to…'

'France. Yes.'

'But you've never been abroad.'

Jenna stared at her sister. 'I know. Isn't it brilliant? It's going to be an adventure!'

'It's going to be a disaster,' said Kat emphatically. 'I can see your leg's playing up and you don't even know what time the trains go from Haxford.'

Jenna turned away, her eyes blinking back tears. 'I know. It sounds mad, even to me, but I have to do this. Don't ask me why, I just do.' She pulled out her passport and wedged it into her handbag.

'You can't go on the train. Not like this.'

'Fine, I'll take the car.'

'That's ridiculous. St Pancras is in the middle of

London, not Haxford with its half empty municipal car park. There won't be any parking for miles.'

'Kat, please don't—'

Val hovered in the doorway. 'Anything I can do to help?'

'Val, you talk some sense into her,' said Kat, throwing Jenna a pointed look.

'Jenna, love, is this really important?'

'Yes.'

'Like regret-for-the-rest-of-your-life-if-you-don't-try important?'

'Yes!'

'Right. I'll drive you. Then you can just hop out right at the door.'

'Val, that's not a good idea,' Kat muttered, but Jenna carefully got to her feet and promptly threw her arms around Val's neck. 'Has anyone told you you're wonderful?'

'Well, I'm coming with you,' announced Evie.

'Ooh, it's just like one of them romantic films,' said Val happily.

'Is no one listening to me?' said Kat loudly. 'This is not a good idea!'

'You can stay behind then and miss all the excitement,' replied Evie.

'Not bloody likely,' Kat huffed. 'Come on then, get a shift on.'

While Val tidied up in the kitchen, the three of them flew into a frenzy of activity. Jenna packed her medication and a few extra clothes, Evie ran into the bathroom to seize Jenna's toiletries, and Kat grabbed a bottle of water and some biscuits.

Two minutes later, they had piled into Val's car, Kat in the front and Evie with Jenna in the back, and heading towards the M40 as fast as speed limits would allow. However, it wasn't long before they encountered traffic and Jenna felt her anxiety levels rise with each hold up.

'Are you sure this is the quickest way to the motorway?'

'Yes, the satnav tells you the quickest route.'

She drummed her fingers against the inside of the door. 'Why is there so much traffic?'

'It's Friday evening. Relax.'

'I can't!'

'Jen, Val's going as fast as she can.'

'And I forgot my phone charger!'

'Why don't we go back and just ring Henry instead?' Kat suggested.

'I tried that. There's no answer. I'll just leave my phone off so it doesn't run down.'

Once they reached the motorway, the traffic moved better and they were soon bowling along. Evie gave Jenna her phone so that she could check the route for herself.

Celia had said the train left at 20:31 but there must be some sort of check-in first. Henry had obviously got a ticket for her already, but as she hadn't showed up yesterday would he have kept it or had he already thrown it away?

The traffic slowed again as they reached the intersection with the M25. Then the M40 became the A40 as they reached the outskirts of London. Even though there were still three lanes of traffic, it was now much slower and the greenery of the countryside was replaced by concrete buildings on both sides of the road. Ahead, Jenna could see tower blocks in the distance and then they were crawling over some sort of giant flyover. Under other circumstances this sightseeing tour might have been interesting but now the sight of cars stretching into the distance just ramped her agitation up another few notches.

She watched the minutes tick by, frustrated by their lack of progress, and regretting not catching the train. Five minutes later, after checking the train times on Evie's phone, she consoled herself with the thought that the planned engineering works coupled with the need to get across London on a Friday night would almost certainly have scuppered any chance of getting there on time. And that was assuming her leg wasn't playing silly buggers. Which it currently was.

As the traffic slowed, the minutes strangely seemed to go faster and now she could no longer bear to look. She chewed her lip, trying unsuccessfully to empty her head.

'It's not far now,' shouted Kat as though she was sitting in another room and not the seat in front. 'That's Midland Road over there. I think that's the closest we're going to get.'

Jenna rechecked her handbag. Passport. Phone.

Money. That's all she needed. She looked at her watch. It was ten minutes past eight. They could still do this.

Leaving Val to park they bundled out of the car; Evie grabbed her case, but even without any luggage to cart around, the pain in Jenna's hip prevented anything other than a slow limp. Still, she gritted her teeth and pushed through the pain. All she wanted was to see Henry, to talk to him, to just be with him. Because there was a Henry-sized hole in her heart that hurt far more than any body parts, and was not dulled by medication.

Kat had run on ahead. If anyone could stop a train from departing, it would be Kat. However, seconds later she was running back towards them pushing a trolley.

'Here you go,' she said, panting slightly. 'This will speed things up a bit.'

Evie dumped the case on the trolley.

Kat pointed. 'Get on! You'll never make it at the pace you're going.'

'The trolley is for luggage, not people,' argued Jenna.

'And it says that where exactly? You're obsessed with rules. Anyway blue badge holders are probably exempt so get a move on.'

Jenna wasn't sure of Kat's logic but gingerly climbed onto the trolley and perched on top of her case. Being designed for the conveyance of suitcases, there wasn't a huge amount of legroom but she hugged her knees with one hand, using the other to grip the tubular metal.

Kat pushed the trolley in the same manner that she drove her car; the only difference was that inside the car, the advice Kat proffered to other motorists and errant pedestrians went largely unheard unless the windows were open, whereas the milling crowds outside St Pancras had no such immunity.

'Honestly, people just don't look where they're going!' Kat puffed as the speeding trolley rammed into another startled commuter.

'Out of the way!' she shouted as she pushed her way through a group of young women gathering for some unknown purpose on the pavement.

Jenna kept her head down and eyes averted, and made a mental note never to let Kat near the steering end of a wheelchair. She sensed, rather than saw everyone's stares of surprise, but as they barged into the station concourse she carefully lifted her gaze, scanning the crowds for a mop of blonde hair. He had to be here. It was just a question of whether he was waiting for her with a ticket, or whether he had already given up hope and got on the train.

The clock display said 20:15. Sixteen minutes in which to find Henry. Jenna felt almost sick with apprehension, and her limbs were jammed together in an uncomfortable position, which was now verging on the acutely painful. The place was a noisy amalgamation of people hurrying in every direction, the majority of whom, it seemed, were obstructing their progress. Jenna dimly wondered how many people would find bruises on their ankles tomorrow morning.

'International departures this way,' said Evie, tugging

Kat's arm and pointing. Thirty seconds later they were staring at a queue of people.

'Is this the check-in?' asked Evie.

'Looks like it. But there are automated ticket barriers.' Kat looked down at her charge. 'Did Henry's mum give you your ticket?'

'No.'

'So you don't have an actual ticket?'

'No. Henry was doing all that.' Jenna's voice wavered uncertainly. She was used to planning things. Organising her own life. Not relying on other people. 'But now I'm here I can still buy one,' she said decisively.

'Wait there, I'll go and find out,' said Kat.

'No you can't,' said Evie quietly, as she stared at her phone.

'What do you mean? Of course I can. There's a man in uniform over there.' Kat jabbed her finger in the direction of the ticket barrier.

'I don't mean no you can't ask; I mean no you can't buy a ticket. It says on the Eurostar website that check-in closes half an hour before departure and it's now twenty past.'

'But – but I need to be on the train!' said Jenna, climbing awkwardly off the trolley and holding onto it for balance. She stared around wildly, looking for someone – anyone – who looked like Henry. If he had checked in, he'd still be looking out for her, wouldn't he?

'Could she get a ticket for the next train?' asked Kat.

'I don't know if there is a next train. And even if she

got to France, then what will she do?' demanded Evie. 'I don't like the idea of her going on her own.'

'Will you two stop talking about me as though I'm not here!' shouted Jenna. She grabbed the handle of her case and ignoring her minders, walked as fast as she could manage over to the ticket barrier. She could explain what had happened. Maybe they could tell whether Henry had checked in yet.

'Excuse me, I need some assistance.'

The uniformed official seemed uninterested in her urgent mission and was unable to tell her whether Henry had checked in, simply confirming that boarding for the 20:31 train to Paris had closed. The next available train was tomorrow morning. Did she want to buy a ticket now?

Jenna felt numb; like when you had a filling at the dentist and your face was still there, but not quite part of you as you remembered it; except it was not just her face but her whole body that felt disconnected. She forced her feet back towards her sister and as she got closer, shook her head. Tears pricked the back of her eyes. She had tried so hard and had come so close. Now Henry was sitting on that train, thinking she had deserted him.

Evie flung her arms around her sister. 'Oh Jen, I'm so sorry, we tried our best. And you can still send him an email tomorrow.'

'Bloody jobsworth!' said Kat loudly. She marched over to the ticket barrier and cupped her hands around her mouth.

'Henry Somners! Can you hear me? Are you there? Jenna is waiting for you!'

Several people stopped to see what was happening and several more got out their phones as if there might be something interesting to record.

'Henry! Henry Somners!' Kat yelled again with the volume control turned up to maximum. 'Where are you?'

Two officials briskly moved over to speak to Kat, and Jenna watched as they engaged in what was clearly a frank exchange of views. 'She's amazing, isn't she?'

Evie took her hand and gave it a gentle squeeze. 'I think it's time to go and find Val.'

Jenna remained rooted to the spot. She couldn't go – not just yet. She had seen those films where the train leaves and then amazingly the hero is left standing on the platform, although admittedly that was in fictional, make-believe worlds, not the real world. In the real world, people got let down, left behind, hurt. But she tried to cling on to the belief that just for once it might be true.

They couldn't see much beyond the ticket barrier, but in her mind she could picture him standing on the platform, waiting for her. He'd be wearing his tired looking jeans and an unironed rugby shirt, and probably sporting a sexy two-day stubble. He wouldn't leave without her.

Kat flounced back, clearly unsuccessful in her attempts to negotiate with Eurostar officialdom, and now all they could do was wait. As the long seconds stretched into long minutes, no one said anything. Jenna climbed back onto her suitcase and her eyes flicked from her watch to the ticket barrier as the words she had read such a short time ago played through her head.

Love is holding fast to your faith in each other...

When you find the person who is right for you, no obstacles, physical or otherwise, will keep you apart...

Right now there was a large metal barrier between them but this time she would trust him; she would not make the same mistake again.

'He will come,' she said quietly, as if to reassure herself as much as the others.

There were no more Eurostar trains leaving that evening. The queues had disappeared and the crowds had thinned, but still she waited as the clock drew nearer to 20:40, then 20:50 ... then 20:55.

Only when it got to nine o'clock did Jenna finally accept he was not coming back. She had almost believed her fantasy, but Henry had not stood on the platform watching the train depart, he had been on it. And he had taken her heart with him. Slow, silent tears trickled down her cheeks as Kat pushed the trolley back out of the station, retracing their steps to where Val was waiting outside with the car, and Evie climbed into the back with Jenna.

No one spoke, and as they made their way back out of London, Jenna turned her face towards the window as the tears turned into loud, gulping sobs of despair. He had loved her. And for the second time she had let him go. If she had left work earlier, she could have bought a ticket and boarded that train. She didn't want her ordinary world anymore, she wanted to explore his. With Henry. Kind, wonderful, funny Henry.

She tortured herself with thoughts of what she wished she had said or done. Was this how her mum had felt when Dad left them? Jenna had often heard her mum crying in her room in the dark, and she had always assumed it was because she was missing their house, her jewellery, her financial security. It had never once occurred to her that what was missing was the person who, despite everything, her mum still loved.

Evie reached out every so often to squeeze her hand or rub her arm, but Jenna was too miserable to respond. Her sister spoke only once, to ask her if she didn't want to switch her phone back on, and maybe she could leave a message? Jenna didn't answer.

It was dark by the time they had escaped the busy-ness of London and they sped along the country roads as if in silent agreement that the quicker they got home the better. There were no streetlights along Nethercott Lane and as they turned up the track towards Farm Cottage, Jenna stared at the place that had become home, but would now only be a temporary one. It had been daylight when they left so no one had thought to switch on the outside light, but for a few seconds until the engine was turned off, the car head-lights threw a beam of light across the front of the cottage.

'I don't believe it,' muttered Kat. 'I think someone's dumped a container. I hope that's not full of guinea pigs like last month.'

'No, it's just the rubbish sacks,' replied Evie. 'I left them round the front so we could take them to the tip tomorrow.'

Jenna sat up and stared. 'It's a rucksack.' She tugged at the door handle. 'It's Henry's rucksack!'

'No, Jen, it's just the—'

Jenna grimaced as she got out of the car. And then out of the shadows a silhouette of a tall, lanky figure appeared in front of the barn.

'What the hell?' said Kat.

'Is that who I think it is?' asked Evie.

'Ooh, it's like *Brief Encounter*!' said Val in a wobbly voice.

Jenna managed two tired steps before her foot slid on the gravel and she grabbed hold of the wing mirror for balance. In a few bounds Henry had closed the space between them.

'How on earth… When did you… But I thought…' The words came out in a jumble as she tried to make sense of what she was seeing.

Henry made no answer but just gently embraced her. His mouth found hers and then nothing else mattered. Not the waiting, not the questions. Just her Henry, holding her close and kissing her tenderly, then with passion as she responded.

Long seconds passed and when the kiss finally ended, Jenna noticed the others had vanished, and lights were on inside the cottage.

'You look exhausted,' said Henry as he gently stroked her hair. 'Shall we go inside?'

Jenna tucked her arm through his but Henry didn't move. 'Oh no. Remember the rules? I'm in charge of the transportation. Jane Austen swoon or Charge of the Light Brigade?'

'Ms Austen please,' said Jenna. 'I don't think I can manage the other today.'

Henry leaned over and she wrapped her arms around his neck, and then for several blissful seconds she was held against his chest.

The front door mysteriously opened as they approached and Henry carried Jenna through the kitchen and into the lounge. He deposited her carefully on the sofa, then removed his boots and sat on the carpet beside her.

Evie fetched her a drink and some painkillers, and there were a few brief seconds of calm before everyone started talking over each other.

'So how long had you been waiting out there?'

'Where's your car? How did you get here?'

'Why aren't you in Paris?'

'Were you even at the station?'

'Whoa!' Henry laughed and held up his hand. 'One at a time, please.' He then took Jenna's hand in his. 'I wanted to go to Paris with you, but then, when I didn't hear back, I didn't know what to think. It was arrogant to assume that I was automatically forgiven, but I booked the tickets, just in case, and went to stay overnight with a friend in London. I had every intention of leaving as planned, but then miraculously, at the last minute, I got your email. I read it a hundred times and realised I couldn't leave without you. If it was a choice between travelling by myself or scrubbing out guinea pig hutches for eternity with you, then this is where I'd rather be. So, I caught the train back to Haxford and then a taxi here.' He lifted Jenna's hand and pressed his warm lips against it. 'Does that answer everyone's questions?'

'Yes,' said Kat loudly.

'No,' corrected Jenna. 'And by the way I still want to go to Paris. But what I don't understand is, what email are you referring to?'

'The one you sent earlier this evening.'

Jenna frowned. She hadn't sent anything. Was this all just some lovely co-codamol-induced dream that was about to evaporate?

'But some of the things that you wrote—' Henry hesitated. 'Sorry, I don't understand.'

Evie and Val were looking similarly baffled but Kat was fidgeting in a distinctly shifty manner.

'Kat, is there something you'd like to share with us?' Jenna asked sharply.

'No.'

Evie looked at her. 'Kat?'

'Yes okay, I sent it,' she huffed.

Several pairs of eyes stared at her in astonishment.

Jenna stretched out her hand and Evie passed her her

phone, which she quickly scanned for messages. 'I don't understand, there's nothing on here.'

'I deleted it afterwards,' said Kat defiantly. 'Look – you love him. He clearly loves you. You two just needed a shove in the right direction. You rushed off, leaving your phone lying on the kitchen table with a half-finished email, so I just … well, I just added a bit.' Kat shrugged. 'I figured it was easier to ask for forgiveness than ask for permission.'

'And here's me thinking fairy godmothers only ever wore floaty, white dresses,' said Henry as everyone laughed.

'Well, that would be completely impractical for looking after a shedload of guinea pigs,' replied Kat, brushing stray ginger hairs from her own black top.

Evie jumped up. 'That reminds me, we'd better go and check on the piggies before we turn in for the night. There are a few evenings meds still to sort out.'

'And I need to get home,' said Val with a yawn.

'And I need my bed,' added Jenna. She stretched out her hand to Henry. 'Is my transportation card still valid?'

Henry leapt to his feet and tugged his imaginary fore-lock. 'It certainly is, ma'am.' He carefully scooped her off the sofa and carried her towards the door.

Jenna relished the warmth of his body, breathed in the smell of him and sighed contentedly. Sometimes being a bit wobbly definitely had its compensations. She gestured with her hand. 'It's the second door on the right.'

As he carried her out, Jenna heard her sister murmur

something to Kat. Evie was too quiet, but she caught Kat's response, which sailed back through the partly closed door with only a mere hint of volume reduction. 'Of course Henry doesn't need the camp bed. What century are you in, woman?'

Jenna blushed furiously but Henry just laughed as he lay her down on her bed and then flashed a cheeky grin. 'No pressure. It's your call, I can get a cab home.'

'Or a lift with Val?' offered a disembodied voice from the hallway. 'She hasn't left yet.'

'Will you two go away!' shouted Jenna, trying not to laugh. 'Honestly, the food here might be good but the privacy leaves something to be desired.'

Jenna waited until she was sure her erstwhile minders had scuttled off before she replied to Henry. 'If it's my call, then I'd like you to stay.'

Henry sat down on the bed next to her, his eyes searching hers. He leaned over and stroked his fingers over her face, then planted fluttering kisses over the same path. His lips moved sensuously over her cheek and along her neck, and Jenna squirmed with pleasure as she slid her hands around his shoulders to pull him closer. 'In that case,' he murmured, 'I'd better go and find my boots and retrieve my rucksack before your sister locks up for the night. I think it's still in the yard. I'll be really quick.'

Jenna reluctantly relaxed her grip as he eased himself away. 'Okay. Just mind the legs of that—'

'Ow!'

'Clothes rail,' finished Jenna.

Chapter Thirty-Six

The first thing Jenna's brain registered the following morning was the sound of chatter coming from the kitchen. The second was that yesterday evening had not been a dream after all. She smiled to herself as she replayed the memories, the majority of which definitely earned a certificate-18 rating. She sighed contentedly and snuggled up to the warm body lying next to her.

'Izzit morning?' mumbled Henry. 'What's the time?'

Jenna lifted her head and peered at her bedside clock. 'Just gone seven,' she whispered.

Henry lifted his arm so that Jenna could lay her head on his shoulder. He smelt warm and sexy, and she stroked her fingers across his bare chest. She recalled how, at their afternoon tea at DeLaneys, she had wondered what lay underneath his designer shirt. She had certainly satisfied her curiosity on that score, but it seemed she was not the only one thinking about items of clothing.

'So you know that T-shirt of yours?' Henry said sleepily.

'Any particular one?'

'The one you showed me at Northlands Abbey.'

Jenna smiled. 'What about it?'

'It was right.'

Jenna giggled and hooked her leg over his.

'You know what?' she murmured after a few minutes. 'This is very comfortable for my leg.'

Henry made a sleepy sort of amused sound. 'Very pleased to hear you are happy with your naked leg rest, Princess Jenna.'

Their quiet intimacy was short-lived as a few seconds later a shriek echoed down the hallway and Jenna sat bolt upright. 'What the—?'

Evie's normally quiet voice yelled, 'Kat, look at this! Look at this!' which was swiftly followed by an even louder shriek and some triumphant expletives.

Jenna grabbed last night's T-shirt, which had been tossed aside, and tugged it over her head. 'I'll go and see what the commotion is about.'

Stepping carefully around the foot of the clothes rail, she made her way into the kitchen to find Evie and Kat huddled in front of Evie's laptop. They were both staring at the Little Paws Go Fund Me Page.

'Did we wake you up? Sorry, sis, but look at this!' Evie pointed at the screen. 'Just look at this! An anonymous donor has just contributed £5500! Five thousand five hundred pounds! Isn't that amazing?

Most people just give a tenner, maybe twenty, but this is insane!'

'It's bloody brilliant, that's what it is,' said Kat, waving the cornflakes box in the air and showering cereal flakes over the keyboard.

Evie shook her head as if she still couldn't quite take it in. 'But why do you suppose they wanted to be anonymous? We can't even send them a thank you card.'

'Who knows?' said Kat. 'Maybe they pressed the wrong button? Maybe they're a celebrity and prefer being anonymous instead of splashing their name everywhere.'

'Or maybe it's someone with a guilty conscience who wanted to make a charitable donation to make up for their previous dishonest activity,' suggested Jenna.

Evie wrinkled her nose. 'Sorry, sis, that doesn't sound very likely. I prefer Kat's idea. I'm going to tell everyone it was from a famous girl band.'

'But everyone will think it's from Little Mix,' said Jenna, trying not to laugh.

'It might be for all we know. Do they like guinea pigs? I bet they do.'

'Who cares who it's from?' said Kat. 'It means we can afford to put down a deposit on someplace else. I'm going to start looking right away.'

'I'm going to tell the piggies they're all safe,' said Evie, excitement written all over her face.

Jenna yawned. 'In that case, I'm going back to bed.'

'Short on sleep, eh?' Kat gave her a sly wink. Jenna looked down as she hurried out, blushing guiltily.

'Well, that's good news,' said Jenna as she shut the bedroom door and edged back under the duvet.

'Yes, I caught the gist of it,' laughed Henry. 'Does Kat have a volume control button somewhere?'

Jenna smiled as she stretched out next to him. 'If she did, it broke years ago. But you know what? She's one of the most kind-hearted people I have ever met.'

'She's also surprisingly adept at composing romantic emails.'

'And that reminds me, what precisely did she write on my behalf?'

Henry tapped his nose. 'Spoilers, Princess Jenna.'

'But I need to know!'

'No you don't. You need to trust the people who have your best interests at heart.'

Jenna opened her mouth to protest, then thought better of it.

'You see, you can do it if you try.' Henry chuckled as he threw back the duvet and stretched. 'I'm going to get ready. What time does breakfast end at this establishment?'

'It's an eat all day sort of place, really. The house speciality is romaine lettuce and red pepper salad,' added Jenna with a knowing smile. 'It's Snickers' favourite.'

'That's good to know. As soon as I'm dressed, I want to go and see my favourite boy. And you need to decide whether you'd still like to go to Paris or whether you want to go somewhere else.'

Jenna sat up carefully and swung her legs over the side

of the bed. 'Paris works for me. But you'll have a problem with Q. We might have to skip that letter.'

'What are you on about?'

'Your idea of trips through the alphabet.'

'But that was just a thing that Isla and I did. I know it was stupid really, and it didn't end all that well so—'

'But I love that idea! I think we should carry it on. It'll be fun looking for places to visit,' Jenna said, now fired up with the idea. 'Although I'm not going to be finishing her cross-stitch project, that's way out of my league.'

'What sort of places did you have in mind?'

Jenna reached for his hand and Henry pulled her gently to her feet and wrapped his arms around her. Jenna thought for a moment. 'Well, obviously it would have to be somewhere scenic and magical.'

Henry grinned. 'Of course.'

'And romantic.'

Henry's hands slipped under her loose-fitting T-shirt. 'You're not asking much are you?' He gently lowered his face until his nose touched hers. 'And what about your job? Don't you need to book the time off? I thought you were always busy?'

Jenna smiled. 'I reckon they owe me a few favours.'

Chapter Thirty-Seven

Kronborg Slot, also known as Elsinore Castle, sits on the north-eastern tip of the beautiful Danish island of Zealand. It is under an hour's drive from Copenhagen (or forty-five minutes by train) and well worth a visit. There has been a stronghold on this narrow strip of water since the 1400s, but in the sixteenth century, King Frederick II turned it into a Renaissance castle. To many people, Kronborg is best known as the setting for Shakespeare's Hamlet. *It is also the resting place of Holger Danske. The statue of Holger Danske is in the dungeons. The floor is cobbled, but manageable with help if you go slowly and carefully.*

According to legends, Holger Danske (also known as Ogier the Dane) was the son of a Danish king who fought many battles in France, before walking home to Kronborg. There he fell asleep for so long that his beard grew through the table and reached to the ground. The legend says that Holger Danske will wake and rise again to save the country if Denmark is in peril.

'Y ou're turning into a proper old romantic,' observed Henry as he sat down on the bench next to her, reading over her shoulder. 'I thought you didn't believe in all these myths and legends.'

'Oi! Just because I don't know as many as you do, doesn't make me an ignoramus!'

'The lady doth protest too much, methinks.'

'And you've got carried away with being Prince of Denmark,' Jenna teased.

'But you can't deny that you like facts and proof.'

Jenna batted him playfully with her notebook. 'You converted me. And anyhow I've got proof.' Jenna held up her left hand to admire the ruby and diamond ring sitting snugly on her fourth finger. 'The maiden of the woods was right, wasn't she? I did find the true meaning of happiness.'

Jenna often thought back to that peaceful afternoon in the woodland glade, making her garland of spring flowers and her whispered request which, just five months later, had been answered when Henry had proposed under the entrance arch of Tivoli Gardens. She had been engaged for four whole days and it still felt like something straight from the pages of a story book. Not bad work for a centuries old lump of stone; one day she would go back there to say thank you.

They had bolted on a quick trip up the coast after spending five days in Copenhagen, sightseeing and exploring. She loved it here in Denmark and had been keeping a diary of everywhere they had been so that she could share it with Evie and Kat when they returned.

A gust of wind blew in from the Øresund and whipped her hair around her face.

It's often windy in Denmark, remember to tie your hair back, she added in her notebook.

This part of Denmark was totally different to the bustling, lively streets of Copenhagen, but it still had a very warm and welcoming feel. And with the castle right on the coast, it was like being inside a fairy tale. Sitting here looking out across the Øresund Sound – the narrow stretch of water that separated Sweden from Denmark – she could almost imagine the sound of cannons booming as they would have centuries ago to ward off intruders.

'So how does Zealand score on the Jenna rating then?' Henry asked as he watched her scribble a few more notes. 'Copenhagen Airport seemed very efficient.'

'Yes, the flight scores highly,' agreed Jenna. 'We can hardly deduct points because the airline staff called me "love".'

'And "sweetheart",' laughed Henry, pretending to dodge out of the way of her notebook.

'And at the Danish end they collect you by wheelchair, not one of those multi-person buggy things. When we went to Venice, if you remember, I had to sit for fifteen minutes listening to some woman telling me how practising mindfulness would help me to walk further, while you jogged behind with a big smirk on your face.'

'I do remember that, yes,' said Henry with a grin. 'But

on the plus side Venice scored highly for the romantic setting. Especially the island of Murano.'

Jenna fingered the necklace of Murano glass beads that hung around her neck. 'So what scores highest on the scenic scale for you?'

Henry thought for a second. 'You know what? I'm a bit of a sucker for all those Welsh hills and castles.'

'So that's nothing to do with the fact that you sold three of your photos from that trip to a publisher then?' she teased.

Henry pretended to look offended. 'Certainly not!'

'Some of it wasn't all that accessible though.'

'True.' Henry looked around him. 'It's easier here, Zealand is very flat. And scenic.'

'And the people are lovely.'

'So ending on a high score, then.'

'Who says it has to be the end?

'Because Z is the end of the alphabet, my illiterate princess.'

'But why can't we start again with A?'

Henry laughed and kissed her cheek. 'Luckily for you, I love you from A to Z and round again. So where do you fancy going on our next trip next then?'

'Somewhere scenic and romantic.'

'Goes without saying.'

'And fully accessible.' Jenna's imagination fired up. 'We can compile an A to Z of romantic accessible destinations and put it all in a blog – there must be loads of people who would find it useful to have access to that kind of information on different places.'

'Sounds good to me. Any pictures required for this blog of yours?'

'Absolutely.'

'Good answer.' Henry kissed her again. 'Are you okay if I go and take a few more photos here before the weather changes? The sky's looking a bit grey over there.'

'I'm fine. I'll check in and see what's happening back at Little Paws.'

Snickers' Facebook page had originally been set up to promote calendar sales, but the loveable guinea pig now had a massive following of his own, thanks to the newspaper articles from earlier in the year. Over the summer, Evie and Kat had posted (on Snickers' behalf) a steady stream of exceptionally cute baby guinea pig pictures, many taken by Henry, and Snickers' offspring had even featured in a couple of adverts courtesy of Henry's photography agency.

Today's post said:

Exciting news! I have another new girlfriend! Chloe can't be rehomed because she's blind, but she's very cute.

Jenna smiled at the pictures. The loveable rogue was building up quite a harem now he was safely neutered. She thought for a few seconds and then added a comment:

Congratulations Snickers! Looking forward to seeing you again soon.

P.S. I've got some exciting news for you too!

Acknowledgments

Thank you for choosing to read my book, and I hope you enjoyed reading it as much as I did writing it. After years of writing and daydreaming about being an author, it's a real dream come true to finally be published. However, this book would never have happened without the help and support of many other people, and perhaps a sprinkling of magic too.

First and foremost, my heartfelt thanks to all the team at One More Chapter and in particular my wonderful editor, Charlotte Ledger, who believed in this book from the very beginning and has been such a great support to me as a newbie author. I am also hugely grateful to Dushi Horti for her comprehensive editing.

My journey to publication has been full of ups and downs, but being awarded the Katie Fforde Bursary in 2020 was a real pinch-me-I'm-dreaming moment, and it gave me the impetus I needed to keep going. I will be eternally grateful to Katie Fforde, and her trophy definitely has some magic in it! The Romantic Novelists' Association has also played a big part, and without joining the RNA's New Writers' Scheme I don't think I would have reached this point at all. Many thanks to the RNA reader who critiqued an early version of the manuscript, to Alison May, book doctor extraordinaire, to Jules Wake for her kind words of encouragement and to the eagle-eyed Julia Williams – she knows what for and is probably still laughing about it. Thanks also to everyone who has made me feel welcome at meetings or just stopped by to say hello on social media. My fellow RNA Surrey Buddies deserve special thanks; you have shared the celebrations and given support during the tough times, and I feel lucky to belong to such a wonderful group of writers.

Writing often involves research, and I'd like to thank Vivien Duval-Steer for answering all my questions about council planning meetings, and patiently explaining how the system works. Any inaccuracies are, of course, down to me. Thanks also to Denise Sutherland for enlightening me on expenses dodges – for avoidance of doubt, this was in connection with other people's, not her own. I also need to thank Sue Tate of Cavy Corner for giving up her precious time to answer guinea pig-related questions. Sue – along with her amazing team of volunteers – does in real life what Evie and Kat do at Little Paws Guinea Pig Rescue (obviously without the baby boom mishap!)

To all my family and friends who have followed the saga: Linda Corbett is trying to write a book – thank you for staying with me on this journey and I look forward to celebrating with you. Occasionally real life makes its way into a book, and I am indebted to my sister, Diana Wood, for giving up entire weekends each year to do our guinea pig calendar photo shoot – so many memories (and so many chewed props!) Last but certainly not least, thanks to my wonderful husband, Andrew, who has cleaned the house, cooked dinners, watered the garden and generally kept everything else running while I sat at my laptop every day. I love you from A to Z and round again.

What Would Jane Austen Do?

LINDA CORBETT

Read on for an exclusive extract from the brand new
novel from Linda Corbett…

Available to pre-order in ebook and paperback now!

Chapter One

There is a stubbornness about me that never can bear to be frightened at the will of others. My courage always rises at every attempt to intimidate me.
Elizabeth Bennett, *Pride & Prejudice*

It was a truth universally acknowledged that being on your own on 14th February entitled one to feel miserable, but being dumped by your employer on Valentine's Day demonstrated a staggering level of mean-spiritedness… and came with an additional financial problem.

Maddy stared at the email on her phone for what felt like the millionth time.

We are sorry to advise…

This was a clearly a business definition of the word sorry that wasn't even distantly related to regret or apology. Why did they feel her column was no longer required for the magazine? Did she even have any right to object?

We *wish you every success in the future*...

So what future were they referring to? The one where she couldn't afford to rent in even the scruffiest part of London and was forced to go back to living with Mum and Dad? Not to mention letting down her best friend who would have to find another flatmate otherwise she would also be in the same pecuniary position.

Once word got around, any requests for blog interviews or podcasts, like the one she was supposed to be doing this evening, would quickly dry up. No one wanted an ex-agony aunt. A few tears escaped and splashed onto the screen, and she wiped them away angrily.

Maddy wouldn't even have minded quite so much if she'd hated her job, but she enjoyed being the love and relationship correspondent for UpClose magazine and especially loved her weekly column, *Dear Jane*. 'Jane' received plenty of requests every week, and many of the emails and letters were actually thanking her for the advice. Now she was effectively jobless with one month's pay in lieu of notice and the barest minimum redundancy payment. A sick empty feeling lodged in her stomach as she turned back to her dressing table.

The voice of her flatmate was therefore a welcome intrusion. 'Can I come in, Madds? I've brought you something.'

'Is it a winning lottery ticket by any chance?'

'Nope, but maybe the next best thing,' Alice said as she pushed the door open and put a glass of chilled white wine next to the eyeshadow compact. 'Here, have a have swig of this.'

Maddy took an appreciative sip before returning to her make-up, which now needed a bit of repair.

'So, you're still going ahead with the podcast interview thingy?'

Maddy paused with the powder brush in her hand and looked at her flat mate Alice in the mirror. 'That's the plan.'

'I just thought that... you know... you might not feel like—'

'—chatting about romance and relationships when I'm single and on top of that I've been sacked on Valentine's Day?' Maddy finished for her. 'There's definitely an irony there somewhere.'

'Still, at least you get to meet that swoon-worthy crime writer,' replied Alice, hugging herself. 'Can you sit together so you can gaze at his gorgeous bod?'

'Nice try. However, in the first place it's not that sort of interview, I just happen to be the next guest on the panel. Secondly, I agree the shop window is extremely well presented, but from what I've heard the customer service needs a bit of improvement.'

'You'll definitely need to channel your inner Jane Austen this evening then.'

Maddy lifted her chin, squared her shoulders and addressed the mirror in a condescending voice.

'He is tolerable, I suppose, but not handsome enough to tempt me.'

Alice laughed at that, and – despite the misery of the day – Maddy found herself smiling.

Maddy took a hurried swig of her wine and then rummaged in her drawer for her waterproof mascara. 'To be honest, I'm expecting the questions to be variations on the usual themes, including the all-too-predictable question of whether Jane Austen is actually still relatable in the 21st century,' she added, widening her eyes as she carefully stroked the mascara brush along her pale lashes. 'Well, at least I suppose it's paid work,' she said with a forced cheeriness.

If she was being completely honest, she also didn't fancy spending the evening sitting on her own in the flat while the rest of the population was off doing romantic things with loved-up partners. Even though Alice didn't have a regular boyfriend she had been invited to make up a foursome at a local Italian restaurant and probably wouldn't be back until late.

Alice gave her a sympathetic smile and a brief hug. 'It's probably a bit late, but I can phone in sick for you, if you like?'

Maddy patted her hand. Even at school Alice had been a loyal friend, and had once smacked a boy over the head with her geography book after he'd called Maddy a carrot top. Rather than being upset, seven-year-old

Maddy had been more amused that the attempted insult wasn't even remotely original.

'Thanks, Alice. Kind of you to offer but it's fine, and anyway, I need the work now.'

She checked the time as she slipped her watch bracelet over her hand. The interview was being recorded live so she aimed to get to the studio in plenty of time to read through her notes. She was not about to let Ms Austen down through lack of preparation.

'Do I look okay?' Radio interviews always felt strange. She knew listeners could only hear her, not see her, but she didn't want to feel under-dressed. Especially not in the company of bestselling author, Cameron Massey. Being a redhead, choosing the right colours was important; she opted for her favourite dark turquoise top, and teamed it with her Jane Austen scarf for luck.

'You look lovely. Now go and charm that gorgeous bloke!' Alice shooed her out the front door.

They had chosen the flat largely on price, plus the proximity of buses and Clapham Common underground station. It hadn't been the cheapest place on the rental market, but with both of them sharing the costs it was just about affordable, as long as they staggered the bills a bit. Now, as Maddy walked in the direction of the bus stop, she experienced an unpleasant stirring of panic.

It had been a bright sunny day with a light breeze; the sort of day where you could snatch a few minutes in the sunshine without feeling like you might catch hypothermia. However, clear skies meant the temperature plummeted after sunset and Maddy tugged her coat around her as she sat on the bus and pondered her job prospects. Being able to pay the rent came significantly higher up the necessities list than liking what she did, but moving back home was definitely last resort –she had worked hard to be financially independent and she loved living in London. In any case, her relationship with her mother improved with distance. In between those two options there must be plenty of possibilities if only she could find them.

Just think of goodbye as hello in a different language; that was one of her Mum's favourite expressions. She had a whole armoury of sayings that were – at least in the early years – intended to either encourage Maddy to try something new or to cushion her from disappointment. In later years there was usually a helping of boyfriend advice in there too, most of it in the large economy size. Mrs Carolyn Shaw had firm ideas on the suitability of the opposite sex, although Maddy had often wondered if things might have been different if she'd had siblings and her mother had been able to spread her maternal advice over a wider population. Today, as Maddy pushed open the doors to the small studio where the interview was being recorded, she hoped her Mum might accidentally be right for once.

A girl in black leggings and a purple floral tunic top who looked like she'd just left school (a definite sign of getting old according to her mother) escorted her through the small reception area into an equally small visitors' waiting area. 'The other guest is already here,' she murmured as they reached the door. 'I'll be back as soon as we're ready for you.'

The walls of the waiting room were painted in a restful pale green colour. Light grey sofa-type seating occupied a large part of one side of the room, with a couple of individual chairs added in vibrant, verging on clashing, colours. In the corner, a spindly spider plant trailed down the side of a tall cupboard in a token nod to office greenery.

A dark-haired man with carefully cultured scruffy stubble and a tan that shouted winter holiday was tapping his phone in an agitated manner and glanced up as she entered the room. She took in the lightly patterned open-necked shirt, tailored navy blazer, and the smart shiny shoes and was grateful she hadn't just rocked up in casual gear.

'I'm guessing you might be Madeleine Shaw?'

'My friends call me Maddy,' she replied with a smile and an outstretched hand. 'And you must be Cameron Massey.' After the merest of hesitations, he shook her hand, made an attempt at a polite smile that was so brief it could have been a facial twitch, and then gestured at his phone. 'Sorry, just got to finish this.'

Maddy tried to ignore what she already knew about Cameron Massey and his reputation for snarky interviews; after all, even her heroine, Jane Austen, would give her characters the benefit of the doubt at the start, and Jane had always been her personal go-to adviser on relationships ever since she'd read Pride & Prejudice for GCSE English. While her classmates were grumbling about being told to read what they considered to be some ancient creaky old story, Maddy had fallen in love with the older Bennett sisters whilst wishing she had one, sympathised with Mary, cringed at their overbearing mother, and no boyfriend – teenage or later – had ever measured up against the fictional Mr Darcy.

Alice was right though about Cameron Massey; he was certainly good-looking, even if his (admittedly sexy) eyes were currently saying *can you leave me in peace?* rather than *well hello there!* She busied herself studying the notes she had made on her phone, which unhelpfully decided that now was a good time to launch into a jaunty ringtone. Cameron looked up at the disturbance.

'Sorry, it's my dad ringing,' said Maddy as she swiftly cancelled the call and put her phone on silent. 'He usually rings for a chat on Thursdays as that fits better round his busy social life; except for last week when he rang on Sunday, but that was because the cat had gone missing overnight,' she explained, being simultaneously pretty sure that Cameron Massey wasn't the slightest bit interested in her family's telecommunications habits nor the whereabouts of her dad's cat.

She gave Cameron a look that was meant to say *parents, eh?*

'Such a British thing, isn't it?' he observed wryly. 'Apologising for something that's outside of your control.'

Maddy wasn't sure whether he was attempting to be

humorous or sarcastic but was spared the need to reply by the reappearance of the same girl who had shown them in. 'We're ready for you now,' she announced to Cameron in a sing-song voice, then looked over to Maddy. 'I'll come back shortly and then we'll get you set up as well.'

Maddy sat back down again and sent a quick message back to her dad:

Sorry, work thing. Will call later

While she waited to be summoned, she spent a bit more time looking over her notes. It was less revision and more distraction really; letting her brain go into free-form thoughts invariably led back to the email from her employer. Former employer, she silently corrected herself.

A few minutes later the girl returned and Maddy was shown into the studio where the presenter Angie Turner was already talking to Cameron Massey, presumably about one or several of his books. As soon as she was miked up she gave the producer the thumbs up sign and started paying attention to the discussion in progress.

'…so given that several of your previous books have topped the bestseller lists, and both *The Dangerous Woman* and *The Cornish Key Cutter* were awarded the coveted crime writers' Silver Spanner, you must have been disappointed that your latest book didn't do quite as well. Why do you think that is?'

Although they were on different sides of a glass

screen, Maddy saw a distinct look of annoyance flash across Cameron's face.

'Clearly, authors hope every book will sell well, but I suspect you'd be better off directing that question to the book buying public, who may or may not have purchased it.'

'Point taken. So, what's next for Detective Inspector Jason Friend? Are you able to give us any hints as to what he might be facing in the next book?'

He did one of those twitchy smiley things. 'Not at the moment. You'll all have to wait a bit longer.'

'O-kay. Sorry folks, looks like the secrets box is staying locked for now. So Cameron, as it's Valentine's Day, perhaps I can ask what your view is of romance in crime novels – and have you ever considered giving DI Jason Friend a love interest?'

'Look, readers of my novels enjoy the challenge of solving a puzzle alongside the detective. They don't need to be distracted by some lightweight romance sub-plot.'

Maddy couldn't believe her ears and just about managed to mute the volume on her voice box as she mouthed the word 'What?!'

'So you're not a fan of the genre then?'

'Not personally. It's hardly much of a challenge to write a story where you know the ending, is it?'

Without waiting to be introduced, Maddy leaned in to the microphone in front of her. 'I think if anything, writing a romance makes it more of a challenge. And whilst it guarantees the reader the emotionally satisfying happy ever after, it's the journey the couple go on that makes the book interesting.' She flashed a smile at Cameron. 'I think many books would benefit from including a bit of a romance.'

'An interesting opinion from agony aunt Maddy Shaw. Cameron, is that something you agree with?' Angie asked. 'Have you ever added a touch of romance to your plots?'

'I don't shy away from sex in my novels, if that's what you mean.'

'But sex doesn't automatically mean there's romance, does it?' Maddy replied.

'And have you actually read any of my books?'

'Yes, I've just finished reading *The Diamond Case*.' Maddy believed in research but tactfully refrained from adding that the story felt very soulless. The brief sexual encounter between the detective constable and the jeweller's wife was more functional than passionate and she had suspected long before the end of the novel that the jeweller's wife had an ulterior motive.

'And?'

'It was interesting,' she replied diplomatically. 'But it didn't give the characters time to develop any meaningful romance.'

'But that's precisely what turns people off. My readers want to see things happen, not just follow two people swanning around the countryside for two hundred pages when you already know they'll get together eventually. It's all the same stuff – it's too predictable.'

'Rubbish! Giving someone the assurance of a happy

ending doesn't necessarily make it predictable. And Cameron may be aware,'—she flashed him an apologetic smile—'that some people who reviewed *The Diamond Case* used the same adjective.' Cameron glared at her as though she'd just made that up; in fact, she'd seen several reviews along the same lines. 'In any case you can argue lots of things are predictable. For example, if you went on holiday to Greece, everyone goes to the same airport, gets on the same plane for a few hours, they mostly stay somewhere in or around the same city for a week, go back to the airport, get on another plane, arrive home tired and minus a chunk of money. But everyone's holiday is different, and the reason for going might be widely different.

'You wouldn't say to a plane load of people they are all doing the same stuff,' she added, borrowing Cameron's earlier phrase. 'When you open that book you go on an individual journey with the characters, whether it's a romantic one, a daring escape, a voyage to the stars. And what's wrong with a satisfying ending? Even you would have to agree that most crimes in novels are solved at the end. It certainly was in the book I read.'

'That's because,' Cameron said with a smug expression, 'the point of the book is usually to find out whodunnit.'

'But you would agree that in real life, police statistics show that only a proportion of crimes are every solved? Whilst the methods of detection might be based on reality there's a huge degree of artistic licence in the resolution.'

'So, is this the crime readers' version of the Happy Ever After?' Angie asked, looking at both of them.

'Absolutely,' replied Maddy.

'Of course it isn't. A crime or mystery is resolved – it doesn't have to have a happy ever after as long as readers find out who did it or why. Romance readers on the other hand just want a bit of frivolous escapism. It's wish fulfilment with—'

'Sorry, but that's ridiculous!' interrupted Maddy, almost vibrating with indignation. 'Just because romance books can be set in any period of history doesn't make it escapism. Whether it's set in the past, present or future, characters can struggle with all sorts of problems. I've read books that deal with family break up, bereavement, domestic abuse, racism – good luck trying to describe that as cosy escapism – but it is real life for many people. These books are no less important just because they can engender a feeling of community and have a romantic relationship at their heart.'

She glared at him through the screen but he seemed to be oblivious to her reaction. If anything, there was almost a hint of a smirk around his mouth as though he was enjoying himself.

'So do you think in some minds there is a stereotyped view of people who read romance novels?' asked Angie.

Maddy nodded. 'It is certainly true that more women than men read romantic fiction, but the idea of the typical romance reader being some bored housewife secretly reading her escapist romance while her husband is out at work is totally out of place in the modern world.'

Cameron held his hands up in a gesture of surrender. 'I wouldn't presume to—'

'And furthermore,' Maddy continued, 'that completely ignores those romances read by and written by men; listeners might be interested to know that a significant proportion of audio books in the erotic fiction genre are downloaded by men.'

Ha! That caught him off guard. Maddy enjoyed the brief look of surprise that flashed across Cameron's face. She wasn't normally this combative but after the day she'd had there was an excess of pent-up frustration waiting for an opportunity to escape. In any case, from what she'd seen so far, Cameron seemed to be enjoying a bit of verbal sparring.

'Now that is interesting,' said Angie. 'Cameron, have you ever been tempted to downloaded a racy romance?'

Cameron refused to be drawn and simply stared at her. It was such a shame he was so testy, Maddy thought, as she mentally redressed him in a white shirt and breeches. Yes, that look definitely suited him better.

Angie looked at Maddy. 'So, do you think that romance books are viewed by some people as inferior because they deal with feelings and relationships?'

'Absolutely. Which is ridiculous as they frequently top the bestseller lists.'

'Although that depends what benchmark you're using,' added Cameron. 'In terms of numbers, they certainly sell well, but how many romances have won the major literary prizes?'

'Oh, not that old chestnut!' said Maddy waving her arm in an exasperated gesture. We all know the answer to that one! So how come in nearly every list of best loved books, the classics like *Jane Eyre* and *Pride & Prejudice* are near or at the top?'

For a brief second their eyes met, both challenging each other. Cameron laughed. 'You don't think people have these titles on their bookcase purely to show off? Look at me, I'm educated, I read the classics!'

Maddy felt a rush of heat to her face, but before she could respond with something suitably witty, Angie jumped in again.

'So while we're on the subject of the classics, what do you think it is about Jane Austen that has such an enduring appeal? It's over two hundred years since her books were written and yet her stories are as popular as ever, and still being turned into films, stage plays and dramas.'

'It's pure nostalgia for the past,' said Cameron. 'Her characters lived in another era and many people view it all through rose-tinted glasses. She has such a huge following that it's now almost perjury to say that you haven't read a Jane Austen book or don't love her characters.'

'I totally disagree. Her books are timeless in their appeal,' Maddy responded. 'People may have dressed differently in that era and they had none of the conveniences of modern life, but the situations the characters find themselves in are still relevant to today's readers. Jane Austen wasn't simply agreeing with the mores and manners of the regency period, she was poking fun at the snobbery of the class system, commenting on social injustices, and – if you know where to look – offering relationship advice that is still as pertinent today as ever. You only have to look around to see that there are just as many Mr Wickhams in today's world as there are Mr Tilneys.'

'And there sadly we have to leave it for today, but I hope you've enjoyed our lively debate.' Angie smiled at her through the glass screen. 'My thanks to our two guests, Maddy Shaw and Cameron Massey for sharing their thoughts on the world of fiction and romance, and do join us again next week.'

'You are off air now,' said a voice in her headphones a few seconds later, and Maddy tugged them off, ruffling her hair in the process. Her fellow panellist left the studio without a backward glance. Good riddance. His book was going to the local charity shop tomorrow.

As she expected, Alice was still out when she returned home. It was only just gone 8:30 so she topped up the wine glass that Alice had brought in for her, took several grateful sips and then kicked off her heels and sank onto the sofa. To avoid thinking about her current jobless situation, she let her thoughts trail back to the studio. So that was the famous Cameron Massey! You couldn't go through an airport or a bookshop without seeing his novels crammed onto the bestseller shelf and it was one of the reasons she had been eager to accept the invite from the radio station.

He looked different somehow in real life; maybe it was because he was smiling in all his publicity pictures, which made him look infinitely more attractive. He was probably ordered to, she thought as she took another mouthful of wine before calling up her dad's number. She hoped it wasn't anything longwinded or cat related – not that she didn't like the cat, she adored Tabitha and it wasn't her fault she was saddled with the world's most unoriginal name for a tabby cat, but she craved a quiet evening and an early night.

'Hi Dad, sorry I couldn't take your call but I was doing a radio interview. Is everything okay?'

'Maddy love, I've just had a very strange conversation with a firm of solicitors.'

A flutter of anxiety shot through her. 'You're not in any trouble, are you?'

'Quite the opposite. You're not going to believe this – are you sitting down?'

We hope you enjoy this book. Please return or renew it by the due date.

You can renew it at www.norfolk.gov.uk/libraries or by using our free library app.

Otherwise you can phone 0344 800 8020 - please have your library card and PIN ready.

You can sign up for email reminders too.

Linda Corbett lives in Surrey with her husband Andrew and three permanently hungry guinea pigs. As well as being an author, Linda is treasurer and fundraiser for Shine Surrey – a volunteer-led charity that supports individuals and families living with spina bifida and hydrocephalus. For many years she also wrote a regular column for Link, a disability magazine, illustrating the humorous aspects of life with a complex disability and she is a passionate advocate of disability representation in fiction. *Love You from A–Z* is her first published novel.

 twitter.com/jcorbettauthor